Court Appointed
By Annmarie McKenna

Jackson knows he needs protection from a stalker, but the last thing he wants is to want his bodyguard.

After receiving several suspicious "gifts", His Honor Jackson Benedict is assigned an agent for protection. He'd be fine with a bodyguard...if he was anyone but the man who enters his courtroom looking hotter than any man has a right to look. Thank God Jackson's robe hides his interest.

Trey London is more than happy that Jackson has practically been handed to him on a silver platter. If his job requires he stay close to one of the country's youngest federal judges, it's no skin off his back. The closer the better, actually.

But someone else is getting closer, too, and when the gifts turn into attacks, Trey is forced to trade his status of new lover for that of protector. He's not about to let anyone come between him and his judge.

Warning, this title contains the following: explicit, nekkid, sometimes robed, m/m judge on bodyguard sex, and graphic language.

For Love and Country
By Mary Winter

Love? Or duty? His choice will damn his country—or his heart.

Vampire Basile Gagnon wants nothing more than to put the United States, its war, and the heartbreak he found on its shores far behind him. He has suffered the loss of one too many mortal lovers, and refuses to risk his heart again, not even for Emil, the mortal he turned away five years ago.

When Union soldier Emil Franks steps aboard Basile's ship, his mission is to try to convince Basile to lend his vessel to the Union cause. But with one look at his former lover, he reveals far more—his lingering love for Basile.

Neither time nor the fires of war have dimmed their passion for each other, but not even the fact that Emil is now a vampire can sway Basile from his course. In two days' time, he leaves for his native France.

On this war-torn Valentine's Day, Emil must choose: Love? Or country?

Warning, this title contains the following: graphic language, and hot nekkid man-love.

Hot Ticket
By K. A. Mitchell

Love's the last thing you expect to find in the trash.

Elliot Graham doesn't make mistakes. So when he ends up serving community service at a recycling plant for inadvertently buying stolen property, he's certain it's the worst thing that's ever happened to him. That is, until he finds tickets to a sold-out concert in the trash, tickets that immediately disappear into the pocket of the hottest—and most exasperating—guy he's ever met.

Cade McKuen has never been one to follow society's expectations. That's why he's serving time sorting trash for destroying his cheating ex-lover's car rather than apologize. Finding those tickets is an unexpected bonus to an otherwise smelly sentence. But when cute, sputtering Elliot claims a share, Cade decides community service might be the best thing that's happened to him all year.

Cade is determined to keep Elliot off balance and tap into the passion he senses is hidden under that buttoned-down exterior. Elliot is fascinated by Cade's outrageous way of thumbing his nose at the world.

Opposites attract, but can passion be the ticket to something lasting?

Warning, this title contains the following: explicit male/male sex, graphic language.

Serving Love

A Samhain Publishing, Ltd. publication.

Samhain Publishing, Ltd.
577 Mulberry Street, Suite 1520
Macon, GA 31201
www.samhainpublishing.com

Serving Love
Print ISBN: 978-1-59998-998-3
Court Appointed Copyright © 2008 by Annmarie McKenna
For Love and Country Copyright © 2008 by Mary Winter
Hot Ticket Copyright © 2008 by K. A. Mitchell

Editing by Sasha Knight
Cover by Anne Cain

Court Appointed, ISBN 1-59998-861-5
First Samhain Publishing, Ltd. electronic publication: January 2008
For Love and Country, ISBN 1-59998-862-3
First Samhain Publishing, Ltd. electronic publication: January 2008
Hot Ticket, ISBN 1-59998-863-1
First Samhain Publishing, Ltd. electronic publication: January 2008
First Samhain Publishing, Ltd. print publication: December 2008

Contents

Court Appointed

Annmarie McKenna

Dedication

To Bianca and Jo~ Thanks for the loads of information! I couldn't have written this without you.

And to Jennifer and John Michael~ Well, let's just say I needed all the help I could get. Thank you.

Chapter One

The door at the back of the courtroom swung open, drawing His Honor, Jackson Benedict's attention despite the defendant's very vocal tirade. A tirade which included something about effectively removing Jackson's balls.

Jackson took offense. He was rather attached to his boys and would prefer to keep them right where they were.

Jesus. The guy had a set of lungs on him that rivaled a herd of elephants in full rant. Jackson barely refrained from cringing at the slew of insults being flung at him. If he weren't already used to it coming from this scumbag, he might get more than just a tad offended.

"That's enough." He slammed the gavel down with a crack, and for a split second, silence reigned.

A slice of black drew his gaze to the back of the room again and this time, he did cringe. What in God's name was *he* doing here? St. Valentine had to be playing with Jackson's peace of mind. Why else would this particular man show up in his courtroom today of all days? That it was Valentine's Day didn't escape his notice and Trey London was a distraction he most definitely didn't need. About the same height as Jackson, Trey—with his rumpled black hair, clear blue eyes and tightly packed, muscled body—was probably the epitome of every woman's dream man. Unfortunately, he was also Jackson's.

His previously threatened balls tightened and his cock hardened in anticipation beneath the zipper of his jeans and the flowing black robe. Jackson was suddenly glad his alarm had failed to go off this morning, forcing him to forgo his usual ensemble of dress pants and shirt for jeans and a long sleeve T.

At least dressed this way, when he stood, the firm fabric would keep his hard-on from tenting the robe, letting everyone know where his thoughts had been.

Of course anyone here would assume he'd been thinking of a woman. Who knew how long he'd be forced to endure the supposedly good-natured ribbing of those he worked with as they tried to guess the identity of his special lady. They'd get nowhere if their brains didn't lead them past the XX chromosomes.

"Bailiff," he said, dragging his brain back where it belonged, "remove the defendant from the courtroom." Jackson kept his tone neutral when he wanted to snarl at the little prick. If it were up to him, instead of the wide-eyed and openmouthed jury sitting along the side, he would have thrown the bastard in prison and swallowed the key during the pretrial.

Fair trial. Even as a federal judge, Jackson sometimes wondered at the laws of his forbearers. If this worm got off— again—Jackson would seriously have to consider a career change.

"You mother-fucking, cock-sucking whore."

Jackson felt his face blanch and his cock soften. Dominic Savanti was nothing if not eloquent. Did he know something few others did, or was he speaking out his ass? For the sake of his sanity, Jackson had to believe the man was spouting anything he could think of.

From beneath his lashes, Jackson saw Trey move in reaction. His hands went to his slender hips and settled there, pushing the sides of his leather jacket open and revealing a holstered gun at his rib cage. Long, lean fingers tapped impatiently. Long, lean fingers Jackson had more than once imagined...

Shit.

"You'll regret this, you come-sucking bastard. My father will destroy you." Dominic continued his screaming diatribe out the door and down the hall. The women on the jury gasped, the men shook their heads, the audience hummed with excitement.

This particular scene was quickly becoming the story of Jackson's life. How many days in a row did this make? How many times had he thrown Dominic out? Too many. Jackson brought the gavel down again, piercing the commotion.

"Order," he commanded. It took three more knocks before everyone settled. "We'll adjourn until tomorrow to give the defendant plenty of time to cool off." *Again.* "Counselor, get your client under control or I'll have him barred from my courtroom." *Should have done it two days ago.* Of course, any man who would gut an undercover federal officer then cut out his tongue and eyes as a warning to anyone else who might think to fuck over the Savanti organization didn't really deserve a trial anyway.

But he was not in his right mind, don't you know, Jackson?

"Yes, Your Honor." The man couldn't quite keep the sleaziness from his tone or the smug look off his face. For God's sake, the man actually looked pleased by the childish behavior of his client.

Jackson sighed. Dominic's lawyer was probably just as crooked as the entire Savanti family. Had to be if he was representing them. And Jackson was damn tired of dealing with every one of them. If this morning's package was any indication though, he wouldn't be seeing their backs any time soon. He'd pissed *someone* off, that much was true, and if he were a betting man, he'd go with the Savantis trying to warn him off putting their golden child behind bars. The messages hadn't yet delved into physical attacks but breaking into his home, as the latest one had done, was close enough.

This morning he'd taken action for the first time and called in the "need to knows". A letter, a photograph, a black rose he guessed symbolized his imminent death—those were things he received on a fairly regular basis. Hell, no criminal liked the man charged with the responsibility of sequestering their bodies to a jail cell. Jackson considered cryptic messages a part of the job. But stealing something from his home crossed into a realm beyond letters left on his windshield in the parking lot.

He let out a breath and stood, ready to get the hell out of there and as far away from Trey London as he could get. Why was he here, anyway? Surely he hadn't been assigned to the case...

Another bailiff opened the door to the hallway leading to his private chambers and nodded. Jackson reciprocated and had his hand on the zipper of his robe before he'd even made it five steps. Jesus, he couldn't wait for this trial to be over. He needed a vacation. Or another line of work. Better yet, could a man retire at thirty-eight?

"How long you been getting gifts, Your Honor?"

Jackson missed a step and hung his head at Trey's deep, gravelly tone behind him. Fuck, but the man's voice alone had the ability to make Jackson's cock swell. His heart thumped. The last time he'd been this close to the agent they'd been at a bar with joint acquaintances, and Jackson had done his best to keep as far back as he could from the man then too.

"Since you probably already know that answer and everything else there is to know about me, I don't really need to answer, do I?" Cheeks hot with thoughts on precisely how much he wanted Trey to know, forced Jackson to keep staring at the wall. It might save him the embarrassment of revealing his true feelings as well. In the courtroom, Jackson had the best of poker faces. This close to Agent London, there wasn't a poker face in all of America that would hide what Jackson felt.

"I only know you got something this morning. The powers that be wanted me to look into it, so indulge me."

If only you knew exactly how indulging I can be. Jackson spun around to face one of the federal agents assigned to keeping threatened judges safe and prayed to whoever was listening that Trey was telling the truth and hadn't been assigned to him, but was instead simply looking into matters. He didn't need a bodyguard. Especially not one he wanted to thrust his cock into until they were both spent only to start over and do it again.

"I'm a big boy, Agent London."

Trey snorted with a shrug and his gaze traveled the entire length of Jackson's body. The flesh at his groin rippled with need. The need to be buried in Trey's mouth.

"You packing under that robe, Jackson?" Trey asked, straying from formality by using his name instead of his title, and meeting Jackson's eyes with a strange look.

Sure. Just not the gun you're insinuating I should be packing. Jackson swallowed without answering and turned, heading for his chambers.

"It won't matter how big you are when you're facing down the barrel of a gun. Although, someone like the Savantis won't have you facing it, they'll have it pressed against the back of your skull. On your knees. With your hands tied behind your back. If this is the Savantis, of course. I'm sure you've made your share of enemies over the years."

Jackson pursed his lips as he reached for the door handle. He wasn't stupid. He knew exactly what the Savantis were capable of. Hell, like Trey said, he wasn't even positive it was the Savantis behind the gifts he'd received. Still didn't mean he needed a babysitter. Especially not one who was six feet four inches of lean, packed muscle with a face to die for and a voice to make Jackson's cock hard enough to pound nails. Or, more importantly, one who would likely turn tail and sprint for the nearest exit if he ever found out which side Jackson batted for.

If the federal government wanted to give him a bodyguard, they needed to find him a nice buff woman, or at the very least, a man who didn't make his hormones go into overdrive. Someone old and grizzled who'd done his time and was waiting for his nice gold retirement watch.

Not that the feds knew he was gay.

He didn't think they did anyway.

"How many?" Trey growled in his ear.

Christ, but the man smelled good. Musk and man and whatever the hell cologne he wore. Trey was so close, Jackson was half tempted to turn into him and show him how he really wanted things to be between them.

"Five," he relented instead, and turned the knob. Trey's hand covered his before he could push the door open.

"See? I don't know everything. When you judges don't report your *gifts*, we don't know about them. Someday one of you will wait too long and there won't be anything we can do to help except carry the casket." His breath whispering across Jackson's ear made more blood rush to his groin when the words Trey had spoken should have permanently removed all thoughts of fucking him.

"I go in first." There was a steel command laced in Trey's voice.

"Fine." Jackson slapped his thighs and stepped aside. He wouldn't win against Trey. The man was known for getting his way in everything that mattered. They might be pretty equal in height, but Trey had the training to take down any sized man. There wasn't a doubt in Jackson's mind he would wind up the loser if they ever came to blows.

Trey drew his gun with his left hand and held it at his side while he pushed the door open with his right and looked inside.

"Stay," he said and entered Jackson's chamber with a caution that made Jackson wonder if there were something he didn't know. Was Trey there for more than a follow-up? Had they heard through their usually reliable set of narks that something might be about to go down involving Jackson?

A few seconds later Trey poked his head out the door. Stuffing the gun back into its holster, he declared, "All clear."

"Gee, thanks." Jackson couldn't help but feel surly. He was a federal judge for God's sake. Federal judges were not supposed to be afraid someone might be lurking in their chambers. He shouldn't have to worry about whether or not the feds had a line on a hit on him. Christ, he was working himself up.

Slamming the door closed with his heel, Jackson yanked the zipper on his robe and stripped it off. "I can take care of myself."

Trey ignored him. "Tell me about this fifth little present."

"I don't want a bodyguard," Jackson snarled. *And I sure as shit don't want to* want *my bodyguard.*

Trey shrugged, stalking closer to Jackson as he hung up the robe on a coat tree. Jackson took a step back, stopping when he hit the wall. Trey kept coming until he pressed his chest to Jackson's. They both hissed at the contact. Jackson swallowed. They might be about the same height, but Jackson could clearly see now that Trey outweighed him by a good fifteen or twenty pounds. All muscle from the feel of his thighs and abs. Not that Jackson was soft, he just didn't have the same amount of physical training Trey did.

"I'm not here in that capacity. I'm only here to follow up because you called us. If or when I get the call to take over responsibility of keeping you alive, then you'll damn well accept it," Trey said softly, his eyes practically gleaming. "I think we need to get a couple of things straight between us."

Jackson felt Trey's erection against his. "I think we've already accomplished that." Fuck. He hadn't meant to say that out loud.

Chapter Two

Trey lifted the corners of his mouth in a loose smile and shifted ever so closer. Jackson was right. They had accomplished getting a couple of things straight between them. He was hard as a rock and getting harder by the second. Anything this particular federal judge did to him would be fine. Except turn him away. Trey wasn't about to let that happen. Not until they'd sated each other about a million times.

If it weren't for the five fucking gifts Jackson had received, Trey would have already shown the honorable Judge Benedict how far past time it was they stopped dancing around one another. The urge to press his lips to Jackson's, to see his gorgeous hazel eyes widen even further than they already had, to hear his breath catch again, was irresistible.

He'd entered the courtroom today fully expecting to look into whatever little present the judge had gotten and then get down to showing Jackson Benedict a thing or two about how he felt. Hell, it was Valentine's Day after all.

Trey leaned in further, his gaze never leaving Jackson's. Only a few inches separated their mouths. What would those lips feel like? Would he open for Trey and let him in or would he seal the delectable pink skin shut and play hard to get? Jackson's breath came in pants and his head pressed against the wall. Trey lifted his hands to the wall to bracket Jackson's head. The judge's nostrils flared.

Shit. Had he been wrong about Judge Benedict all along?

No. No fucking way. He'd watched the man. Been around him if only as an acquaintance for as long as he'd been in this division. While he'd never actually pulled a detail with Jackson, he knew other people who had. This morning, fresh off another case, he'd practically jumped up and down to be assigned the job of taking Jackson's statement. Trey could have said with an almost ninety-nine point nine nine percent certainty that he knew which direction Jackson's tastes ran. And it wasn't to breasts and a vagina. Now here they were, right where he wanted them to be, with two things straight between them, yet not nearly close enough.

Jackson swallowed, his gaze jumping between Trey's eyes and mouth. Trey attacked, seizing Jackson's lips with his own. He coaxed Jackson into opening his mouth with his tongue and insinuated himself inside.

Sweet Jesus, the man tasted good. Tentative at first, Jackson licked back. Then he moaned and tilted his head to the side, giving Trey better access to the recesses of his mouth. His hands fisted in Trey's leather jacket. Their tongues melded together, swept across velvet softness so they tasted and fed off each other. Trey pressed his body along Jackson's, capturing his gasp as their cocks ground together. They were the perfect size for one another.

Fuck. He had to stop now or he'd have the good judge thrown on the floor and their cocks out of their pants and in hand before they could count to ten.

Trey pulled back, kissing along Jackson's lips and up his jawline to the lobe of his ear.

"We'll finish this later, Judge," he growled before biting down gently on the flap of skin. Nothing would keep him away now.

He grasped Jackson's hands, which were still twisted in his jacket, and tugged them loose, then backed away, leaving the other man breathless.

Jackson's heart pounded. What in the hell had just happened? He hadn't known Trey was gay. He'd hoped and suspected, but hadn't been sure, and he sure as shit hadn't known that Trey knew Jackson was gay. He'd tried to be so careful all these years not to broadcast his preferences, in order to protect not only his privacy but his family's too. Not to mention his status as a homosexual would most likely get him kicked off his seat so fast his head would spin. Wouldn't his father love that?

His past lovers had hated him for his insistence they keep their affairs strictly confidential, but he'd been adamant. And extremely selective of lovers. One scent of this kind of scandal and Jackson could kiss his fast track to the Supreme Court goodbye, powerful family or not. Hell, his father had once flat-out told him, "I don't care what you do with your dick, boy, but you better fuckin' keep it zipped in your pants in public. Even the President won't be able to save you, you get caught sniffin' another man's balls."

Crude. Allenton Benedict was the epitome of snobby crudeness. It was his way or the highway.

Not that Allenton mattered. Lately, the Supreme Court, which Jackson at one time had thought was the be all and end all, had been looking less and less appealing. Not even hints of his name coming up in the nomination process had sparked his desire. He was tired and getting to the point of being burnt out. He was definitely tired of the bullshit that convicts routinely got away with, tired of letting people like Dominic Savanti threaten him because they thought they were above the law, but mostly he was damn tired of being in the closet. He wanted a lover. Someone to share his life with instead of hiding. Maybe it really was time to get out. He could always look at the smaller courts.

Chest heaving, he stared at Agent London. The man's lips were red and puffy from the smashing kiss they'd shared. Jackson lifted his hand to his own mouth, knowing he must look the same way. You don't attack another man's perfect mouth and not look disheveled.

Cool blue eyes assessed him and begged Jackson to say he hadn't wanted it.

"I'm not done with you, Judge. Not by a long shot. I've skated around us for too long. We *will* finish what's between us. Preferably in a bed, with your lips wrapped around my cock, or mine around yours, I don't give a fuck who tops, but we will have each other."

Jesus, if that wasn't the sweetest goddamn thing Jackson had ever heard. He swallowed, feeling like a fucking teenager looking at his first wet dream.

One of Trey's eyebrows quirked. "You have an objection to that, Judge?"

And the truth shall set you free. Jackson inhaled and finally moved away from the wall. "No." One thing he knew for certain, he wouldn't have to sweet talk this lover into keeping things behind closed doors. Surely Trey had a job to protect too. And Jackson knew he could trust the man with his life.

Even if he didn't want to do so now.

"Glad you see it my way. Now tell me about the reason I'm here other than to declare my intentions to you," Trey growled, breaking the tension.

Jackson let his gaze travel the length of Trey's body one last time, taking in the rather impressive bulge beneath his black slacks. He licked his lips.

"Later, Judge," Trey commanded softly, a hint of amusement laced in his tone. "Trust me, there won't be much of you I won't get to with my tongue."

"Damn. Anybody ever tell you to shut up?" Jackson scoffed, snapping out of the last several minutes of stunned disbelief in what was happening. He adjusted his cock inside his jeans. Why bother trying to hide it now?

"All the time."

Jackson strode past Trey, blatantly brushing up against the man and not excusing himself. Might as well get all the touches in he could. Who knew how long their little tryst might last. Besides, the man smelled incredible. He couldn't remember the last time his cock had gotten so hard just from looking at a man. Fully clothed no less.

Okay, the kiss helped. Big time.

He slipped into the leather chair at his desk and yanked open the middle drawer on the right side. Inside lay the object he'd found on his desk this morning. It had been delivered to his secretary and she had placed it on his desk, not knowing what it was. She figured if it had gotten through security—they didn't let just any package in to a federal judge—then it must be all right. And it *had* been a safe enough package. Meaning it hadn't exploded or been laced with a mysterious nerve-eating powder. However, what had been inside had been no less shocking to Jackson.

Lifting it by one corner, he flipped it face-up onto his desk.

Trey sauntered—there was no other word for it—and stuffed his hands in his jacket pockets before leaning over to take a closer look.

"What is it?"

Jackson gave a snort of impatience. Was the man American? "It's a baseball card. A nineteen fifty-two, Topps, Mickey Mantle rookie card, mint condition."

Trey rolled his eyes. "I can clearly see it's a Mickey Mantle baseball card. I also know it's worth a lot of money. But it's not really a mob kind of mentality if you catch my drift. They tend to drift more toward the breaking of fingers or sinking your feet in cement blocks before throwing you off a bridge to feed the fishes. So what kinds of things did you get before this?"

Jackson slumped back in his chair. "The typical cut-out newspaper letters that said, 'Things aren't always what they seem.'"

"Huh?"

"Exactly. I had no clue what it referred to so I discounted it like I do ninety percent of the things I get."

"Okay. You keep it?"

"Yes. I've got it back at home with all the rest of the lovely letters I've gotten."

"Nice keepsakes."

"I like to think I've affected someone's life somehow," he half joked. The truth was, he had no clue why he kept them. They served to remind him he was doing the right thing by removing the scum so they couldn't hurt anyone else. It wasn't like he had cabinets full of them, just a file folder. An overstuffed one, but still, a file folder. He wasn't popular enough to warrant the hardcore death threats some of the other judges he knew had received.

"All right, what else?"

Jackson sighed. "A black rose, a paper mock-up of my headstone."

"Very original."

"Yep."

"And..."

"A photo." *With a nice little message on the back.*

"I feel like I'm pulling teeth here, Judge. You're going to have to fill me in a tad bit more. What's in the photo?"

"A picture of me with my face scratched off and some...friends." Including a past lover who probably wouldn't be too happy to find out there was a picture of them together, even if it was a group photo.

Trey stared hard at him for long seconds, and Jackson suspected he was wondering what exactly he and his friends were doing in the picture.

Trey swallowed and sucked his lips in before saying, "Is this the kind of picture you wouldn't show to your mother?"

Yep, Jackson had guessed correctly. Was that a hint of jealousy Jackson detected in the agent's voice? He could have pushed to see just how jealous Trey was, but he didn't.

"Not at all. It was taken at a baseball game and there was nothing the least bit incriminating going on between us, unless you consider kicking back and having a beer at the ball game incriminating."

Trey nodded. "So who are these friends and why would someone send you this particular picture?"

"A couple of longtime buddies and two men from my father's law firm, and I have no idea why this one. I'd never seen it before. I don't even know who took it, but I remember it because it was one of the few times we went out in public."

"We, who? And I assume by your comment about not going out in public that one of those men was someone you were seeing as more than a friend?"

Jackson grimaced. "Yes, and had my father found out I had taken a boyfriend into plain view of everyone, he would have had a coronary. I can't imagine what would have happened if it had hit the papers."

"If it's just a pic of some guys at a game, why would it matter if it hit the papers? You said yourself there was nothing incriminating."

"Nope, but to Allenton, my being seen with another man could only mean we were fucking."

Trey raised an eyebrow. "Would he think you were fucking all four of them at once?"

Jackson snorted. "Probably."

"Can you give me some names?" Trey took a small pad of paper and a pen from an inside pocket on the jacket.

"Sure. Two of my closest friends, Eric Kinder and Daniel Gardner and Caleb Murphy and Michael Green from my father's firm."

"Which one were you seeing?"

"Caleb, but I got the feeling he was just trying out the lifestyle anyway." It had pissed Jackson off and left him feeling used, but then Caleb had broken things off and practically disappeared. He'd never felt comfortable seeing Caleb anyway because he worked for Jackson's father, but there'd been something about the man that drew him in enough to take a chance. In the end, Jackson had decided to view the few months they'd been together as a live and learn experience. Not every man Jackson saw as partner material had the same thing in mind.

"Any reason he'd feel the need for revenge or blackmail, maybe? Would he have hired someone to take the picture, only to produce it now?" Trey pointed to the baseball card. "Is it possible *he* could have sent this? Or more importantly, what made you call us for having received what amounts to a birthday present?"

Jackson shrugged. "My guess would be because it's mine." He lifted his gaze to Trey's, ready for the man to explode. What he got was a fair share of confusion.

"You want to tell me what you mean by that?" he asked with deadly calm.

"Exactly what I said. It's mine. Two days ago it was tucked up in my wall safe at home, and now it's here—"

"They fucking got into your house?" Trey roared.

Jackson sat forward in his seat. He wasn't any happier about this than Trey was. Finding the card, still in its protective plastic case—the one with the tiny crack on one corner that confirmed the card was indeed his—on his desk this morning had made his stomach plummet to his toes. Realizing whoever the bastard was had not only gotten into his house, but into his safe without him knowing it or setting off the alarm was unthinkable. There weren't that many people who knew his codes. He'd thought only two, so unless his father had broken into it, there was obviously someone else.

Trey tore his jacket off, revealing a less-than-crisp white dress shirt, sleeves rolled up to the elbows, and shoulder holster. He tossed the black leather onto one of two chairs across the desk from Jackson while loosening a red tie with his other hand, and then yanked the open chair closer before settling his frame in it.

He ripped a cell phone from a clip at his waist and a second later barked into the mouthpiece, "They've been in Judge Benedict's house." Trey's narrowed-eye gaze caught Jackson's.

Damn if the man wasn't sexy as all get out when he was pissed. Jackson was prepared to rip the rest of the suit from Trey's body and bend him over the desk. His dick twitched. Any more of this subtle foreplay and he'd have to excuse himself to the bathroom to relieve the pressure with his own hand.

"He received a package this morning, one that came from the safe inside his house." Based on Trey's white-knuckled grip on the small silver phone, he was more than agitated. "I'll follow him there and go through everything he's received recently."

Trey dared Jackson with his eyes to contradict him. Jackson took it in stride. He could handle the man coming home with him to check things out. So long as they weren't going the whole bodyguard route, Jackson was good. He wasn't about to let some scumbags run him out of his own home.

Trey flipped his cell closed and snapped it into its holder. "I need a list of everyone who knows about the safe—family, friends, *boyfriends*. If you weren't aware it had been broken into, then it had to be someone you know. Or, at the very least, a person hired by someone you know. When do you have to be back here?"

"Tomorrow morning, why?"

Trey nodded. "We'll go to your house, get whatever you need and head someplace safe for the night."

"No." Jackson stood and collected a few papers scattered across the top of his desk.

"I'm not asking you, I'm telling you."

Jackson lifted his gaze to Trey's. They were by far the most gorgeous blue eyes. The same color as the sky on a cloudless day. "Have you been assigned as my bodyguard?"

"No."

"Then I'm not running from this. You can follow me home just like you told whoever was on the other end of that call and we can go over everything I have but if the decision hasn't been made to give me a babysitter, then I'm staying put."

"You sure as shit are running from this, Judge. You'll have to give me the codes to your systems because tomorrow I'll be sending a team to your house to find out just how the fuck someone got in without you knowing it. In the meantime, you're with me."

Any other time, Jackson would love to hear Trey say those words to him. Now that he knew Trey's sexual preference, he couldn't wait to spend some time with the man. But not under these circumstances. Not if it meant being holed up somewhere with no contact to the outside world. Jackson knew from a few friends who'd been in similar situations what would happen. Trey would take him either to a safe house or an undisclosed hotel, and he'd be trapped.

"And what'll you tell your boss, huh?"

"That he fucking needs to assign me to you because this guy sure as hell got about as close to you as a person can get without touching you."

Jackson shook his head, making no move to grab his jacket. "I've got a dog, London."

"You've also got a staff."

"I have a maid who comes in three times a week and she isn't responsible for Corky."

Trey pressed his lips together and looked suspiciously like he was trying not to laugh. "Corky?"

"You got a problem with my dog's name?"

Trey smiled. "Nope." He scooped up his jacket. "Give him to your sister."

Figures he would know about Jackson's little sister. "Tammy doesn't do dogs and leave her out of this. I'm not bringing this shit to my family."

"You think it's not already affecting your family?"

Jackson sucked in a breath. Christ. Getting fan mail of the perverse kind wasn't new, but Trey was right. Things had never gone this far and Jackson hadn't thought about them getting to his family.

Jackson sat back down. If they could get to him so easily, they could for damn sure get to Tammy and his niece and nephew. He wasn't as worried about his parents. His uber-wealthy father surrounded himself and Jackson's mother, Maria, with all sorts of bodyguards, something Jackson had been quick to discard the second he'd moved out of his parents' house. Remembering the stifling security he'd lived with as a child made his head spin. He wouldn't go through that again.

He glanced up at Trey, who watched him with a knowing look. "I'll call them and let them all know to be on guard just in case." He'd never forgive himself if anything happened to them because somebody had a bone to pick with him.

"If the only thing stopping you from leaving your house is...Corky, then bring the dog." Trey swung the jacket over his arms. "Let's get going."

"I can't take a dog to a hotel, London," Jackson argued, but stood and collected his own jacket from the coat tree.

Trey opened the door and stuck his head out, his hand on the butt of his gun. "Who said we were going to a hotel? Not official means no money for lodging," he threw over his shoulder and ushered Jackson out with a hand on his elbow.

Chapter Three

Five minutes later Jackson stood inside the glass doors at the rear of the courthouse watching like a nancy-boy while Trey searched Jackson's prized black Acura TL. The agent had ripped the keys from Jackson's hand the second he'd pulled them from his pocket just after leaving his office.

His "What the fuck are you doing?" had only garnered the irritable response, "Searching your car before you go out there and start pushing buttons on a car that might have been tampered with."

"Tampered with? We've leaped from stolen baseball cards to cut brake lines?"

"And/or bombs, but yes, that's the usual progression."

Jackson had balked. This sort of thing was exactly what he hadn't wanted to happen. Aside from an occasional escort to his car by one of the guards, he'd never had to stand inside and watch while someone *else* searched it for him. How pathetic. Trey was treating him like a woman. His life was being taken over with no say-so from him. Then a part of him said, "Be smart, the man's only doing his job, protecting you from whatever someone *might* have done to your car."

That was a big *might have*. And what the hell was Jackson supposed to do if there was a bomb? What if Trey triggered it? He would have to stand here and watch the man of his dreams go up with an inferno. His stomach rolled.

Every ounce of original anger fled the second Trey dropped to his knees to peer under the car. Stupid, stupid man. He'd either get killed or cause Jackson to have a heart attack. Even from this distance Jackson could see Trey's ass clearly defined by the cut of his slacks. Jackson ceased to breathe, let alone think about possible impending danger. Did Trey have any clue what he was doing to him? No, of course not, because he flipped to his back and proceeded to shimmy beneath the car's undercarriage to get a closer look. His shirt had come untucked and ridden up, exposing a three-inch wide gap of tanned, hard abs. Jackson wondered who was getting the most out of Trey's search and thanked God his parking spot was so close to the doors.

He was still staring—and probably drooling—like a fool when Trey scooted back out and stood, wiping one hand on the fine butt Jackson had been admiring. He reached into his jacket pocket and flipped something out, opening it. Then he tossed something Jackson hadn't seen him holding in his other, gloved hand—when the shit had he put a glove on?—into the baggie and stuck the whole package in his pocket. What the hell had he found? He swallowed back a curse, his face draining of blood. Had there been a bomb on his car? Surely not. Trey wouldn't have been so careless with it. Unless he'd disarmed the damn thing.

Fuck. Beads of sweat popped on his upper lip. Throwing one last look over his shoulder, then shaking his head, Trey walked back toward the courthouse, tucking his shirt in as he went. Holding the door open, he withdrew the baggie and tossed it at Jackson, who instinctively flicked his hand out and caught it in midair. Inside was a small black box, about an inch and a half square, which had a tiny red light on one side and a sticky tab on the other.

"I'm assuming you wouldn't throw a bomb at me, no matter how miniscule it might be." Jackson's heart thudded.

Trey grinned at him. "You assume correctly. Not a bomb, though I've seen some smaller than that do a hell of a lot of damage. It's a tracking device." He pointed at it. "Whoever planted it has known exactly where you've been for however long it's been on your car."

"Son of a bitch." Jackson tried to remember the places he might have gone over the last several days. At least since the Savanti trial had started. Nowhere exciting for sure. The grocery store, work—Christ, it wasn't like he had much of a life outside the bench.

So who would care? Right now the only person who came to mind was Dominic Savanti. His family would do anything to keep one of their own out of prison, including having him tailed. Perhaps trying to dig up some dirt? Jackson was halfway sorry he hadn't given them something more interesting to use. If they'd seen him in some gay strip club they'd at least have something on him other than watching him skip over the fresh fruit and vegetables in favor of the frozen foods.

"Follow me. We'll hit your house, look over your *items*, pick up some clothes and head out. Don't even think about trying to evade me on the way. I'll have your ass pinned to the ground so fast..." As they walked to their cars, Trey handed back Jackson's keys but not before pushing the unlock button himself.

As for having his ass pinned to the ground, Jackson couldn't really see what problem he could possibly have with the scenario.

Jackson shook his head. "What about this?" He held up the tracking device.

"I'm going to drop it off with another agent who's still in the building. He'll take it back to the lab to see if there are any prints to be gotten off it," Trey said, taking it back. He unlocked the door to his own car, conveniently parked next to Jackson's, and got in.

Jackson crossed his arms over his chest and shifted his weight to one foot. "How come you're not checking *your* car for bombs?"

"I don't have a reason to. I'm here to follow up on your call to us. No one else knows about it and like you pointed out, I haven't been assigned to you. Yet." He jammed the key into the ignition and started the car. "Don't make me get out to tuck you into your car."

After handing over the device to an agent he'd called to the car, Trey led them from the lot. Because he half expected Jackson to try and evade him, he couldn't resist frequent peeks in the rearview mirror. Surely the man wouldn't run now. Not after the mind-blowing kiss they'd shared back in his office. Trey shifted in his seat, trying to alleviate some of the pressure on his cock. Thank God for the suit pants. They allowed for a bit of mobility.

He stopped at a busy intersection and drummed his fingers on the steering wheel, wondering about the tracking device he'd found stuck to the undercarriage of Jackson's car. If someone wanted the judge dead, they would have left something meant to go boom, not a GPS unit. So maybe Jackson had a stalker. Someone who didn't want him dead, but did want to know where he was at all times, which would exclude the Savantis, wouldn't it? Stalking wasn't really their style.

Trey slapped the wheel. "Damn." If the presence of a tracking device didn't get his bosses to issue a need for Jackson to have a bodyguard, Trey didn't know what would.

Jackson was on the phone when Trey looked at him through the rearview mirror. He looked tense for a moment, then a smile split his face, and suddenly Trey found himself wanting the smile to be directed at him. His cock, which had softened with his thoughts of Jackson being watched, hardened again.

Now, beyond getting back to his place with Jackson and spreading him wide open, Trey couldn't think. Not good. He needed to have every bit of his focus on keeping Jackson safe from here on out. Trey had already decided to leave Jackson's car at the judge's house. If this thing with the gifts was progressing as quickly as it seemed to be, Jackson didn't need to be driving anyway.

The light turned green. With another glance in the mirror, Trey accelerated. Something caught his attention to his right. A sudden movement when there shouldn't have been any. A black SUV bore down on the intersection. No way would it be able to stop and with Jackson on the phone, he might not see the imminent danger in time to avoid it...

"Fuck." Trey stomped on his brakes.

A split second later the SUV slammed into the passenger side doors, T-boning him hard enough to push Trey across two lanes of oncoming traffic. Horns blared, tires squealed, a second car smashed into the right front of his car, sending his company-issued Taurus into a spin.

Smoke hissed from beneath the crumpled hood and his vision wavered. His head pounded. Trey lifted his hand and swiped at a point on his forehead where the pain radiated. His fingers came away bloody.

Damn. He must have hit the wheel. Or perhaps the shattered window next to his head. The radial pattern of broken yet intact glass made a kaleidoscope of the street around him. Sluggish, he turned his head, trying to make heads or tails of the scene around him.

Two men dressed in black jumped out of the SUV and ran somewhere behind him. Trey turned to find them headed straight for Jackson, who so stupidly had gotten out of his car.

"Son of a bitch." It was a setup. He shoved his door open and stumbled from the car, quickly regaining his faculties. Someone screamed, another one yelled that they'd already called the cops, was anyone hurt, they'd send an ambulance too.

Trey drew his gun and aimed. The two goons were too close to the judge for him to fire, not that he needed to. Jackson threw a punch at one of the men as the other one grabbed him from behind. His other fist slashed backward, catching the guy clinging to his back in the nose. Blood spurting from his face, the man howled and doubled over, giving Jackson the chance to spin and knock the first man off his feet with a sweep of his leg.

Trey knelt and slapped a pair of handcuffs on the man still writhing and holding his nose. He didn't take too kindly to having his hands wrenched from his face and fought like the devil.

Sirens sounded.

"I've got this one," Jackson stated calmly from his seat on number one's back, as if he hadn't just fought off two thugs who'd tried to kidnap him.

Breathing heavy, Trey stood, swaying when a wave of dizziness passed over him.

"Whoa. You all right, London?" Jackson started to come to Trey but the idiot beneath him moved and he plopped back down. "Somebody help him. He's a federal agent."

Trey held up a hand. "I'm fine."

"Right. Is that why you look like you're ready to fall on your face?"

"What's going on?" A police officer strolled through the mix of cars. Two more had rear-ended the car which had collided with the Taurus's front end, and about twenty people milled about. No one else seemed to be hurt, thank God.

Trey flipped open his badge and pointed at Jackson. "Make sure he's okay. And arrest the man he's sitting on. These two are the ones who caused this whole accident."

A paramedic appeared and lifted a gauze pad to Trey's head. Trey ducked and shrugged him off. "Him first."

"Right." Jackson stood, letting the police take care of the swearing man. "You should look at me first because I wasn't in any of the cars involved and I don't have blood running down my face." The judge turned to Trey. "Stop being a pussy and let them look at you."

"Did you just call me a pussy?" Trey moved to stand toe to toe with Jackson.

"I did."

Goddamn if he didn't want to lean in and kiss the smirk right off Judge Benedict's face. "Don't push me, Judge," he whispered so only the two of them could hear. "Are you sure you're okay?" Fuck, this whole thing had been too close for comfort.

"Yes."

Trey watched Jackson's lips move and his cock hardened. "I can think of so many better things you could be doing with your mouth."

"You're the one making us stand here by not letting the paramedics clean you up."

"I'm going to fuck you."

"I can't wait."

"Sir." The paramedic broke the spell. Trey whipped around too fast and nearly collapsed. "Maybe you should sit."

"Yeah, maybe. For a second." He heard his voice wobble and cringed. Some bodyguard he was turning out to be.

Jackson took one elbow, the paramedic the other, and they escorted him to the back of the ambulance. His knees felt like Jell-O. He must have taken a harder knock than he thought. Cold wetness touched the cut, making him hiss in pain.

"Do not move out of my sight, Judge."

"Who, me?"

Trey looked at him from beneath his eyelashes while the sadistic medic stabbed at him with a Q-Tip. "Ow."

"Baby," Jackson muttered, lifting his gaze and whistling into the air.

The medic snorted.

Another policeman joined them. "Any idea what happened here?"

"I believe it was an attempt to—"

"I was smashed into by the SUV driven by one of those idiots," Trey interrupted the judge. "They ran a red light. And while you're questioning them about it, ask them why they were targeting a federal judge." He wanted to be in on the questioning but right now his number one priority was getting Jackson to his condo. He'd felt things were escalating. But was this the kind of thing the Savantis would do? Possibly, if they were abandoning their modus operandi for the sake of making this look like an accident.

The policeman's eyes widened and his gaze shot to Jackson, who shrugged.

"They might not have been, but it is true I've received a few *gifts* recently and Agent London found a tracking device on my car just before we left the courthouse," he told the officer.

Trey could just imagine how those two idiots' interrogation would go. Total denial on their part with a little bit of "The guy attacked us when we tried to help out" thrown in for good measure. Made Trey want to be present even more. If they had been hired by someone it was unlikely they'd give up their moneyman.

"I don't think you'll need stitches." The medic stuck a bandage on his forehead. "I put a butterfly on this. Keep it dry for a couple of days and you'll be good to go."

"Great." Trey jumped up, wobbling less this time.

"Did you lose consciousness at any time?"

"No." They really needed to get out of here. Too many people. If anyone else had followed them, they had ample time to make a move. Taking out a federal judge in a crowd like this would be easy. A sniper on a rooftop... Trey turned in a circle, scanning the buildings around him, one of which was the courthouse. A number of lawyers and court personnel he recognized had ventured outside to see what all the fuss was about.

He picked out Dominic Savanti's lawyer watching with extreme interest. Bastard.

"Time to go, Your Honor." They were sitting ducks out here.

"You should probably go in and have an x-ray done." The medic stuffed his equipment back in his bag.

"No time."

"But you could have a concussion."

"I don't." He'd had a few in his lifetime, he knew what they felt like.

"I'll watch him," Jackson offered. The medic didn't look happy but sighed.

"You'll have to sign a release form. Watch for signs of a concussion and get him to a doctor if he exhibits anything. Nausea, not being able to wake him..."

Jackson nodded.

Christ. They were talking about him as if he wasn't even there. "In the car, Your Honor." Time to get the fuck out of there.

"Everyone okay?" Sleaze oozed off Savanti's lawyer, David Bergdorf, when he sauntered over. "Wouldn't want anything to postpone the trial, would we?"

"Say another word and I'll have you disbarred," Jackson snarled.

Bergdorf smiled. "You can try."

"Your Honor." Trey led Jackson to his car. The police would have to deal with having the unmarked Taurus towed. He wasn't sure the judge wouldn't throw another punch, this time directed at the lawyer defending one badass family in his courtroom. "Fucking bastard. Hundred bucks says he's not real upset about what happened. Give me your keys."

Jackson laughed. "I don't think so. You have a bump on the head and nobody drives my Acura."

Damn it. The man was right. He shouldn't drive. Trey acquiesced and slid into the passenger seat. After Jackson slammed his door shut and started the car, Trey said, "I will drive *something* of yours."

"Fuck. Don't say shit like that until we're in a more convenient place." Jackson paused for a second. "Like my house."

"How long?" Trey fidgeted in his seat thinking about the ways he could take the man next to him.

"About twenty minutes."

"Then I think I'll have to improvise." He ignored the throb in his head and the little voice telling him he shouldn't do this, it was wrong—especially now after what they just went through—and slid his hand over the bulge in Jackson's jeans. Trey squeezed, savoring the long hiss that escaped Jackson's clenched teeth.

෴

Bergdorf watched them walk away and get into the good judge's car. Too bad the accident hadn't succeeded in ridding the planet of Jackson Benedict. The man was quickly becoming a thorn in David's side and the sooner he was out of the picture, the sooner the Savantis would be off David's back. He wasn't winning the trial and it was becoming apparent the Savantis weren't happy with his performance.

He had to assume the accident had been the Savantis doing. He'd overheard a phone conversation just the other day between Dominic's father and an unknown person, where the elder Savanti had mentioned Judge Benedict being the bane of their existence. One could only assume the man was planning to do something about it. As long as David was kept in the dark, he could say he'd known nothing about the judge's demise.

David sucked in a breath as Benedict's car rounded a corner and disappeared. When had he stopped caring about another human's life? But he knew. It was the second his wife had been hit by a drunk, leaving her quadriplegic. Her 'round the clock care was expensive, but to keep her comfortable, there was nothing he wouldn't do for the woman he loved more the anything in the world. Even sell his soul to the devil named Savanti.

He'd done so the day he took over for the previous attorney who'd never been seen or heard from again. His ulcer flared with a vengeance. As soon as this trial was over, or dismissed because something had happened to the judge, David would be done. He'd be free to take his beloved Ellen and retire someplace warm and exotic.

Chapter Four

Jesus Christ, he wouldn't make it. Jackson did not want their first time to be in a cramped car. Trey's fingers moved, pushing the buttons of Jackson's fly through their slots one by one.

"I need to see you, Judge."

Jackson licked his lips. What could he say to that? No?

"You go commando beneath your robe? For shame, Your Honor." Trey lifted Jackson's cock. Not that it needed lifting. The damn thing sprang out, begging for Trey's attention, which it got when lean fingers wrapped around his circumference near the base.

"I have to taste you."

The car swerved. "Shit. Sorry."

"No problem." Trey's head dipped.

"You do realize everyone can see you?" *What the fuck are you doing? Let him suck you off if he wants to.*

Trey sighed. "Damn. You're right. Not to mention, now we know you're in real danger so there's no doubt in my mind I'll be assigned as your protection." He sat back and Jackson watched him check out the side mirror as if he hadn't just had his head in Jackson's lap.

Unbelievable. "You can't just stop."

"I can. I am. I shouldn't have gone there in the first place. Not until I've got you stashed somewhere they can't get to you again."

"You left me fucking hanging here," Jackson growled. He covered his erection with his shirt. Ten more minutes. In ten more minutes he'd have Trey plastered against the wall in his foyer the same way Trey had pressed Jackson to the wall in his office. He didn't care what kind of danger he was in.

"Very unprofessional of me. I'm here to protect you, not fuck you. I don't need the distraction right now." Trey turned in his seat to glare out the back window. "One look at you and everything I've been trained to do goes out the window."

"I'm having the same problem." All these years Jackson had kept his gay lifestyle a secret, and now he wanted more than anything for Trey to suck him off in the car while he drove. Maybe he was the one with the head injury.

Trey's cell phone rang, dispelling the sexual tension in the cramped confines of the car.

"London."

Jackson did his best to tuck his shrinking cock back into his jeans one handed. Didn't do any good.

"Say that again?" Trey snarled. He wrenched his head in Jackson's direction. "Yeah. I'd like to know that too. Go through his life for the last six months. I want to know everything the bastard's done." He flipped the lid closed.

Jackson noticed Trey's white-knuckled grip on the phone. "What was that about?"

"Caleb Murphy."

"Caleb? What does he have to do with this?"

"They caught him trying to break into your office. I think you and I need to have another talk about him, find out what the hell he might want with you after all this time."

Jackson swung the car to the side of the road and slammed on the brakes, throwing both of them into their seat belts. "I have no fucking idea. I haven't heard from him since the day he left. In fact, I haven't laid eyes on him until that picture arrived in the mail. He left me, remember? Not the other way around. He used *me* to test the waters. If anyone should feel the need for revenge it should be me."

"Shit, Judge, let's not stop on the side of the road."

"What the fuck kind of game is he playing? And why?"

Trey whipped his gaze to watch the cars go by. "I don't know, but I plan to find out. Now get moving."

Jackson punched the steering wheel, fury rolling through him as he pulled back onto the road. His and Caleb's affair, if you could even call what they had an affair, had been brief. Very brief. A few months at most. Why then, goddamn it? What had he done to Caleb to deserve this? And what did he hope to gain by stalking him?

"We'll find out what's going on, I promise. He's already being detained and questioned."

Jackson fought the urge to jump from the car and kick something. A few minutes passed before he had himself reasonably controlled enough to drive without killing them both.

"Had he seemed like the type of man out for revenge?"

Jackson shook his head, his fingers twisting on the steering wheel. "Like I said, I'm sure he was trying to decide if he wanted to be gay or not."

"Ahh. One of those, huh?"

"He always had a ton of questions, like he was fascinated by the lifestyle or something. I think he saw it as a novelty. I didn't realize it until he was gone. Left me feeling used."

"Been there, done that too. At least I had people to help me through the rough patch. What about you?"

Jackson barked out in laughter. "Allenton Benedict has done everything in his power to try and convert me. Parading women left and right, leaving *Playboys* in my room, forcing dates on me. I thought he'd finally gotten tired of it all when he came out and said he didn't care where I put my dick as long as it never came out to ruin my chances for a bid to a Supreme Court nomination. That picture would have been my complete ruination in his eyes."

"Must have been a rough life, growing up like that."

Jackson passed the slower-moving car in front of him. "Sometimes, but I've known since before high school. Hell on a boy's ego to know you're different but can't do anything about it, ya know? Do *your* parents know?"

"Yep."

"And?"

"And nothing. They support me. I have a sister who's married and given them three little grandkids. As long as I'm happy, they are."

"Yeah?"

"Yeah." Trey looked at Jackson. He could feel the agent studying him. "They'll like you."

Jackson did a double take. "What?"

"They'll like you. When you meet them, they'll accept you for not only *who* you are but *what* you are to me."

"What am I to you, London? We practically just met today."

Trey grunted. "Do you really believe that?"

Did he? He had to. No matter how close he'd wanted to get to Trey in the past, he hadn't done anything about it, hadn't known for sure whether Trey wanted him in the same way. Could he accept him as something more than a possible lover this quickly?

"How much further?"

Jackson glanced at Trey. "You in a hurry?" Payback could be a bitch.

"I nearly sucked you off while you were driving after you were nearly kidnapped. Does that answer your question?"

"What will your boss say?"

Trey leaned closer and laid his arm along Jackson's shoulders. "You gonna tell him? Because I gotta say if the director of the FBI finds out one of the top federal judges is gay, there might be some negative kickbacks."

"Are you blackmailing me, Agent London? There's got to be some kind of law against that. Not to mention blackmailing a judge can bring hard time."

Trey chuckled and angled even closer. "What if I said I can guarantee if my boss finds out you'll never feel the slide of my tongue on the cock currently tenting your shirt?"

Jackson clenched the steering wheel and swallowed. "Five minutes," he rasped, already anticipating the feel of Trey's mouth on the head of his erection.

"Make it four," Trey growled, squirming in his seat. "And by the way," he whispered, "you asked what my boss would say?"

His teeth scraped along Jackson's earlobe. "He'd say, 'Be discreet.'"

Shit. Jackson nearly choked on his tongue. Must be nice to be out, even if Trey still had to be *discreet* at least he didn't have to hide it from his boss.

The car slid to a stop in front of the judge's house. Trey had never been inside, though he'd once waited in the car for another agent while he talked to Jackson. There were no other cars in evidence. He was damn glad. Trey was out of the car before the engine stopped running and around the hood in five strides. He yanked open the driver's door and hauled Jackson out. A heartbeat later he had the judge plastered against the car and their lips locked.

"Not here," Trey grunted, pulling away from heaven. Damn it. He should at least have enough control to wait until they were inside.

Jackson's freed cock prodded Trey's still-covered one. He wanted to take them both in his fist and pump his hand until they both came, shooting into the air.

"We need to get inside," Trey panted, hoping like hell he made it to the door and didn't spread Jackson out on the stairs of the porch to have his way with him. He'd been serious when he'd said he didn't care who topped as long as one of them was buried in the other.

"Yeah." Jackson's hand traveled to Trey's chest and flicked at a nipple standing taut beneath his shirt. His finger and thumb pinched at the nub, making Trey's breath catch in his throat.

He moved his lips from Jackson's mouth over his chin, up his jaw and covered the lobe of his ear. "Now, Judge. That's an order." Because he sure as shit couldn't wait and Jackson wasn't safe out in the open. Trey covered Jackson's cock and tugged slightly, ready to lead him by the dick if he had to.

Somehow they made it to the front door, hands wandering over each other's bodies, mouths roaming, grunts, groans and moans breaking the silence of the afternoon.

Jackson got the door unlocked and open and a second later, Trey backed him against the wall, turning the deadbolt as he did. "Stay right here," he commanded, slapping the judge's chest and turning to survey the house. He'd be fucking stupid not to check the place out before it got too hot and heavy between them. The last thing he wanted to happen was for them to be ambushed because he hadn't done his job first.

Trey made his way through every room of the house, thanking God along the way Jackson had chosen a more modest home over what his wealth might have afforded him. There were only three bedrooms and closets, four bathrooms, the kitchen—where he found Jackson's dog in a big kennel, asleep and not caring there was a stranger in the house—the living room, dining room, family room and an open, finished basement to search instead of a mansion-sized twenty-six bedroom place that would have been a nightmare to go through in his current, hard-as-a-rock condition.

He returned to the entry foyer to find Jackson still standing where he left him, his cock protruding from his groin as hard as it had been when he'd left him hanging there.

Without a word, Trey clasped both of Jackson's wrists in one of his hands and raised them above his head, trapping them on the wall and pinning Jackson from shoulders to knees with his body. They matched in every way.

He wrapped the fingers of his free hand around Jackson's erection. His cock was as firm as steel yet soft as silk, and somehow felt different than any other lover he'd ever held. Like perfection and forever. It was the forever thought that shot through him. An awareness and immediate acceptance that this particular man was the one he'd been waiting for.

He bit down on the flesh of Jackson's neck. "I need you, Judge."

"Have me. Wait. How's the head?" His gaze flicked to the butterfly bandage. "If you need to wait—"

Trey had forgotten about his head. He realized now there was a dull ache but nothing that would stop him from being with Jackson. And since he knew for a fact there was no one in the house, there wouldn't be any other distractions.

Trey let his lips wander down the length of Jackson's neck. God the skin of his throat tasted like man, musk and lingering aftershave. Made Trey want to move lower and find out if he tasted the same all over. So he did.

"Keep these here." Trey pressed on Jackson's wrist to punctuate his command and used both hands to lift Jackson's shirt up and off.

He knelt, running his hands down Jackson's chest and abs. His tight, muscular pecs were covered in a splash of light brown, curly hair, the same shade as on his head, which tapered into a straight line leading to the ultimate reward.

Jackson's fingers speared into Trey's hair. He glanced up at his soon-to-be lover's eyes. "Put the hand back up, Judge."

Jackson's eyes widened, his nostrils flared and he swallowed. "I need to touch you."

"You want my lips around this?" Trey wrapped his hand around the circumference of the thick erection staring him in the face and gave a slow stroke from base to tip.

Jackson hissed. "Fuck. Don't play with me, London."

"You don't like this?" He rubbed his thumb over the rubbery head, spreading the drop of pre-come.

A long, drawn-out groan rumbled from Jackson's throat.

"If you don't want to play though, I can st—"

"You stop now, and I'll have you arrested for torturing a federal judge."

"Ooh, pulling out the judicial guns." Trey leaned in and swept the flat of his tongue through the weeping slit. Goddamn. He did taste mighty fine all over. Trey unbuttoned and unzipped his own fly, needing to ease the ache pounding in his own cock.

Flicking his tongue over the sensitive head, he lapped up the salty essence beaded there, teasing Jackson. The judge's head rolled back and forth on the wall, but his hands remained where Trey had commanded.

Without warning, he engulfed Jackson's cock, swallowing him until his nose touched Jackson's abdomen.

"Holy shit!" Jackson's hips shot away from the wall, almost knocking Trey off his feet.

He grinned around his mouthful. His lovers were always surprised by how much he could take. He slowly withdrew, hollowing his cheeks out as he sucked.

"Oh my God." Jackson's hand left its position to tangle in Trey's hair again and Trey let him.

It wouldn't take long for the judge to come.

No one had ever sucked his cock the way Trey London was currently trying to draw his balls through his urethra. Holy shit, the man had a mouth of a god. Never had anyone taken his entire length, deep-throating him with the ease Trey seemed to have naturally. No gagging, no choking, just pure swallowing as if he'd done it a million times.

His vision swam with a green haze. He didn't want to think about Agent London being with another man. If he were ever introduced to any of them, he was liable to end up the defendant dressed in orange in his own courtroom, because Jackson could easily see himself killing any man who touched Trey.

In the space of a few hours, Trey had gone from someone Jackson desired from afar to a man he wanted as more than a temporary lover. And if he could think at all while Trey's tongue licked a heated path up the vein underneath his cock, he might be able to look more into the notion.

Later. Jackson tensed when Trey shoved his jeans off his hips and cupped his balls, tugging and rolling them in his hand almost like they were a pair of those musical balls used for de-stressing. A long finger prodded his anus, not entering, just teasing the rim, making it pucker open.

"Fuck." Jesus, he'd been reduced to using less than three word phrases. Some of them not even intelligent, more grunts and groans than actual words.

His balls drew up tight and the tingle began, growing more and more persistent. Trey swallowed him whole, moaning as if he couldn't get enough. Jackson couldn't help the way his hips jerked forward. Trey disappeared.

"Fuck no," Jackson growled, reaching for Trey's head. "Finish me."

Trey chuckled. "Relax, Judge." He took his finger into his mouth, wetting it until it shined with spit, and resumed his ministration.

That long, lean finger slid into Jackson's opening effortlessly to the palm.

Sweat beaded on Jackson's forehead. Trey's finger deep inside him nudged his prostate and the fireworks started. Or the eruption did anyway. His balls unloaded, releasing their come in a series of mini explosions. Trey sucked him dry, milking every single drop from his cock. His finger slipped from Jackson's anus and he covered Jackson's hips to keep him still while he licked him clean.

Jackson's knees collapsed, sending him sliding down the wall to the floor in a heap. Purring, Trey kissed his way from Jackson's softening cock, over his navel, paused at his nipples where he tugged them deep into his mouth, and finally to his lips where Jackson tasted himself on his lover.

Still panting, he pushed his tongue into the agent's mouth. It wasn't enough. He needed, no, wanted to reciprocate.

"As soon as I catch my breath, you're mine."

Trey laughed. "As much as I'd like you to, there's no time. We shouldn't have gone this far even." He sat up and Jackson saw for the first time Trey's cock was hanging out of his fly. It glistened and Jackson knew Trey had found release with him.

"We for damn sure needed the release, Trey. Don't tell me you regret it."

"Hell no." Trey's chest rumbled against Jackson's where he lay atop him. "But we came to get your shit and your dog, not fuck. I need you at a safe house."

Jackson snorted. "You don't think we were safe here with the front door standing open?"

Trey leapt to his feet and swore.

Jackson laughed out loud and stood. "Got you." He winked at his new lover and pulled him in by the back of his neck for another mind-blowing kiss.

"I'll get my shit, as you so nicely put it, and my pooch, but before we go anywhere, I have to go talk to my father. He needs to be made aware of the situation." Jackson nestled his sated penis back in his pants and grabbed his shirt off the floor. Trey followed him through the house to the kitchen.

"The situation between you and me?" Trey came to a standstill behind him.

"Hell no," Jackson retorted. "About the possible danger following me. Besides, he might be able to shed some light on Caleb."

"This isn't your fault. Even if it isn't Caleb, you know better than anyone there are some sick fuckers out there. You just happened to catch the attention of one."

They stopped in front of Corky's crate. The dog sat up, thumped his tail on the rather impressive bedding Jackson had put inside and gave a sharp bark in greeting. He was one of the mangiest looking mutts Trey had ever seen. Missing an eye and half a front leg, Corky was a piss-poor excuse for a dog. Yet the second Jackson opened the gate, it bounded out to dance, three-legged, around him, tongue hanging out and tail wagging so hard Jackson was amazed the damn thing didn't fall off.

"Meet Corky."

Trey snorted. "That's not a dog."

Jackson crouched down and rubbed the scruff of Corky's neck. "Don't say mean things. You are too a dog, aren't you? Aren't you, boy? Yes Corky's a good boy."

"Please tell me you don't talk to him like this all the time."

Jackson stood, his hand still reaching for Corky's head. "If you hurt his feelings, he may eat you while you sleep."

Trey raised an eyebrow. "Be kinda hard from the confines of his crate."

Jackson looked down at the kennel. "Oh, he's only in there when no one's home. At night he sleeps with me."

"Not in my fucking bed he won't."

"And why would he be sleeping in your bed?"

Trey stepped closer, only stopping when they were toe to toe. "Because in my bed is where *you'll* be."

The corner of the judge's mouth kicked up. "Where will you be while I'm sleeping in your bed?"

He grazed Jackson's lips with his own and rasped, "Spooned against your naked body."

"Sounds good to me."

"You still gonna sic Corky on me?"

"Absolutely not." Jackson wrapped both hands around Trey's face and sealed their mouths together.

Minutes later, after they'd staggered clear across the kitchen to end up pinned against the counter, the kiss ended. Eyes glazed, cocks rubbing each other, chests heaving, they broke apart.

"I can't fucking stop touching you." Jackson spun on his heel and stormed to the master bedroom. He looked over his shoulder. "You have cuffs, right?" he asked, changing the subject completely.

Trey's answer was drawn out. "Yesss. Any particular reason you need to know if I have cuffs?"

Jackson shrugged and started throwing shirts and pants from his dresser into a suitcase he tugged from the closet. "You might have to make an arrest."

"Your father won't do a damn thing in front of a federal agent, Judge. Whether or not you're his son."

"Probably not."

Trey cocked his head. "Then what—"

"He might not, but I can't guarantee I won't. Things tend to get a little volatile when we're in the same room."

Chapter Five

"Where is he, Cordelia?" Jackson strode briskly through the front door of the mansion he'd grown up in, right past the housekeeper who'd practically raised him. Partially because he was pumped up and ready for a likely confrontation with his father and partially because Corky was dragging him full force. The second Jackson dropped the leash, Corky bounded off straight to the kitchen where he knew from previous rare visits he would be given scraps from the cook.

"Oh, Jackson. He's not..."

Jackson rounded on the small woman. "Don't tell me he's not seeing visitors, Cordelia. I'm his son and he'll see me whether he wants to or not." He spun back around and headed for a closed set of doors.

"But I, bu..."

Jackson stopped and looked over his shoulder at the woman closer to him than his own mother. Maria Benedict loved him in her own way, despite the fault she perceived him as having, but she'd always been less than...motherly.

"Cordelia, is it?" Trey took hold of her elbow. She smiled up at him and he grinned back. "It's a fine time for Daddy and son to talk. Don't worry. We'll be out of your hair in a few minutes."

Cordelia raised a hand to her hair and Jackson snorted a short laugh. Trey had played right into the older woman's hands.

"You're him, aren't you?" she asked, a look of wonder in her eyes.

Trey raised an eyebrow and Jackson turned more fully to face them. He could hear his father's voice through the door but nothing would take him away from Trey facing Cordelia.

"I am who?"

"Jackson's lover," Cordelia said matter-of-factly. "You two are perfect for each other."

Trey let go of Cordelia and retreated. He cleared his throat and jerked his gaze to Jackson.

Eyes wide, Jackson took a step toward them. If anyone outside his family knew of his affinity for men it was Cordelia. Hell, she'd probably known it longer than Jackson had. But how had she known about Trey? Were they broadcasting that much? If so maybe Jackson should talk to Allenton on his own, because he sure the fuck didn't want to get into a discussion with him about Trey.

He glanced at his new lover, wondering what Trey wanted him to say. He didn't need to wonder.

"I am."

The housekeeper grew giddy. She actually jumped up and down and clapped her hands. "Thank God he found you. I know he's been waiting for the exact special man."

"Cordelia," Jackson groaned, feeling his cheeks go red.

"No, it's all right, Judge." Trey gave her another one of those award-winning smiles. The one that melted Jackson in his spot and hardened his cock.

"Jackson and I have just started this relationship. But we'll be sure to let you know how it goes."

"That's great. Jackson's such a nice boy."

Shit. She might as well pat them both on the cheeks and tell them they were good boys for playing so well together. He shook his head.

"Jackson is thirty-eight years old," Jackson grumbled.

"What happened to your head?" Cordelia reached for the cut on Trey's head, ignoring Jackson.

"Car accident. Nothing to worry about, ma'am."

She clucked her tongue at him. "Be more careful next time."

Trey nodded. "I will."

Jackson chuckled.

"Let me know how the deal goes." Allenton's voice sounded behind him. "I've got to go now," he continued after realizing he had an audience.

"Mr. Benedict." Trey lowered his head slightly, giving Jackson's father more respect then the man deserved.

"Father."

"Why are you here, son? Don't you have court today?"

"I did, but some issues have come up."

"What kind of issues?" Allenton huffed. He was good at huffing. His chest puffed up as if he were the most important man alive. He jerked his chin at Trey. "Who's he?"

"A federal agent," Jackson said dismissively. "Issues such as him finding a tracking device stuck to the bottom of my car, someone getting into my house to steal out of my safe, and pictures. Oh, and there's the *issue* of Caleb Murphy trying to get into my office at the courthouse. I hear he'll be needing some representation fairly soon."

Allenton's eyes narrowed. "Pictures of what?"

Jackson bristled. It was just like Allenton to disregard the fact that one of his underlings had done something wrong and hit on the one thing that perked his pea-sized brain. He knew exactly what his father was envisioning at the mention of pictures. He should have left them off.

"It's not important wh—"

"It is if it's of you and one of your fags."

Jackson advanced on him. "Don't even fucking say one more word."

Allenton's top lip curled into a snarl and his eye twitched. To Jackson, it was a dead giveaway to the disgust he felt over his son.

"And don't *you* dare talk to *me* that way, boy."

"Cordelia, would you excuse us?" Trey asked, stepping between Jackson and Allenton. He gestured them into the room his father had vacated and followed them in, shutting the door behind him. "Maybe I should get us all a drink."

"Are you one of his fag whores?" Allenton shouted, miffed no doubt for having been called out by his own son.

"What I am is the man charged with keeping your son's life intact. Or have you already forgotten about the threats he just told you about? Surely you're not more worried about his chosen lifestyle over his safety, hmm? Or could it be you're the one sending them? Did you decide to try and scare your son straight?"

Christ. Jackson hadn't thought about that. Surely it wasn't true. He'd done a lot of dirty things in the face of Jackson's preference but still, he wouldn't stoop so low as to stalk his own son or hire someone else to do it...say, Caleb?

Would he?

Jackson sat in one of the two leather armchairs facing his father's desk. Allenton marched around the hundred-year-old piece of furniture as if he couldn't do anything without its protection.

He looked Jackson square in the eye. "I asked you if you were fucking him. I'll have his ass kicked out of the agency so fast his head will spin."

Jackson catapulted from the chair.

Trey chuckled. "Fucking my charge would be against agency policy, wouldn't it?" Something in Trey's voice alerted Jackson. He wasn't trying to hide what was happening between them, he simply didn't think Allenton Benedict needed or deserved to know a damn thing.

Jackson wanted to kiss him. He wanted to lay him across the antique desk and fuck him until they both came.

Allenton lifted his chin. "All my son needs is a real woman."

"You mean like mother?" Jackson sneered. "A woman who cowers behind her husband because she's afraid of what you might do to her should she stand up for herself?"

Allenton's ears glowed red. "I will not have you speak about your mother that way," he spat.

"But you'll talk to me any way you want too? Tell me you don't know anything about the tracking device, *Dad*."

"I don't know what you're talking about. Trust me, son, I don't need a tracking device to know whose ass you've dipped your wick in. I have eyes and ears all over the place."

The blood leeched from Jackson's face. Allenton truly was one sick bastard.

"They help me by making sure the whole world doesn't find out you're a queer by running interference and I pay them well. A fucking Benedict, for God's sake," he sneered.

Trey took a step and Jackson saw his hand fisting. He held up a palm to stop him. No need to get into a knock-down, drag-out fight. Not with a man who looked apoplectic. Trey subsided and leaned a hip against the desk to watch the show, ignoring Allenton's gasp. Trey crossed his arms over his chest, looking good enough to eat.

Jackson dropped his hand to his side, tired of having the same old argument with his father. His own fucking father had been having him followed. Which meant he *could* have been the one to take the picture of him and his friends. At least he hadn't been having him followed today or he would have known that he and Trey had hardly made it through Jackson's front door before Trey had sucked him dry.

"Your spies must be bored out of their minds then, since I haven't had a lover in over a year, don't you think?"

"I've tried to give you a life," Allenton snapped, slapping his hands on the desktop and sending a few slips of paper fluttering into the air. "Woman after woman after woman I handed to you on a silver platter."

Jackson knew firsthand how some of those women came packaged. One he had found nude in his bed upon returning home late one night. Another had mysteriously appeared in his car, countless others had been thrust on him at various social functions.

"How the fuck do you think you made federal judge as young as you did?"

Jackson saw red. For years he'd wondered about this. How someone his age could be appointed a federal bench. He'd tried to believe it was because he'd graduated so young from law school but Jackson wasn't stupid. He knew it had something to do with his family connections, but he liked to believe he'd gotten so far on his own merit.

Apparently he'd been deluding himself.

He ground his teeth until they hurt. "If I ever catch you having me followed, I will resign from my bench and never look back."

Allenton laughed.

Jackson smiled. His father didn't think he would ever give up such a prestigious lifestyle. What Allenton didn't know was how much thought his son had already given the idea.

"Just tell us about Caleb."

Allenton's chin rose haughtily. "The only thing I know about Caleb is that the partners have been watching him closely."

"As one of those partners don't you think you can give me a little more info?"

His father's nose flared as he sucked in a breath. "He's been losing cases left and right and there's been talk he's doing so on purpose."

"For what purpose?" Trey interjected.

Allenton barely flicked a glance at the agent. "Money, what else?"

Trey cleared his throat. "So you say you had nothing to do with the device—"

"Then why the hell did you accuse me of it?" Allenton snapped, still not gracing Trey with his eyes.

Trey ignored his outburst. "Because it hasn't been proved that you didn't do it. What about the other warnings?"

Allenton finally looked at him. "I don't know anything about them either. If I want my son to do something, I tell him."

"Does he listen?" Trey asked with a hint of amusement.

"If he knows what's good for him."

Jackson didn't even try to hold his snort of laughter back. Allenton was one delusional man.

"So you have no clue who might have broken into your son's house and taken a baseball card from the safe, or anything about the two men who attempted to kidnap the judge from his car today?"

His father regarded Jackson in silence for a moment with an odd look on his face. "No," he finally said, and walked out of the room, concluding the discussion.

℘

"You and your old man put on a good show." Trey pulled into his assigned parking space and cut the engine. Jackson had handed him the keys to his Acura—apparently having abandoned his previous notion of not allowing anyone to drive his car—after leaving his parents' house without saying a word. Trey had let him stew in the car, thinking Jackson would talk when he was ready. He was tired of the silence.

"You don't know how bad I wanted to put my fist through his face."

"Uh, yeah I do. I wanted to, too. You stopped me from doing it, remember?" He stared at his place, his heart racing as he imagined what would happen inside. Very few people outside the agency knew of his condo and it would be almost impossible to trace him here since it was mortgaged under one of his distant cousin's names.

"I'm hard as a rock."

Trey turned in his seat and faced Jackson. There was a predatory gleam in his eye. "Me too."

"Then perhaps we should get inside and do something about it."

Trey reached over and swiped the lock of hair from Jackson's forehead. "You mean, you didn't have a date all lined up for tonight?"

"Not until you smashed me against the wall in my office and kissed me within an inch of my life. Then it was kind of clear what I'd be doing tonight." His head advanced ever so slowly, his lips parted.

Trey palmed Jackson's cheek and rubbed a thumb across the prominent bone beneath one of his beautiful hazel eyes. "I think I can make it worth your while."

"Yeah?"

Corky whined from his position in the backseat.

"Oh yeah." Trey ignored the strange beast and touched his lips to Jackson's, savoring the softness.

"Agent London," Jackson breathed, "as much as I like this, I'd much rather have you in a bed instead of out here in the open where we keep starting these things."

"Let's go then, because there is nowhere I'd rather be either."

Trey couldn't remember the trip from the car to the front door or Jackson stowing Corky in his crate in the front hall for the time being. Could be because he'd been so busy studying Jackson's very fine, taut ass hidden behind the thick denim of his jeans.

Maybe that's also how he missed walking down the hall with their lips locked together while trying to divest each other of their clothes. Less than a minute later Trey found himself staring at more than six feet of tanned muscular body complete with major, mouthwatering hard-on.

"Where's the lube?"

Trey raised an eyebrow. "No foreplay?"

"Fuck foreplay. I need you. Now."

"Top drawer," he said with a flick of his chin.

By the time Jackson retrieved the lube and turned back around, his hand was already glistening and slick. When it wrapped around Trey's cock without preamble, he hissed and thrust into the fist.

"On your bed, Agent London."

Trey swallowed. This was one Valentine's Day he'd remember forever. He withdrew slowly from the fingers curled around his erection and sauntered to the bed. Placing one knee on the mattress, he started in on giving Jackson a little show of his own.

Waggling his ass, he crawled toward the headboard and looked over his shoulder.

"What now, Judge?"

Jackson took hold of his cock and stroked it from root to tip. He knelt on the bed behind Trey, straddling his calves until the front of his thighs touched the back of Trey's. "Now I bury my cock inside you."

His hands wandered over the globes of Trey's ass, making him shiver. He wanted to beg Jackson to grab his balls, but bit his tongue. Jackson seemed to want the control.

"Spread your knees." Jackson's thumbs centered on the ring of muscle shielding his anus and spread his cheeks apart, opening him for Jackson's gaze.

Trey scooted his knees further apart and gasped when Jackson reached between his legs to fondle his sack.

"Shit."

The hand on his ass disappeared, leaving Trey feeling somehow empty. There was a slurping noise, like someone slathering lube on their cock.

Trey clenched his ass and his nipples hardened. The anticipation was killing him. He dropped his head. "Any time," he growled.

A hard slap rent the air a split second before a sharp sting flared across his right butt cheek.

"What the fuck was that for?"

"This is my turn. You had yours back at my house," Jackson said simply.

Goddamn if the spank hadn't made his dick harder. The fingers at his balls squeezed, adding another warning. It only served to make him hornier. One finger traced his crack, pausing to swirl the tight ring of muscles and deposit some of the lube.

The tip of Jackson's finger entered him to the knuckle. It was a start, but not near enough.

"Wait 'til I get the chocolate out, Judge."

"Chocolate? Sounds intriguing." His tongue followed the path of his finger.

"Stop fucking teasing."

"Turnabout is fair play. God you taste good."

Fuck the control issue. "Inside me, now, or I flip us and suck your balls dry."

"Hmm. Sounds like a win-win for me."

"Judge," he snarled.

"Fine."

The next thing touching his ass was much bigger than a fingertip. Trey knew exactly what the mushroom-shaped, velvety-soft head currently pushing against his anus tasted like.

"Shit."

"What? Don't stop," Trey panted, anticipating what was to come.

"No condom."

"Damn." Trey lowered his face to the bed. He'd been so caught up in Jackson he hadn't even thought about protection. How much did that say about the way he felt about his judge?

Trey looked back over his shoulder, decision already made. "I'm clean," he rasped. "Physicals at the agency every six months. I'm good if you are, Judge."

The muscle along Jackson's jaw twitched and he jerked his head in a nod. "I'm good with it." His fingertips stroked Trey's spine. "And I'm clean too."

Trey's gaze connected with Jackson's. Damn but he wanted him for more than the sex they were about to share. "I believe you."

Jackson returned to Trey's opening, pressing against him once again with the head of cock. "Sure you don't need me to open you up a little?"

Jesus, don't let Jackson start going soft. Trey wanted hard, he wanted fast, and he didn't want to wait. He shoved his hips back, impaling himself on Jackson's cock.

"Guess not," Jackson gasped. He withdrew then hammered back in, nicking Trey's prostate.

Trey gritted his teeth against the sensation and fisted the comforter. His eyes rolled when Jackson touched the spot a second time. Then Jackson took hold of Trey's cock to pump it in time with his thrusting and Trey thought he might die. Sex had never felt this good before. Another sure sign that His Honor Jackson Benedict was more to him than a passing lover.

"Christ, I'm not gonna last." Sweat dripped from Jackson's forehead to land on the small of Trey's back.

"Me...either," Trey grunted. His balls drew up tight, signaling his impending orgasm. It couldn't come soon enough. He didn't want it to come too soon.

They cried out together, Jackson's come shooting deep in Trey's rectum, Trey's spurting anywhere from his stomach to the comforter.

Jackson continued stroking Trey's penis as he leaned over his back. His head rested between Trey's shoulder blades and his mouth pecked small kisses on his sweat-slicked skin. They both breathed heavily.

For long seconds they stayed in this position, unable to speak, only to feel each other's bodies, skin to skin. Then Trey's elbows started to wobble and down he went, face first into the mattress, taking Jackson with him. The action caused the judge's softening cock to slip from the shield of his body.

Jackson's lips moved to the crook of Trey's neck and wandered up, over his jaw and onto his earlobe. "When can we do it again?"

Chapter Six

Darkness had completely fallen by the time Jackson woke up. It took him a few minutes to remember where he was, who he was with. He smiled when he did and turned onto his side, seeking Trey's warm body.

He didn't find it. His hand encountered cold sheets instead. Jackson rose up on his elbow and glanced around the room. He hadn't seen any part of Trey's room earlier, only the nude body of the man he'd wanted for so long he could hardly think straight when they were in the same room.

Corky stirred in his crate. They'd carried it into the bedroom so he wouldn't feel so lonely in the night.

"London?" No one answered his call but there was noise coming from somewhere in the house. He groaned and rubbed his face. Priority one, use the john. His self-appointed bodyguard was number two on the list.

After making use of Trey's restroom, Jackson tugged on his jeans and ventured out of the bedroom and followed the sounds of...Trey singing? He chuckled. Just his luck that the man he loved did not do Bon Jovi any justice.

Love? Jackson came to a standstill in the hallway and propped his hip against the wall. Where the hell had the word love come from? And why did it feel so goddamn right?

More important, did Trey feel anything close to the same way?

"You give love..."

"Stop!" he yelled, jerking out of his musings. "Your singing leaves much to be desired." Jackson laughed and moved through the door.

And almost swallowed his tongue.

His lover stood in the opening of the refrigerator, illuminated by the light inside it, buck naked.

"Hungry?"

Jackson couldn't look away from Trey's impressive package. He nodded. "Uh-huh."

Trey snorted. "Not for that." He closed the door and padded to the table. "Well, not yet, anyway. I was thinking more along the lines of sandwiches and chips. We missed dinner."

"We *were* a little busy, weren't we?" Jackson glanced at his watch. Not as late as he thought. Only ten twenty-four. Still, must have been the orgasm of the century—and it had been— for him to zonk out for a few hours.

He pulled out the chair across from Trey and took the plate offered him. Trey had no problem stacking a huge sandwich with turkey, ham, cheese, lettuce, tomato, with a smattering of mustard on the rye bread, and taking a huge bite.

A squirt of yellow oozed from the corner of his mouth. Jackson put his hands on the table and bent over.

Trey leaned back. "Want a bite?"

"Nope. Come here."

Eyes wide, Trey brought his face closer, the sandwich forgotten in his hand between them. Jackson pulled him in with a hand around his neck and licked the spot of mustard.

"Spicy," he whispered, still nibbling Trey's lips. With his other hand, he flicked at a raised nipple.

"Shit." Trey rested his forehead on Jackson's. "So much for eating."

"I think I'm in the mood for something a little sweeter."

"Yeah? What's that?"

"Where's that chocolate sauce you were talking about earlier?" Jackson pushed his tongue inside Trey's mouth when he started to speak, sealing their lips. Trey tilted his head, giving him better access, and parried with his own tongue. The kiss was sweet, passionate, and led to a raging hard-on needing to be dealt with immediately.

"Somewhere in there." Trey thumbed over his shoulder.

Jackson shoved away from the table and threw open the refrigerator door. He was expecting the empty shelves of a traditional bachelor's fridge, instead he found fresh fruits and vegetables, meats, and various other, *real* food that Jackson's housekeeper kept his own stocked with.

There it was, right behind the ketchup.

Aaaa-lleluia, alleluia, alleluia, alleeee-lluuu-ia.

Several things tumbled to the floor, one shattering when he yanked the brown bottle of the gods out and flipped the cap open with his thumb. Eyes narrowed, he turned to face Trey. His lover sat in his chair, legs sprawled apart, one arm propped on the table, the other lazily scratching his chest, and his cock at full staff.

"You broke my pickles."

Jackson ran his tongue around the rim of the chocolate. "I'll buy you a new jar." He stepped between Trey's legs and upended the chocolate, drizzling it over his lover's six-pack abs. Trey hissed as the cold touched his skin. Both hands went behind his head and pure lust glittered in his eyes.

Jackson lifted one corner of his mouth and trailed the sauce further south to trickle down the smooth tip of his cock. When he was satisfied with the amount of chocolate coating Trey's tanned skin, he tossed the bottle over his shoulder.

"Add chocolate sauce to the list of things you owe me," Trey murmured.

"Done." Jackson kneeled before his feast and ran his palms up Trey's thighs. He'd planned on starting at the nipples, but he couldn't resist. Without breaking eye contact, he bent and licked Trey's chocolate-covered cock like it was a popsicle.

Trey's knees locked, his heels dug into the tiled floor, one hand slapped the table, and the other gripped the seat of his chair with white knuckles.

"Christ." Trey's hips lifted, thrusting his cock deeper into Jackson's mouth.

Jackson knew he wouldn't be able to take it the same way Trey had taken his. Just because he couldn't deep throat wouldn't make it any less enjoyable. He sucked in what he could, licking the chocolate from Trey's erection and teasing him with flicks of his tongue.

Trey groaned and bit his lip. His eyes closed, his nostrils flared with his quick intake of breath.

Jackson took hold of Trey's balls. They were pulled up tight. Trey wouldn't last long. Taking one last draw on the mushroom-shaped head, Jackson released him.

"Why are you stopping?" Trey growled.

Jackson chuckled. "Because I'm not ready for you to come." He wrapped his fingers around Trey's cock and smoothed his thumb through the slit at the top. "I want you to suffer." Jackson jumped to his feet and looked around the kitchen. There had to be something else to add to his dessert.

Ooh. Just the thing. He crossed the room in three strides and snagged what had caught his attention.

"My own fondue." Jackson slowly peeled the banana he held and took a bite. Trey's cock twitched.

"Mmm. Nice and ripe." He swiped the banana through the stream of chocolate running from Trey's navel to the base of his cock and bit down again. "Even better. Bite?"

Trey nodded, his jaw bunched tight.

"You eat this and I'll work some more on this," he said pointing at Trey's groin.

Trey swallowed. "Seems like a good tradeoff."

Jackson ran the banana over one of Trey's nipples, coating it with chocolate again before handing it to him and kneeling once more.

He returned to feasting on his lover, pulling on his cock and teasing his balls with one hand. The other he let wander along the sensitive length between his sac and anus. He stopped at the opening and rimmed it with his fingertip.

Trey shifted, scooting his butt closer to the edge to give Jackson better access. Jackson slid his finger through the pool of chocolate in Trey's navel and returned to his anus, easily penetrating the ring of muscle.

"Ah, fuck." Trey's hips shot upward, impaling Jackson's mouth with more than he could take.

He fought the gag reflex and lost. Tears sprang to his eyes but he held on until Trey sagged in the chair. He took control, pressing Trey down with his forearm while bobbing his head up and down along his length and plunged his finger in and out, tapping the small gland that would send shockwaves through Trey's body.

"If you don't swallow," Trey growled, "you better release me now."

Hell yeah he swallowed. Wouldn't trade this experience for the world.

"Judge," Trey warned again.

Jackson didn't release him. He hollowed his cheeks and doubled his efforts, ready to taste London's come for the first time. He was rewarded with a hot spurt against his throat and a firm squeeze on the finger inside Trey's anus.

He worked Trey until the man's entire body went limp and he started to slide from the chair. His eyelids drooped, his chest heaved with every breath, and Jackson was pretty sure Trey's toes were curled.

Jackson nibbled and licked his way up from the still chocolaty puddle in Trey's bellybutton, between his pecs, along his throat, over his chin and settled on his lips. Banana and chocolate and Trey all rolled into one.

"That was by far the best Valentine I've ever received," Trey rasped, grabbing Jackson's hair and holding him still for a deep kiss.

"It was pretty nice for me too."

"What time do you have to be in court tomorrow?" The gleam was back in Trey's eyes and Jackson got the feeling it would be a really long night.

"Eight."

Trey groaned. "I was hoping to have breakfast in bed."

"You still can, it'll just have to be an early one."

"Oh, I intend for it to be, Judge." Trey palmed Jackson's cock through his jeans. "Reciprocation is definitely in order."

"Now's good for me." Jackson nuzzled Trey's cheek. He felt like they were a part of one another, that they'd been together for years and couldn't bare the thought of being separated from him. In actuality it had been what? Seven or eight hours?

Trey's mouth moved on Jackson's ear. "I think I need a shower to get all this sticky off."

"Need help?"

"Absolutely."

Trey made sure the water was warm before dragging Jackson into the spacious marble-walled shower behind him. Water sluiced down his back, massaging his neck and shoulders. He wrapped his arms around Jackson's torso until they were skin to skin.

Their entire bodies were pressed together. Knees, thighs, cock, abs, chests and lips. Nothing would ever feel more perfect than the man in his arms. Their mouths melded, their tongues dueled and they were reduced to grunts and groans.

Trey found himself thrusting his hips, looking for the friction he desperately needed for a cock that seemed insatiable. Jackson's hand slid between them and took both their cocks in his fist. Trey fell forward, moaning and pushing Jackson up against the wall.

"God damn, Judge." His penis swelled as Jackson's thumb rubbed over the head, spreading the drop of pre-come. How the fuck could there be any come left in his body when Jackson had just drained it not ten minutes ago?

Up and down he stroked them, bringing them to a peak in less than a minute. No foreplay, no teasing, no need to build it up. They both stared down at their erections snuggled tightly together in Jackson's fist and watched them erupt, shooting spurts of thick white come on their bellies.

Trey rested his forehead on Jackson's. "How many times do you think we can do this before they fall off?"

"Oh, at least a lifetime's worth or more."

"You think?"

"I know." Jackson kissed Trey's forehead and turned him around. Trey found a softening cock nestled in the crack of his ass.

An arm reached over his shoulder to grab the shampoo and then magical fingers worked through his hair—ever so careful of his wound and not getting it wet—rubbing his scalp until Trey thought he might melt.

"Turn."

Trey did and tilted his head back, allowing Jackson to rinse the suds from his hair. Somehow he managed not to disturb the bandaged area. Soapy hands wandered down his torso, cleaning every inch of him down to his toes.

"Turn again," Jackson murmured and continued washing Trey from the back this time. When he was done, Jackson spun Trey in a slow circle, dousing his body.

The cleansing exploration had hardened him. "Down," he commanded his cock.

Jackson laughed. "I feel like I'll be telling myself that a lot around you."

Trey twirled his finger in the air. "Now it's my turn to wash you."

Jackson held his hands in front of him. "By all means."

Lathering his hands, Trey soaped Jackson's hard body, taking particular care to stay away from his groin. His erection would come last. It needed the most attention.

"Rinse," he murmured, kissing the tip of one of Jackson's peaked nipples.

Hands in the air, Jackson did a three-sixty, washing the soap away. "You forgot an important part."

"I didn't forget it." Trey slowly dropped to his knees, pressing kisses everywhere on Jackson's body he could reach on the way down. When he looked up, Jackson's eyes were glazed with heat. His cock bobbed against his chin. "I was saving the best for last."

Trey took the fat purple head into his mouth and sucked. Jackson's hiss could be heard above the roar of the shower. He lapped at the slit, tasting the creamy pre-come, then licked his way around the head, flicking at the nerve rich spot underneath.

Releasing him, Trey explored the vein running the length of Jackson's penis with his lips, nipping and sipping at him. With one hand, he fondled the sac between Jackson's legs. Jackson stepped farther apart allowing Trey better access. Still cupping his balls, Trey pressed on his perineum, massaging the nerves with the tip of his finger. Jackson stood on his tiptoes, his knees bowing out, and his hands flew up to the walls as an anchor.

Trey smiled and gripped the base of Jackson's cock with his free hand a second before taking what was left into his mouth.

"Shit."

He loved reducing the judge to one word grunts. The tip of his finger easily slipped past the ring of muscles, and Jackson impaled himself as he dropped to his heels again.

"Fuck."

Trey worked his lover's cock with his mouth and his hand, knowing he wouldn't last long despite having come a few minutes earlier. He loved the taste of Jackson, loved the way he squirmed trying to get closer yet trying to prolong things at the same time. Trey didn't allow retreat. Removing his hand, Trey took Jackson to the back of his throat. He couldn't see Jackson's face since he had his head thrown back.

With the combination of penetration, massage and sucking, he had Jackson coming down his throat in seconds. Trey licked him clean, making sure all the tremors were gone before he stood.

"I can't even think when you do that," Jackson rasped.

Trey grinned. "Then I've done my job well."

Chapter Seven

Trey watched Jackson roll his head on his neck, working out the kinks their sleepless night had probably given him. Trey had a few of his own. Damn, it had been a long time since he'd gone that many rounds with someone.

Security had been tight at the courthouse, like always. They'd each flashed a badge at the guard and then succumbed to the wand. No one got in with weapons, except those in law enforcement like himself, and no one got by without going through a metal detector and having their bags or briefcases checked. You could hardly go anywhere nowadays without encountering heightened security.

Trey was still weary over the conglomeration of items the judge had received thus far. Thank God they hadn't walked into his office this morning to find something else waiting for him. Trey still sported a headache from his run-in with the car window yesterday. Finding another package would have caused it to go supernova.

Last night between serious bouts of lovemaking, he'd laid awake, wracking his brain for clues. He'd learned there weren't any fingerprints on the tracking device so there was no way of knowing, short of a confession, who'd placed it. Was it possible they were looking at more than one suspect? It seemed almost too much of a coincidence if they were. Especially based on the trial Jackson was currently trying and the family involved. The Savantis were notorious for their mob-like mentality and these were precisely the type of things they'd use to intimidate a judge before moving on to a more physical approach. The Savantis were the obvious choice for culprits. What better way to get the prodigal son a get-out-of-jail-free card then by harassing or threatening the judge into dropping the case.

Yet Trey couldn't and wouldn't discount Caleb Murphy either. Until he got the full dossier on the man, Murphy had to remain high on the list of suspects. Had the previous boyfriend cared more about Jackson than he'd led on? Had he hired someone to take the picture of them together to use as blackmail? For what purpose? What could he possibly hope to gain? Money was always an issue and Jackson had money in spades. Other than that, about the only thing Murphy could hope to gain from a federal judge was clemency. What lawyer needed clemency except one on the take? And if what Allenton had said about Caleb losing cases was correct, then Caleb was probably in need of both.

Then there was Allenton Benedict. The man rubbed Trey the wrong way. If Allenton Benedict hated his son's lifestyle enough, maybe he wasn't above sending threats to somehow scare Jackson out of it. He'd have to be pretty wacked out to think the tactic might work but then from what Trey had seen, the man wasn't really running on all cylinders. Of course, if he hated his son enough, he only had to disown him. Trey believed Allenton was using Jackson as his nonstop ticket to Washington D.C. He clearly had his sights set on the Supreme Court through his son. Trey had a suspicious feeling Jackson wasn't on the same track. Then there'd been something about the look on Allenton's face in his office yesterday. The one that said he knew more than he was willing to tell. So just what the hell did he know?

Jackson had given Trey a list of people he knew were aware of the safe in his home office. Originally Jackson had told Trey he was aware that besides him, only his father knew the actual codes, but the list contained eleven names of those who knew exactly where it was. His father, of course, and other family members, the maid, and an assortment of friends and acquaintances, including three of the four men from the photo. Caleb Murphy was one of them. Jackson had said Caleb had left him and that he'd felt used by someone trying out the lifestyle. Had Murphy decided being gay was dirty? Did he think he needed to cleanse Jackson the same way the judge's father did? The other two, Daniel Gardner and Eric Kinder, were lifelong friends of Jackson's.

There were also two past lovers, one of whom was in a permanent relationship and the other had more to lose than Jackson did. Causing some sort of scandal would be the last thing he'd want to do. If Jackson had had any more recent relationships, they hadn't gotten to the point of him taking them home.

Trey had excused himself from the judge's chambers earlier, leaving Jackson alone to get ready to step up to the bench for the continuation of Dominic Savanti's trial, and gotten on the phone. He'd wanted to hurry the background check on Caleb. The sooner he had the information, the better. He hadn't wandered far from the judge, despite leaving him secluded. With the attack yesterday, Trey wanted to be as close as possible to his lover. Now he stared across the courtroom at the man he wanted to stay in his life.

Jackson's gaze lifted and met Trey's. A dull blush graced the judge's cheekbones and Trey could very well guess what images brought the color forth. His heart pounded. His Honor, Judge Jackson Benedict, had captured Trey, body and soul. If it took him forever to find the culprit behind these latest threats, he'd do it.

His cell phone vibrated in his front pocket, providing a reason to finally break eye contact. He flipped it open just as the bailiff called out, "You may be seated." Trey stood and stepped outside the doors, making sure to stay near the small window inset in the door so he could still see the judge while he talked, without disturbing everyone in the courtroom.

"London."

"This is Crenshaw. No fingerprints on the baseball card."

"Damn it." Trey fought the temptation to punch the wall. They were hitting dead ends everywhere they turned. "So we're still at square one." They still had no clue who was stalking the judge. Outside of Murphy, who for whatever reason felt the need to get back in touch with his previous experiment—Jackson.

Trey glanced at Jackson, whose face was impartial as he listened to another witness's testimony. Dominic Savanti, the little slime-ball weasel, twiddled his thumbs and smiled like a Cheshire cat.

They had nothing. Five anonymous gifts with no real meaning beyond, "I hate you and look how close I can get to you," and one botched kidnapping attempt.

"What about the two idiots from yesterday?"

"Nothing. They were trying to help, don't you know? Just wanted to make sure the judge wasn't hurt, when he jumped them. Of course they had to defend themselves."

Trey snorted. "Why the fuck didn't they ask about my well being, since I was the one they rammed?" Something Crenshaw said stirred in his head. "Wait. Back up. What exactly did they say?"

"They had wanted to make sure the judge was not hurt when he jumped them. They cried self-defense, for what, I don't—"

"How the fuck did they know he was a judge if they weren't there specifically for him? I was very careful not to say anything in their presence. They might have known who I was, but they shouldn't have known who Judge Benedict was." Trey's gaze swept over the visitors watching the proceedings. There was momentary silence on the other end of the line.

"Shit. You're right. I'm reading the statement right now. It says word for word, 'We didn't know the judge was gonna jump us, we was just making sure he wasn't hurt.'"

"Go back there and find out who the fuck they're working for." As soon as they knew who'd hired those two idiots, they'd have their stalker.

And Jackson Benedict would be free to walk out of Trey's condo.

Not if Trey had anything to say about it.

"Will do. Everyone else from the photo checks out. Well, sort of. Daniel Gardner's ex-wife says she hasn't seen him since their divorce."

"When was that?"

"Let's see." Trey heard the rustling of papers. "According to the report she says it was final in August. She doesn't seem to be too heartbroken over their dissolved marriage."

Trey made a mental note to ask Jackson if he knew anything about Daniel, not that the man's divorce should have any bearing on Jackson. "What about the other guy? Eric."

"Clean. Married with two kids and a steady job. They live in Seattle. Nothing hidden in the closet as far as we can tell."

"Thanks," he told Crenshaw and slapped the flip closed before bracing his hands on his hips.

The shrill scream of the fire alarm sounded throughout the building. Pandemonium broke out in Judge Benedict's courtroom as everyone jumped to their feet, first looking confused and then panicked. Trey threw open the door, and while winding his way through the people, thoroughly followed every movement Jackson made. The guards did a good job of settling everyone down and getting on their radios to find out what the hell was going on. A few seconds later they started ushering the crowd through the doors. Evidently this wasn't a false alarm.

He ignored the agitated crowd and kept heading for Jackson, who had stood slowly and pounded his gavel to help get everyone's attention. "Follow the guard outside, people," he shouted, trying to be heard over the shrieking of the fire alarm, and banged the gavel again. The loud clanking did little to sway the mass exodus of people from the room. Trey only knew he was doing it because he could see him. A bailiff stepped in front of Trey before he could reach the judge.

"You'll have to leave the room, sir," he yelled, trying to turn Trey around.

"Let him through, Pete." Jackson winced and Trey sympathized. His ears were already ringing. "Take Savanti into custody." He needn't have said anything. Two bailiffs had already started the process.

The bailiff who'd stopped him stepped back, eyeing Trey long and hard, then turned to help secure the prisoner. Two other bailiffs stood behind Savanti. Their prisoner rocked back and forth on heels and balls of his feet, his thumbs twiddling where he had his hands cuffed and manacled to a chain around his waist. The smile on his face made Trey think he had something to do with the fire alarm going off. What he hoped to gain, Trey didn't know. A fire could cause a distraction but anyone with a lick of sense would know he'd be surrounded by guards, none of who would fall for the ruse. "Let's get out of here," his lawyer barked. "I assume we'll be heading outside with the others?"

One guard nodded and pointed while two others took hold of Savanti's elbows.

Trey couldn't shake the sleazy feeling about Savanti's smile. His lawyer's wasn't any better. It was almost as if they...knew something. Dominic winked, confirming Trey's suspicion. The little weasel had set this up.

He opened his mouth to warn Jackson when the sprinkler system came on. A woman stuck her head in the doors.

"It's on the second floor," she yelled and disappeared.

Dominic smirked at Trey as he was led out. The lawyer straightened his tie, walking as if he wasn't getting soaked.

"Let's go, Judge," Trey spat.

"Right behind you." Jackson came around the bench, water dripping from his nose and chin.

"This is a set-up," Trey said, jogging to get out of the building.

"Probably."

When they hit the lobby, firefighters were storming in, dragging heavy hoses and shouting to be heard over the shrill bleating of the alarm and the sprinklers. Trey could smell the smoke, so at least there was a real fire somewhere like the lady had said and this wasn't a total false alarm.

People scrambled as the police directed them where to go. When Trey looked back, smoke poured from a second story window.

They slowed to a walk and Jackson unzipped and yanked the soaked robe from his body. Trey didn't have the luxury since he'd left his coat in the car so he'd suffer with being wet until they could get the hell out of there. He was supremely conscious of everything happening around them. As diversions went, he'd been right in thinking this would be a good one. Fire trucks, police cars, ambulances, sirens, hundreds of people running, yelling, and in general, panicking. A perfect opportunity to bust someone out.

Or to take out a federal judge.

"Where the hell did Savanti go? Do you see him?" Jackson barked.

Trey turned a circle. "No."

"A hundred bucks says he's gone."

"Could one of those bailiffs have been paid off?" Trey hated to think about it, but it happened on rare occasions.

Jackson hung his head. "I wouldn't have thought so, but I guess just about anyone can be bought for the right amount of money."

"I don't like this. We have to get you out of here."

Jackson nodded. "I'm all for it. There won't be any more court today anyway. Let me speak to the man in charge and make sure Dominic hasn't already been taken into custody. They got out before us. They could have secured him without us seeing."

He started toward a command post they spied to the right of the building. Trey kept a constant vigil, scanning the rooftops, the vehicles and the pedestrians.

"Well speak of the devil," Jackson said, coming to a standstill at the feet of Dominic himself, sprawled on his ass, his hands balled into fists at his waist. Two added policemen, guns drawn, stood above him. Dominic scowled.

"Didn't work out for you, did it?" Jackson asked.

"Cocksucker." Dominic spit on Jackson's pants.

One of the cops planted his booted foot in the middle of Dominic's chest, forcing him to lie on the ground. "Watch your mouth, kid. That's Your Honor to you."

"Where's his lawyer?" Jackson asked.

The second cop nodded toward a patrol car. "In the back. He cracked one of the bailiffs over the head with his briefcase." He grinned. "They had him pinned to the ground and handcuffed before he even knew what hit him. Dumbass."

"Great. Since you've got this under control, I'm escorting *His Honor* off premises." Trey nudged Jackson forward. The hairs on the back of his neck stood up and he swung around.

"Have a good afternoon, Judge Benedict," Trey heard the first policeman say.

He walked backward, scanning the parking lot, but not finding anything out of the ordinary.

"What's wrong?" Jackson turned around with him.

"Don't know. Just a feeling. The quicker I get you away from here, the better."

"Now what?" Jackson threw the drenched robe in the backseat of his car and looked across the roof at the...puppy dog eyes of Trey? "What the hell is that look for?"

"I should be driving," Trey grumbled. He'd searched the car again and found nothing. Jackson wasn't surprised. An agent had been assigned to watch the damn thing while they were inside. As soon as he'd finished his search, Trey had called off the babysitter. It was just them now since everyone else was in the front watching the fire get taken care of. No doubt the majority of people needed to go back inside and get pertinent items.

Jackson laughed at the pitiful sound. "Why? Because you're the federal agent?"

"I do have the evasive driving experience and you don't know where we're going *and* because letting me drive your car would tell me I mean something to you."

"Are you kidding me? I let you drive from my parents' house yesterday." He paused. "You don't think you mean something to me?" Jesus. The muscle ticked along Jackson's jaw. He thought back to all the times they'd fucked last night. Had he ever said anything other than I need, I want? Hell, had Trey?

"I realize we've only been together for twenty-four hours or so, but I kinda thought there was something between us."

Hell yes there was something between them. He hoped it lasted a long-ass time. Like, forever. Jackson tossed the keys into the air and caught them. "So my letting you drive my car says...I love you?"

Trey squirmed, but the corners of his mouth tilted up in a grin. "Yeah. Letting your lover drive your car is the ultimate 'I love you'."

"Hmm." Jackson pretended to think about it for a minute. "Fine, *lover*, you drive." He threw the keys over the car. Trey caught them with one hand, smiling like a kid in a candy store. He strolled around the trunk of the car, passing Trey along the way. His hand brushed Trey's, and he linked their fingers, stopping his progress so he could give a quick kiss on the lips of the man he loved. When they parted, Jackson's heart hammered. For the first time ever, Jackson hadn't looked to see if anyone was watching. He hadn't cared. That's how he knew for sure Trey was the man he needed in his life.

Wasn't hard to admit something that was true.

"Wouldn't want you to think I don't love you," Jackson murmured as they moved again and got into the car.

"I could never think anything else after this moment." Trey leaned over and kissed him gently then started the car.

"What's special about this moment?" Jackson asked as Trey backed them out of the space.

"We're in the parking lot in front of your building. I believe you could have just outed us both."

Jackson smiled. So he could have. He didn't care. He was more than ready to have a real relationship as opposed to a secret one. He didn't see anyone around but that didn't mean someone couldn't have seen them from a window somewhere. "Oops. Sorry."

"I'm not. I'd hate to have to keep what's happening between us a secret."

"Great. So we'll both be jobless."

"Nah. Remember, my boss knows about me. I won't lose my job. Might get razzed or beat up by a few of the agents but if I'm more or less discreet, I won't lose my job. Now if I got caught fucking on the director's desk…"

"Good. Then I guess you can support me when I'm relieved of my bench." God, why did coming out make his chest feel so much lighter? Not that he'd actually "come out" per se, but if by chance anyone had seen them, by tomorrow morning the entire courthouse would know he'd been caught smooching in the parking lot with his bodyguard. Kind of made him feel like he could take on the world.

"You never know what'll happen."

"Right." Jackson took hold of Trey's hand and gave it a squeeze. The action felt right. "So where are we going?"

"Dinner. At my parents'."

"Your parents'? Why the hell are we going there? In light of everything that's happened don't you think that's unwise? Aren't I still in danger? Don't you need to sequester me *alone* somewhere? You know, show me how it's gonna be."

Trey smiled. "Oh, trust me, I will have you sequestered before the night is over. In my bed, in my arms, in my mouth. There will be no part of you I haven't sequestered. But first, it's family dinner night at my house. Besides, there'll be enough law enforcement there to stop an army."

Jackson swallowed back the anxiety growing inside him. "Why?" Was he ready to meet his lover's family? His parents?

Trey accelerated through an intersection when the light turned yellow in front of them. "Damn this is a nice car," he said appreciatively. "My dad is a detective, my older brother is an MP, my younger brother is a U.S. Marshal, and my sister...well, she isn't a cop, she's a doctor."

"A house full of high achievers, huh?"

Trey snorted. "And you're not, Mr. Very Young Judge?"

Jackson sighed and slouched in his seat as Trey took a turn on two wheels. "Mostly my dad's doing, so I'm discovering."

"I doubt your dad gave you the brains to get through college like you did."

"No, but it was his connections that got me to the federal bench quicker than most men."

"All right. What is it you want to be doing?"

Jackson looked at Trey. "Right this second I'd like to buried balls deep in your ass."

The car veered to the right. "Don't fucking say shit like that while I'm driving."

"I seem to recall your head in my lap yesterday while my hands were on the wheel."

Trey laid his hand on Jackson's thigh. "Balls deep, *after* dinner."

"Count on it."

"I'll be there." Trey groaned, shifting in his seat and adjusting what Jackson was sure would be a rock-hard cock.

Chapter Eight

Twenty tense, painful minutes later, Trey turned into a suburban, typical middle-class neighborhood. He'd nearly bypassed it and headed straight for the condo to feel the effects of balls deep, but he didn't. His mother's disapproval for not showing up two weeks in a row was not something he wanted to deal with right now.

There were always extenuating circumstances, especially since they all had jobs that might take them away at a moment's notice, but if they were in town, he and his brothers and sister were expected to come to dinner on Friday night. To reconnect, his mother would say. Besides, Trey wanted to show Jackson off. He wanted to see the look on his mother's face.

"This is where you grew up?"

Trey squeezed the steering wheel. "Yep. Born and raised in the same house my parents still live in."

"I couldn't wait to get out of the mansion. Actually the truth is, I wanted out from under my father's thumb."

"In that respect, we are totally different. I can't imagine my parents not being around." Trey pulled up in front of a brick ranch and parked at the curb. In the summer it always sported a nice arrangement of pretty flowers around the walkway leading from the porch to the driveway. Right now the flowerbeds were bare.

"Hmm. Are we going to sit in the car all day?"

"No. Time to meet the parents." Trey stepped out of the car.

Jackson followed him, wiping his sweaty palms on his thighs, Trey saw when he looked back.

They stopped at the front door. "Hey." Trey turned, grabbed hold of the back of Jackson's neck and planted his lips on his mouth. He swept his tongue against Jackson's, and felt how stiff he was. Trey was determined to ease his anxiousness. "No sweat tonight, right? Dinner, chitchat—"

"Family, dads with shotguns, big brothers with bigger fists."

Trey laughed out loud. "Jesus, Judge. You make it sound like we're in high school. My brothers are the same size as you, and I promise Dad hasn't taken his shotgun out of the closet for years."

"Not helping."

The front door swung open before Trey could turn the knob.

"There you are."

Trey smiled at his mom. "Here we are. Did you doubt me?"

Her gaze went between him and Jackson, and Trey's smile turned into a grin.

"Mom, this is His Honor, Jackson Benedict. Jackson, my mom, Meg."

"Your Honor." She reached a hand out to him, looking genuinely pleased to meet him.

Jackson took it, his cheeks pink. "Jackson, please. Nice to meet you, Mrs. London."

"Jackson," she repeated and stepped back, a smug expression on her face when she looked at Trey. She knew. "Such nice manners."

Trey rolled his eyes.

"Come in, come in." She ushered them in and closed the door behind them. "Your dad's in the living room. There's a basketball game on, I think. Paige is in the kitchen and Cameron and Kurt can't make it."

"Yeah, I thought Kurt was on a witness detail or something."

"He is. So," she said, turning her attention to Jackson.

Trey pursed his lips, trying not to laugh. Here it came, the third degree. The woman could drag information out of the toughest of crooks.

"You're a judge?" Meg took his hand and looped it through her elbow. She started walking into the living room.

"Yes, ma'am."

Lord, he was in another dimension. Trey's mother was June Cleaver-ish. She was talking his ear off, but oddly, Jackson didn't mind. It was nice. Peaceful.

The smirk on Trey's face he could do without. He'd work it off later. In bed.

Trey's mother spoke after leading him into a family room filled with worn furniture and a big screen TV. "Jerry, this is Jackson Benedict. *His Honor* Jackson Benedict."

A man stood from his spot in a La-Z-Boy and Jackson forced himself not to look for a shotgun. Jerry came forward and pounded Jackson on the shoulder. "Your Honor."

Trey was a spitting image of his father.

"Jackson." No way would he stand on precedence in Trey's home. He wanted to be an equal here.

Jerry quirked an eyebrow. "Are you a job for my son, or something else?"

Jackson's jaw dropped. "I'm a j—"

"Something else," Trey interrupted and grabbed his hand.

Stunned, Jackson stared at Trey's father, waiting for the meaty fist they'd talked about on the porch. Instead the man beamed and clapped him on the shoulder again.

"I knew he'd find someone soon. Didn't I tell you, Meg?"

"You did, dear," Meg answered and plumped a pillow before leaving the room.

Jackson looked at Trey, who shrugged and said, "I told you so."

"Hey Trey-head." A woman Jackson could only guess was Trey's sister walked in, chewing on a carrot stick, and smacked Trey on the back of the head.

"Paige." Trey wrapped his arm around her neck and rubbed the top of her scalp with his knuckles.

"Get off me, you Neanderthal." They wrestled for another couple of seconds, neither of them winning.

"Who are you, stud?" Paige asked, facing Jackson.

"Jackson Benedict. I'm a jud—"

"Jackson's my lover."

Jackson's face flamed and he nearly choked on his spit. *Oh. My. God.* He suddenly pictured the fist again. *His* going through Trey's nose.

"Hmm. 'Bout time, Trey-head." Paige walked away and flopped onto the couch.

Unbelievable. Jackson felt dissed somehow. She was supposed to turn her nose up, call him names, sneer, something. Not accept him no questions asked.

Trey squeezed by him, murmuring, "Don't mind the brat." He sat next to his sister, leaving Jackson standing alone. "Where are your little minions?" he asked her.

It was the strangest feeling. Like watching a family the way it was supposed to run instead of the kind his dysfunctional family had.

"Parker's bringing them."

"Parker is late and dinner is served," Meg announced from the doorway.

Jackson's cell phone rang as they followed his mother through the door. He unclipped it from his belt and looked at the number. It wasn't one he recognized and the caller's name was blocked. Trey turned and crossed his arms over his chest, ready to wait for him if need be.

"Don't know who it is." It rang again.

"Answer it."

Jackson shrugged and flipped it open. "Hello."

"You won't get away with it, Judge." The voice was distorted so Jackson couldn't get a bead on who it might be. He nodded at Trey, who scooted closer, and held the phone at a slant so Trey could hear too.

"Who is this?"

"Does it really matter?" the man snapped. "I'm rather positive you don't give a rat's ass who I am anymore. You've ruined my life, *Judge*. Now it's time for a little payback. I wouldn't turn your back if I was you."

The phone call disconnected and Jackson stared at the phone, wondering who the hell that had been.

"Whose life have you been ruining, Judge?" Trey tsked. He was making light of the situation, trying to relieve some of the tension.

"I ruin lives on a daily basis, if you call putting murderers and thieves in prison for life, ruining them."

Trey's hand looped around Jackson's neck and massaged. "It's your job. Did you recognize the voice?"

Jackson shook his head. "No, he was disguising it somehow."

"Give it to me." Trey took the phone from Jackson's hand and retrieved his own, punching in a stored number and talking to whoever answered. "This is Agent London. Is there any way to trace a call placed to this cell phone?" He repeated Jackson's phone number. "Yeah. ASAP. Thanks." He handed the phone back and Jackson clipped it on his waistband again. "We'll get him, Jackson. I promise."

"Maybe we should leave." Jackson wanted no part of endangering Trey's family.

"You did meet my family, right? You did get the part of almost all of them being in some branch of protective services? Hell, even my mom went through basic and did her time in the service. That's where my parents met. I'm telling you, you're almost as safe here as you are at the courthouse."

Intellectually Jackson knew Trey was right. Didn't make it any easier to stick around knowing he might somehow be putting his lover's family in the line of fire.

৪০

"That was by far the most interesting dinner I've ever been a part of." A hell of lot better than any meal he'd ever shared with his own family which were often quiet, pristine affairs with only the clink of silverware against the dishes for listening pleasure.

Jackson slid into the passenger seat without even thinking about driving. The phone call Trey had received halfway through the meal had garnered no information on who his caller had been. The cell phone had been one of those prepaids, which meant it was virtually untraceable. But then Trey had gotten another call. Caleb had been released without being charged. They couldn't prove he'd done anything wrong and he insisted he'd only been at Jackson's office to talk to him.

"Nah, totally normal. Actually tonight was pretty mild. Usually things turn to sex. Tonight Paige was tame."

"Her kids were there."

"Doesn't faze her. She has a subtle way of throwing down the gauntlet. She must have really liked you."

"Actually, I think she was totally indifferent to me."

Trey smiled. "Yep. That's how I know she likes you."

Time to change the subject. Trey smelled so damn good and he was trapped in this box on wheels with him. All thoughts of Trey's family and his stalker fled. "Dinner's over."

Jackson watched Trey's hands tighten on the steering wheel and the muscle bunch in his jaw. "Yes it is," Trey ground out.

"And we're heading to your condo, right?"

Trey swallowed. "Most definitely."

Jackson could hardly hear him, but he saw his tongue come out to lick his lips.

A cell phone rang, breaking the sexual tension surrounding them.

"Damn it," Jackson growled, semi-afraid it would be *him* again. He unclipped the gadget and glanced at the Caller ID. "Perfect."

"What?"

"It's my father."

"Well there's a damper on the evening."

"What?" he growled into the phone. He was in no mood to be nice. Trey had been right. Nothing could make his cock deflate faster than talking to his condescending father. He should have ignored it.

"Is that any way to talk to the man trying to apologize?"

Jackson pulled the phone from his ear and stared at it. "Apologize for what?"

There was a heavy sigh on the end of the line. "For talking to you the way I did yesterday."

"What?" Jackson couldn't be more confused. His father had never apologized to him, so why now?

"What, what?" Trey grabbed his thigh and Jackson lifted a hand to hold him off.

"I lied to you," Allenton continued. "Caleb Murphy isn't on the take. The miserable little bastard's been asking around about you. I told him months ago if he got anywhere near you again, I'd kill him myself. Didn't you wonder why he stopped seeing you?"

"You bastard."

"He will ruin you, keep you from the Supreme Court if you start fucking him again. You know I have your best interest at heart. No way will I let some fag keep you from that."

Son of a bitch, here it was. There was no apologizing, just more working for his own ends. "What about *this* fag, Allenton?"

"My son is no queer," he barked.

Jackson banged the cell phone on his forehead. The man would never get it. He held the phone in front of his face and spoke very succinctly and loudly. "Did you take the picture of us together?"

"Of course I did. Had to let him know—all of them know—I was always watching you. I sent each of them one. No way will I let some *man* hurt your chances."

"So, because of that picture of me with what looks like a group of friends at a fucking baseball game, I have a goddamn bodyguard." *Well, not technically and not that I mind the bodyguard in the least.* He peeked at Trey from the corner of his eye.

Apparently his lover took offense. "I'll show you bodyguard."

"Jackson," he heard his father say. "This rebellion needs to end. I understand you're lashing out, shirking authority, but it needs to stop. You've got to find a wife and settle down, get ready for Washington."

Jackson was surprised his grip on the phone didn't break it. "Listen. To. Me," he said with dead calm. "I am gay. I have a lover. And no matter what stupid things you do to make it different won't work. I will never marry a woman and have two and half kids and become a Supreme Court justice or a senator or anything else political. I will not take you on my coattails to D.C. or the White House."

"Jackson Montgomery Benedict. Do not talk to me in that tone of voice."

"I'll talk to you any way I want to. You attempted to change my life to fit yours. What exactly did you think would happen by doing what you did?"

"I was trying to convince you being a homo is wrong."

"Wrong for you," Jackson hissed.

"Wrong for my son. Whenever you decide to do the right thing, you can come home. Until then, you are not welcome in this house."

"I'm shaking in my robe." Jackson slammed the flip closed and threw the phone to the floorboard. It might have made him feel better to see the plastic shatter into a million pieces, but it wouldn't solve the real issue.

"I'll take your family over mine any day," he muttered. Trey squeezed his thigh and Jackson only just realized he hadn't ever moved his hand.

"I knew it," Trey exclaimed. "You liked them."

"Of course I did. What's not to like?"

"They liked you too. I thought my mom might tackle you in hugs before we left." Trey's hand wandered higher up Jackson's thigh, getting dangerously close to a part of Jackson that quickly forgot his father's shenanigans.

"At least we know who sent the picture. Damn him." Jackson punched the dashboard.

"Did he say he sent it?"

Jackson thought back to their conversation. "No," he said, slowly. "Shit. No, he said he'd taken it and used it to warn Caleb off."

"So what reason would Caleb have for sending it to you?"

"Rekindling old flames? Hell, I don't know. That doesn't explain all the other things I've gotten though. What now?"

"Now we go back to the condo and wait for my team to find him."

Since they were in a holding pattern, nothing sounded better to Jackson. "I *was* kind of looking forward to the hot tub."

"Oh yeah." Trey groaned. "Balls deep."

"I know for a fact my car can go faster than this."

Chapter Nine

"God I've been waiting for this since...well since you mentioned it earlier today." Jackson dropped his towel, ignoring the chill of the February night. The sight of Trey standing naked at the hot tub adjusting the controls was more than enough to keep him warm.

He stepped closer and set his beer in one of the cup holders, then stroked his hand down Trey's flank.

"You're giving me goose bumps, Judge."

"Then we better get in and work them off."

Trey turned into Jackson's arms. Their cocks rubbed together, bobbed against each other, adding to the building tension surrounding them.

"I can't wait any longer." Trey trailed his lips down Jackson's neck. Now it was him with the goose bumps.

"Climb in," Jackson growled.

"So you can get a good look at my ass?"

"Absolutely."

Trey climbed the two steps and threw his leg over the side, separating the cheeks of his ass and giving Jackson the sweet glimpse of his anus. His cock swelled and spasmed in anticipation. He wet his finger in his mouth.

"Stop."

Trey paused where he was, one leg in, one out, and looked over his shoulder. Jackson rimmed the tight ring of muscle with his spit-slicked finger, penetrating him to the knuckle, smiling when Trey moaned and hung his head. His fingers were white where they gripped the tub. "Fucking tease."

Jackson withdrew and patted a butt cheek. "Get in and I'll stop teasing."

Trey slid into the water, the bubbly heat covering all of him from his shoulders down. "You know what?"

Jackson slipped into the tub and stood in front of Trey, letting the water lick at his erection. "What?"

"I think it's my turn." Trey held a hand out and Jackson accepted it, allowing Trey to pull him into his lap.

"Sounds good to me."

"Oh yeah." Trey held his cock in hand as Jackson spread his knees on either side of his thighs and lowered himself, ending up face to face, chest to chest with his lover.

Trey enveloped both their cocks in his hands, squeezing and rubbing until Jackson began to thrust his hips. Jackson sighed. This was how they were meant to be, together as one. He knew it to the bottom of his soul. He held onto Trey's shoulders and felt his lover's hands work their magic on his cock.

"I can't wait to get inside you, Judge."

"It's been awhile. Might take some major preparation on your part."

"Oh yeah? How long?" Trey asked, slipping the tight pocket of his hands up and down.

Jackson dropped his head back. "Mmm. A year. At least."

"I'll take it as slow as you want."

"Keep doing that," Jackson rasped, squeezing his ass as his balls tightened almost painfully. He leaned in and seized Trey's lips in a forever kind of kiss, sucking his tongue into his mouth, then slid his hands down so he could manipulate Trey's hardened nipples.

"Jesus, Judge."

"What?" he said innocently. "If I move, I'll blow and I'm not ready to just yet." Jackson compressed his ass again and nipped Trey's earlobe.

"Fuck it." Trey worked their erections in earnest, stroking them until Jackson couldn't sit still any longer. He thrust his hips forward. The action splashed water out of the tub and lit fireworks inside Jackson as the head of Trey's cock made contact with his over and over.

"Shit." Jackson bit his lip. Trey was right about fucking it. Why in the hell had he even thought about keeping still? He raised and dropped, up and down, causing a series of tidal waves in the tub. They were both sweaty within minutes, from a heat having nothing to do with the hot tub.

"I'm close, Judge," Trey warned, his neck taut, his breath coming out in pants.

"Me too." Jackson ground his ass on Trey's lap, his eyes rolling at the tingling starting in his lower back. Trey swept his thumb over the head of his cock and down around the bundle of nerves underneath. It pulsated, ready to spill.

"Come with me," Jackson snarled, wanting this to be special for both of them.

"Now," Trey yelled.

The force of Jackson's orgasm was explosive. It contracted again and again like it never had in the past, drawing itself out. Hot spurts of their come shot into the water as both of them gyrated, their pelvises wringing out every drop.

Jackson collapsed on Trey, burying his head in the crook of Trey's neck. Trey's arms wrapped around his torso, hugging him close, almost as if he were afraid to let Jackson go. Jackson sure the hell wasn't inclined to be let go.

"I think we lost about half the water." Trey's lips pressed against Jackson's forehead.

"You complaining?"

"Nope."

"I can't move," Jackson groaned, licking Trey's neck. "I love the way you taste."

"Don't want you to move. And I love the way you taste too." Trey tilted Jackson's chin and delved into his mouth with his tongue.

Long, breathless minutes later, they separated and Jackson slid off Trey into the seat next to him.

A loud crack, like the limb of a tree breaking off from the weight of snow bearing down on it, split the night air.

Trey watched the man jump from a tree above his six foot privacy fence line into his yard with a barbaric yell. He rolled to his feet none too gracefully as he got caught in his jacket, stumbling forward, arms waving. Moonlight glinted off metal. Trey and Jackson reacted at the same time.

"Get down," Trey shouted, shoving Jackson aside.

Trey vaulted from the hot tub. His gun was on the table next to the tub. He'd wanted it closer but drowning it in water wouldn't have done him any good. A few splashes it might handle, but he hadn't known how much water they'd displace.

"Don't move."

Trey froze, his hands in the air, looking like a naked runner mid-stride.

"Daniel?" Jackson's voice was full of incredulousness.

"Yeah, it's me, Jackson. Surprised? Don't be. I've been waiting for this moment since the day you ruined my life."

Trey moved, inch by inch, slow enough Daniel wouldn't see it and become more alarmed than he already was. How hard would it be to lunge, grab, turn and fire? His mark would be dead on, but risking Jackson, who was standing at the edge of the tub, getting shot wasn't an option.

"Ruined your life? What the hell are you talking about?"

Daniel laughed. "You caused my divorce, *friend*."

"Doreen divorced you?" Jackson's shock was genuine since Trey hadn't told him about it yet.

Trey made it to half a foot away from his gun. Through the glass door, he saw Corky chomping at the bit to come outside. His ears were pinned back, and his top lip was snarled, revealing dangerously sharp teeth. The dog might only have three legs but what he lacked in feet, he more than made up for in teeth.

"When?"

"The same day she found me jacking off while looking at a picture of you. Then I got that picture of us at the game in the mail and it sealed the nail in my coffin."

"So you sent it to me after scratching my face off?"

"Yes. Everything that's happened to me is your fault." There was a wild look in his eyes, one that said he didn't care what happened anymore.

"It's my fault you got caught masturbating? I didn't even know you wanted me. Jesus, Daniel, we've been friends since the third grade. Don't you think you could have mentioned it sometime in all those years? You're the one who drifted away after your marriage. How often did we see each other besides that day at the game?"

"Which was exactly when I'd decided to tell you how I felt, but then you were too busy seducing some punk little lawyer who would never have been good enough for you."

Water splashed over the side of the tub as Jackson jumped out, providing the distraction he needed. Trey kept an eye on each of them as he stood taller and hid the gun behind his back. Glorious in his complete nakedness, Jackson took a wide stance and put his hands on his hips.

"Daniel, put the gun down. Used to be you wouldn't have gotten within twenty feet of one. Do you even have any clue how to use it?"

"I do, Jackson Benedict. There's a lot of things you don't know about me."

Trey took a step back toward them. He'd have to have a little talk with Jackson about antagonizing a suspect, friend or not.

"Why would you do this? Why not come to me instead of breaking into my house and sending things?"

"I wanted you to be scared. I wanted you to come to me, your best friend, for help, advice, so I could comfort you, make things better for you. Then I was going to let you know how I wanted it to be between us."

"Christ, Daniel, that's a little farfetched don't you think, when we haven't seen each other much? Why would you assume I'd come running to you? Let's just say we were friends, Daniel. *Still* are friends. You couldn't be a lover to me because I wouldn't allow it. I'm not willing to be a guinea pig."

Daniel swung the gun back up and pointed it straight at Jackson's forehead. "And therein lies the problem. Was I not good enough for you? Didn't I fit your mold? Am I not man enough? Like him." Daniel swept the gun in Trey's direction. "I watched you fucking him. Why wouldn't you do that with me?" he cried.

Jackson crossed his arms over his chest. *"You're not gay."*

"But I want to be."

Jackson threw his hands in the air. "For God's sake, man. We went to dinner one night and you couldn't stop talking about the pair of college girls who sat next to us. And you were engaged at the time. To a *woman*."

Daniel sniffed. "No. I wanted you. And you denied me." The gun shook in his hand.

"Put the gun down." Trey stepped to Jackson's side.

Daniel snorted. "What exactly are two naked men going to do?"

"I don't need clothes to take you down." Though a jacket might have been nice because the heat from the hot tub was gone and now it was just plain cold. "Plus I have one of these." He aimed his much steadier hand at Daniel. "Threatening a judge is a federal offense."

Daniel lifted his chin. "My Jackson would never put me away."

Glass shattered behind them, and they all jumped. One hundred pounds of beast came bounding at them, growling and barking. He headed straight for Daniel, catching the man on his arm and pushing him to the ground. Daniel screamed, more in fright than pain. His gun flew out of his hand and skittered across the patio.

"Corky. Off." Jackson snapped his fingers and immediately Corky released the still shrieking Daniel.

"Go get my handcuffs off the counter, Jackson."

"Sure. Corky, come."

"Daniel Gardner, you have the right to remain silent..." By the time he finished reading Daniel his rights, Jackson returned.

"Here." Jackson handed him the cuffs. "And here's your pants."

"Thanks."

"Figured you wouldn't want to meet the backup in the buff."

"Jackson. Don't do this. You know we could be good together."

Jackson squatted down next Daniel. "Get yourself another wife, Daniel, or go back to your ex and explain things. As your friend, I'll be here for you, but not as your lover." He glanced at Trey. "I'm already taken."

℘

"God, I'm tired." Jackson stripped off the T-shirt he'd thrown on before the police arrived and dropped it on the chair in the corner.

Trey pressed up against his back and kissed his shoulder. "Too tired?"

"Mmm. For you, I'll never be too tired." Jackson turned in Trey's arms, savoring the feel of the man he couldn't imagine not being involved with for the rest of his life. Love at first sight? Was it possible? Maybe not first sight, more like first touch.

"I love you," he murmured, nuzzling Trey's cheek.

"I was just thinking the same thing." Trey pushed Jackson's pants over his hips and they fell to the floor. His lips blazed a path down Jackson's chest, his abs, and along his erection to envelope the head of his cock in wet heat.

Jackson grasped Trey's hair, holding him there, wanting this act of love more than anything. Trey sucked him all the way with his magical mouth, drawing on him and tugging at his balls.

Holy shit, the man could suck cock like no one else on Earth. Jackson thrashed, wanting it to end, yet wanting it to go on forever. Trey's throat closed on the head, practically squeezing the come from his balls.

Stop. They had to...shit.

"Up," he grunted, passed the point of speaking straight. "Want you with me."

He shuffled them closer to the bed and reached for the lube. Somehow they made it crosswise on the mattress facing each other on their sides. Jackson wanted to be able to see Trey's face as they erupted together.

Smearing a glob of lube first on Trey's hand, then his own, he guided Trey to take hold of both their cocks. Jackson did the same. They both started pumping with their fists, in perfect sync with each other. Their lips locked, their tongues dueled. Trey rolled them so they lay on their opposite sides, never breaking their rhythm.

Jackson swung his leg over Trey's, holding him still as they fought for release. Sweat clung to their skin. The tingle started low and grew until nothing could stop it.

Trey's eyes widened and his breath hitched a second before their orgasms hit. Strings of come spurted onto their hands and bellies, coating them with their essence. It was beautiful.

"I love you, Agent London."

"I love you, Judge Benedict."

About the Author

Annmarie McKenna lives with her husband and four kids just outside of St. Louis, MO. She spent years reading romances before deciding to try out the other side—writing. After joining RWA and MORWA, she discovered all the things she'd done wrong with her first story. Then she tackled her second, *Blackmailed*, which she very happily sold to Samhain Publishing. During naps and shuffling kids to various activities, she is working hard on her next project.

To learn more about Annmarie McKenna, please visit www.annmariemckenna.com. Send an email to Annmarie at annmarmck@yahoo.com.

For Love and Country

Mary Winter

Chapter One

Baltimore, MD, February 1862

Gray clouds scuttled across the not-quite full moon, casting the inky waters of the Atlantic into total darkness. The splash of water against ships anchored in Baltimore's Inner Harbor reminded Emil Franks of the ebb and flow of the ocean, a tide he'd lived with all his life. Behind him, the sounds of drunken revelers and ship hands working late into the night faded as he neared the boats on which men slept or gambled. Either way, it was a lot quieter than the boisterous noise that came from the street a few blocks behind him. The tang of salt water filled the air, and he breathed deeply the seductive aroma even though he no longer needed to take air into his lungs. God, he loved the smell of the ocean.

The large French ship, *Commerce de Souverain*, sat moored near the center of the dock where the harbor was at its deepest. Emil's steps faltered. He stared at the large ship, the sails slack in the absence of any breeze, and his heart pounded in a purely human reaction. Basile Gagnon captained this vessel. His tender, yet firm hand on the wheel guided the ship from port to port, just as at one time he had coaxed Emil's body to heights of ecstasy he hadn't known since. Emil hoped Basile would soon sail somewhere along the southern Atlantic coast as part of the Union blockade of the Confederate states.

Emil swallowed and ran his tongue along the fangs in his mouth. The last time he'd seen Basile Emil had been human. His humanity had driven them apart. Now, he came with new knowledge and with a plea for his country. Squaring his shoulders, he strode across the dock, his boots echoing on the wooden planks as he made his way to the rope and rung ladder thrown over the side of the ship.

Darkness shrouded the man standing at the top of the ladder. Emil's keen vision saw his short, white-blond hair and baggy clothing. A young lad, maybe nineteen, without even a hint of stubble covering his face. Basile always did have the habit of picking up lost young men, and Emil fought the stab of jealousy that perhaps this boy, barely into manhood, shared the vampire's bed. No, not when the rich aroma of coppery life poured off the young man like ambrosia. Basile turned away from mortals, or at least that was the excuse he'd given when he'd left five years ago. Emil's mouth watered, reminding him it'd been too long since he'd fed. He tugged at the rope.

"You there, what do you want?" the youngster called down, his voice hardly dipping into the lower registers.

"I have an appointment with your captain." A lie, of course, but if he announced himself as waiting to see Basile, no doubt the ship's captain would turn him away. He had before.

"No one told me," the boy yelled back. "Go away."

"Now is that any way to treat a guest?" Basile's rich voice, smooth with his French accent, drifted to Emil's hungry ears. He strained toward it, like a dog toward a tidbit in his master's hand. It'd been too many years since the honeyed tones played across him, and in his trousers, his cock hardened. Basile peered over the edge of the ship. "Emil, I didn't expect to see you here."

"I didn't expect to be here, Basile. I hope you've been well. I come as an emissary from the Secretary of War. May I come aboard?" Emil asked, not worrying about who might hear about his Union leanings here. Sure, Baltimore harbored Confederate sympathizers, this close to Washington D.C., how could it not? But he had no doubt he could take on any who threatened him. A stint in the Union Army and training after his near death at Bull Run had given him an edge over most street thugs.

Basile hesitated.

Emil waited, knowing better than to interrupt Basile's inspection. He stood there, the moon coming from behind a cloud to illuminate his muscled form. He knew what the vampire would see, had seen, and knew what he would sense. Forcing his body to the stillness of a predator watching prey, he waited for Basile's response. Some unspoken signal passed between Basile and the young man on deck, for the French vampire turned and walked away.

"Come on up." The young man gestured to the ship.

Emil wasted no time in climbing the ladder. No sooner had his feet touched the wooden deck of the ship when the young man grunted.

"Follow me," he said, his thick Boston accent even more evident. Turning on his heel, he led Emil across the gently rocking deck.

Emil ignored the stares of the sailors on board. He recognized several of the men from five years ago. Basile had, and still, inspired fierce loyalty. No angry glares, only curious looks, came in his direction, a fact which relieved Emil. Though Basile had been the one to leave, Emil worried about the reactions of those who worked with and protected his former lover.

The boy led Emil down the stairs to the captain's cabin. Emil drank in the sight of the polished wood, the love and care that had obviously gone into the ship. It was Basile's pride and joy, and Emil knew all too well that the vampire prized the vessel above all else. He closed his eyes as memories threatened to swamp him. Right here at the foot of the stairs, one dark, August evening, Basile had pressed him against the wall and taken him, quickly, furiously, his cock plowing into Emil's body, making the man come with such fierceness he blacked out for a moment. And there, the Captain's office, a room full of maps and navigation equipment where the table created the perfect surface to bend Basile over and show the Frenchman the meaning of control. Emil's body vibrated with the force of his memory, his shaft thick and hard. In the low light the human leading him wouldn't be able to see it. Basile would, and the thought quickened Emil's blood.

Business. Forcibly, he reminded himself of the reason why he was there, the young man's discreet knock on Basile's door drawing his thoughts away from sex.

"Come in." Basile's voice wrapped around Emil and compelled him forward.

He stepped into the captain's quarters, a low room under the slope of the deck, a large bed in the corner, shutters open on the windows to reveal the inky water beyond. The vessel swayed back and forth. Emil stepped into the room and firmly into Basile's sanctuary. The vampire's scent surrounded him, as salty and clean as the fresh ocean air. The young man closed the door behind him, leaving Emil alone with the man he still loved.

"Thank you for seeing me," Emil said. "I apologize for the lack of notice."

Basile waved his hand dismissively. Light gleamed on his blue-black hair. A bit of ribbon held it away from his face and Emil's fingers itched to run through the silken strands. A dark blue waistcoat highlighted the darkness of Basile's hair, as did the matching trousers. His white shirt was unbuttoned, revealing a large expanse of his hairless chest. His flat pectorals invited touch, and Emil remembered long nights doing just that, tracing the contours and planes of Basile's body with fingers and tongue.

Basile remained quiet. Emil stumbled, acutely feeling his far younger age. His former lover was at least two hundred years old, and such experience tended to widen the gulf between them, especially when he was mortal and Basile hadn't been for quite some time. Emil opened his mouth to speak and closed it quickly. With a small shake of his head, he clenched and unclenched his fingers. He forced his shoulders to relax.

"The years have treated you kindly." Basile turned to face Emil, his gaze sweeping over the insignia on Emil's chest and the slightly visible uniform. If he noticed Emil's erection he gave no sign, instead, looked dismissively away. "I thought I made my views on our acquaintance clear." He pursed his lips.

"Things have changed since then, and you know I wouldn't seek you out if I didn't have a good reason," Emil countered. He sensed the walls Basile built around himself. Ten years ago Emil'd carefully torn them down, emotional brick by emotional brick. The vampire had grieved for his long-time human lover who'd succumbed to illness and had vowed never to get involved with a mortal ever again. Until Emil.

"Your reasons are not my reasons. I've had a long night. Say your piece and then leave. I have no desire to reopen old wounds." Basile rubbed the back of his hand across his eyes.

Emil's heart leapt. He drew in a lungful of Basile's scent, filled his pores, his very spirit with the essence of the man he still loved. A grin twitched the corners of his lips, and he relaxed his hands. "Neither do I. I wouldn't be here except our need is vital. We need ships and men to help us with the blockade of the Confederate states. Your ship, a French gunboat, one of the first and finest models, would be a great asset to us. We need the *Commerce de Souverain*. We need you." Emil hadn't intended to blurt out his mission. He hoped to warm Basile to it, to maybe talk about old times, about the change Emil had undergone. If Basile had noticed Emil's transformation he gave no sign.

Basile stared at Emil, his eyes blank. Lips drawn tight, he turned away and strode to the windows. Curling his fingers around the sill, he stared over the glassy smooth waters of the Atlantic. His back was ramrod straight, shoulders square, though Emil sensed the heavy weight settled on them.

Emil stepped forward before he could stop himself. His feet carried him across the cabin, past the heavy oak desk in the corner that was older than the vampire, past the bed rumpled from sleep and redolent with memories. He stopped behind Basile and rested his hand on the man's shoulder. "I'm sorry. I wouldn't have come had we any choice. But when I found out you were in port... We need you, Basile. The Union needs you."

"I have no need of the Union. These shores have brought me nothing but heartbreak. In two days I return to France. I hope never to see the United States ever again." Basile released the sill and balled his hands at his sides.

The uncharacteristic show of emotion startled Emil. He gently squeezed Basile's shoulder. "Things are different now. The nation is at war. I cannot tell you how important your help would be." *And that war nearly killed me.*

Basile whirled around. He stood toe-to-toe with Emil. "For you or for your precious country?"

"Both of us," Emil answered. "I've—"

"If you're going to tell me about how you've lain awake at night thinking of me, missing me, how you still love me, spare us both the vapors." Basile held up his hand. "I'm sorry, Emil. I'm going home for good. I'm not going to change my mind. Not even for you." Pain laced his words, a soul-deep pain Emil also felt.

At least he still made Basile feel something. The vampire hadn't gone completely dead inside, though he wanted to. Oh, Emil knew how much Basile wanted to die inside, to be as cold and unfeeling as the frigid waters of the Northern Atlantic. But even there, the waters held life, hope, and Emil prayed that his former lover did the same.

"I'm sorry you came all this way for nothing. Goodbye, Emil." Basile turned to the desk.

Emil remained standing by the window. Words escaped him. He watched Basile bend over the charts, consulting courses, or maybe looking over shipping manifestos. "Please," Emil implored. "Just hear me out."

Basile shuffled papers. "No. I leave in two days, Emil. Goodbye."

Emil refused to budge. He opened his lips, feeling his fangs itch with the need to reveal themselves. Perhaps it would make a difference if Basile knew about Emil's transformation. The Union officer hoped so, but also suspected Basile held the ability to sense other vampires. If he said nothing about Emil's change, well, then that was that, and their relationship well and truly was over. A memory clicked in his mind and he smiled.

"I remember lying on the deck of this very ship, bundled up in blankets and staring at the stars. You told me then of your dreams for your country, how you hoped France would rise to greatness and how, in some ways, you felt she had. If I stood here and held the means for your country to achieve that greatness, to heal the rifts between the classes, and make your nation whole, would you not listen to me? Or would you throw me out without so much as an acknowledgement of our past relationship?"

Basile's hands stilled.

Sensing his words having their desired effect, Emil continued, "I am not asking you to sweep me into your arms and proclaim your undying love for me. I wouldn't mind. I've thought of you, and I'll confess you still hold my heart. But I'm here purely on a political mission, one of expediency and need. The Confederate ports are her strength. Through them supplies, ammunition, the very things she could use to spread her poison could arrive and help defeat the Union. Do you really want to see the United States broken in two? I know you hate us. I understand why. Your former lover died on our shores. But do you hate us so much as to sail away when your assistance could keep us from being ripped apart?"

Basile barked mocking laughter. "And you think my ship, my *single* ship, can turn the tide? If you do, you're more naive than I thought." He straightened and turned his attention fully on Emil.

"No, but it'll help. The Union needs all the help it can get." He spoke the plain truth, not covering it up in ideology wrapped in flowers. Leaning forward, Emil braced his hands on the table. His stare bored into Basile's face, searched it for any trace of sympathy. He saw none. Swallowing hard, he kept his fangs well hidden, a trait he'd practiced in the several months since his turning. The man who transformed him promised a bold new society, a place where powerful beings, no longer men, could shape the course of history. And in his youthful exuberance, Emil had believed. Now, staring into Basile's eyes, he saw the true cost of his vampirism in the long and cold years where he continued and everyone around him died. Emil suppressed a shudder. It didn't have to be that way, if only Basile could see reason.

"I don't think you know what you're asking. You see only your glorious upstart of a country torn in two by war. You forget I've lived through wars. They end and the people go on. I return to my lands in two days. From there, I'll run my business and no longer sail the high seas. I just want to go home, Emil. Surely you can let me do that one, simple thing." Basile rested his lean hip against the edge of the desk and crossed his arms over his chest.

"We are two men at cross purposes, I'm afraid. I'm charged by the Secretary of War to find us more ships to aid in the Confederate Blockade. I've used my knowledge of the docks, the secrets they hold, and the world in which I grew up to ask everyone, and I do mean everyone. You're the last hope. All have turned me down. To them, money is superior to country. You know that's not true. You know the right thing to do is to join me, join the Union in this blockade." Emil paused and moistened his dry lips with his tongue. His heart thudded, sweat trickled along his spine. Where the coat barely kept the chill from him on deck, down here, so close to Basile, warmth radiated from his body. "When it's over, then you can go home."

"Or will you find another task for me just so you can keep me here on your damned American soil?"

Emil reared back from Basile's words as if he'd been physically struck. "I'd never keep you against your will."

"Then why ask now? Go back to your government and tell them this Frenchman is going home." Basile slammed his fist onto the desk.

Emil jerked at the sharp blast of sound. His sensitive vampire ears rang. He held one card, a card he always played close to his vest. To come out with it now, would it make him look like an amateur or would it tip the scales? Emil refused to be cowed. He stepped forward, so close he smelled the hint of coppery blood on Basile's lips. The vampire had recently fed, and Emil wondered from whom. Thinking about the man's mouth on a neck, a wrist, the skin of a human, licking, sucking, brought back memories in a flood. His flagging erection surged hard once more. Emil remembered what it was like to have the vampire's tongue sliding across his flesh, his fangs piercing skin to draw crimson blood into his mouth. The gentle suction would force Emil's cock as hard as a railroad spike, and then, Basile would turn Emil on his stomach and take him over and over again until they both lay limp and sated. Had he breathed, his breath might have caught in his chest at the mental images.

"Because things have changed, Basile." With those words, Emil unleashed the beast he kept close inside. His eyes darkened, turned an angry red. A curl of his lips bared his fangs, and his fingers changed, nails lengthening into talons. For long moments he stood there, the true extent of his vampire nature revealed.

Basile's eyes widened. He uncrossed his arms and studied, really studied, Emil from head to toe and back again. His deep blue eyes churned like the depths of the ocean, darkening to the color of the water outside the window, flecks of red visible in the nearly black irises. A shake of his head and they were gone, but for a moment, a precious, beautiful moment, his vampire had risen to greet Emil's.

Slowly, Emil drew his beast back within himself. The bloodlust faded, the need for flesh and hunger sinking beneath the surface like a diving whale. He stepped back to give Basile some room. Fingers curled with the need to touch the Frenchman, to stroke the planes of his cheekbones, explore the hollow of his throat. Instead, he moved another step closer to the door.

"Things have changed, Basile. I'm no longer mortal and your arguments about not continuing our relationship because I'm human aren't true any longer. So pardon me if I come to you to ask you to help out my country. Because you see, these shores might hold more possibilities for you than you ever knew." Emil waited for a heartbeat, two, but Basile said nothing. Taking his silence as a dismissal, Emil turned on his heel and strode from the cabin.

Long, angry strides carried him up the steps and onto the deck. Salty spray hung in the air, clouds churning with the promise of a storm. Rain or ice, Emil smelled the potential for both on the wind and a part of him prayed for ice, anything to keep Basile in port for a few days longer. He left in two days. Valentine's Day. Nodding to the young man standing watch, Emil bit back his angry chuckles as he descended the ladder. Once his feet stood firmly on the dock, he looked up at the ship. He stared at the gunboat's sleek lines, the sails slack in their rigging. Memories upon memories filled the ship, and frankly, once it left port, he didn't know whether to be relieved or sad.

He turned his back to the vessel just as Basile had turned his back on Emil and strode back to the boisterous streets lining the dock and his cold, barren rooms. Tomorrow he'd tell the Secretary of War his news. Tomorrow he'd tell him that he had failed in his mission. He expected to be back on the front lines before the end of February. And Basile would be back in France, where a part of Emil wished he could follow.

Instead of returning home, Emil stopped into a corner pub frequented by dockworkers. With ships coming and going on a daily basis, perhaps there would be a chance to speak with other captains and redeem himself. He found a chair at the bar, the cloying scent of cigarette smoke and unwashed bodies strong enough to make him gag. The too-loud conversation of drunken men who didn't care about tomorrow rang in his ears. The bartender, a balding man who'd seen nearly everything on these docks, shoved a mug of thick beer at him. Emil passed a few coins across the bar at him in payment, and the man knew enough to leave Emil alone.

Emil nursed his beer. Strong hops sat bitter on his tongue, the foamy head reminding him of other beers he'd shared as a mortal. His vampire constitution allowed him only liquids, and the beers he drank here were precious reminders of the life he'd once had. Behind him, snippets of conversation about the war yielded little information that Emil didn't already know. Talk of a new ship, an English vessel coming into port in a few days perked his interest, though Emil knew the Brits traded more with the Confederates than they did the Union nowadays. All depended on the ship's captain, and Emil knew enough to be wary of the incoming vessel. The *Marengo* held Confederate sympathizers, and Emil made a mental note to tell his superiors to monitor this ship closely.

His beer nearly finished, he watched the clientele change as those who had families drifted home and those who didn't ordered another round. Tongues got looser and louder, but still no talk of any other ships of which Emil wasn't aware. He frowned and ordered another beer. Going back to his rented rooms seemed futile at the moment, not when his heart remained on Basile's ship. Damn. Even now, after five years apart, the sight of the Frenchman with his lustrous dark hair and piercing blue eyes had him hard and ready for action. He wanted nothing more than to finish removing his shirt and waistcoat, pull those tailored slacks down his lean legs, remove his boots and show the vampire how much he missed him. And the bastard had to leave for France on Valentine's Day. Not enough to simply rebuff him and go back, but to do it on the one holiday devoted to love. Emil hid his derision by downing his beer.

The bartender returned and Emil waved him away. Rising from his bench, he made his way into the cold, damp night. Several hours before sunrise meant several more hours to try and ferret out information about additional ships coming into Baltimore's harbor. Perhaps by the time the sun rose, he'd have enough information to save face with his bosses in the War Department. Perhaps, he'd have something on which to focus so he wouldn't have to think about Basile's leaving.

Chapter Two

Basile stared at the portrait showing him and Emil during their first year together. The young man looked so fresh-faced, so innocent, and it had been that youth and vigor which had drawn the vampire to the mortal in the first place. As a vampire Emil would retain those qualities for many centuries to come.

He shouldn't have let Emil leave. Basile frowned and shoved the traitorous thought away. He needed to return to France, get away from the mortal world and all its dangers. Hiding in his chateau for a decade or two sounded lovely, and nothing prevented him from running his business from there. That living in isolation prevented him from being hurt only made the deal that much sweeter. He'd leave in two days on Valentine's Day. Basile snorted inelegantly. How fitting that on the day devoted to love he'd leave the man he still loved behind for the country he'd always loved. Too much love and yet, not enough. He replaced the picture in a drawer, not wanting his men to see him maudlin.

Sounds of a scuffle easily penetrated the decks to his room below. Raised voices and the solid thud of a fist against flesh propelled Basile out of his cabin. He took the stairs two at a time, emerging on deck to find the young lad with a bloody nose and a thunderous look on Emil's face. The man scowled. "I'm sorry, lad, but I have to see him."

"No—" the lad protested, spitting globules of blood and a broken tooth onto the deck.

"Yes, and clean that up." Basile's nostrils flared at the scent of blood. He strode over to Emil. "I told you to leave and yet, you're here."

"Since when have I followed your orders?" Emil grinned.

Basile's heart melted just a little bit more. His other traitorous organ stirred, and Basile ensured he stood in shadow as to hide his body's physical reaction. "We have nothing more to say to each other." Basile crossed his arms over his chest.

"Oh, but I think we do." The tang of badly brewed beer rolled off of Emil. Swaggering forward, he stopped in front of Basile. "We have a lot to talk about. Would you like to do it on deck or shall we have some privacy?"

"I've said everything that needs to be said. I'm leaving in two days. I can't help you." Basile drew on the well of patience he worked to cultivate deep inside. When one dealt on a regular basis with mortals, one needed as much patience as possible. Emil might not be a mortal any longer, but he still thought like one.

"You may be done, but I'm not," Emil bantered as the moon emerged from behind clouds. Pale light glinted off his elongated canines.

Basile kept his reaction hidden. Perhaps if he ignored the fact Emil was a vampire, then he'd go away. Not likely. "Yes, I think you are. We are." He struggled to keep his features dispassionate. Let the man think Basile no longer had any feelings for him. Let him return to his home. If it weren't for a shipment to arrive tomorrow and the fact that most of his crew were on shore leave, he'd weigh anchor right now and leave Emil and his ceaseless demands behind.

Emil moved closer, so close had he still been mortal his breath would have caressed Basile's skin. Cupping Basile's chin, Emil stroked his thumb across the small cleft. "We're not finished. Not by a long shot."

Basile couldn't stop the shudder that raced through his body. His cock tightened painfully. "Let's go to my cabin," he snarled past his clenched teeth. No need for the few men who remained on board to see their captain kissing another man. Basile worked to keep a low profile, both in the fact that he was a vampire and that he preferred men. Only a few trusted members of his crew knew his secrets. Basile wanted to keep it that way.

Triumph, quickly masked, filled Emil's face.

Basile turned away, a bad taste in his mouth. That he'd succumbed to Emil's wishes, even for just a few moments longer, galled. He hurried downstairs, regretting even bringing Emil below decks. As soon as he entered his cabin he slammed the door shut behind Emil. Tired of having to face Emil and risk his perfect plans going astray, Basile released the frustration bottled up inside him. "What will it take for you to go away?" he snarled.

"Prove to me you feel nothing for me. Prove to me that we're really over. Then I'll accept your unwillingness to help the Union cause and go away quietly."

"Fine," Basile growled. Curling his fingers over Emil's shoulders, he shoved him against the wall. Before Emil could protest, Basile slanted his lips across his, hard and urgent. His tongue thrust into Emil's mouth and struck the point of one fang.

Blood welled from the tiny wound.

Emil moaned, his throat working to try and swallow Basile's crimson essence.

He really was a vampire.

Control fled along with Basile's anger. Spearing his fingers into the man's short hair, he marveled at once again feeling the silky strands against his hand. With lips and tongue he devoured Emil's mouth. He stroked each of Emil's fangs with his tongue, up and down as if they were miniature cocks. For so long, Basile had cut himself off from the man he'd loved because he feared the inevitable pain of his lover's death. Now, with Emil a vampire, his greatest dreams could come true.

Except he still intended to leave for France in a couple of days. Getting out of the states before the war grew any more violent seemed like a prudent move. Emil wanted him to support the Union blockade. He wanted Basile to get his ship, his property, directly involved in the heinous battle. Basile fought for control. Blood pounded in his veins, hardened his cock like one of the masts of his ship, and demanded he take this man over and over again in an attempt to make up for lost time.

Emil flattened his palm on Basile's chest. His fingers fumbled as he opened Basile's shirt. A button flew off, pinging against the wall. Reaching into the opening, Emil traced the contours of Basile's pectorals. He flattened his hands over the nipples, clenching and releasing like the paws of a purring cat. With his fingertips, he teased Basile's nipples, drawing them into tiny, hard points.

Basile feared he wouldn't last. Their tongues tangled. The sweet feel of Emil's skin brought back so many sweet memories that Basile soon had Emil bared to the waist. His caresses found pathways across flesh both old and new. Several scars on Emil's chest testified to his near-fatal wound, a battlefield somewhere, Basile guessed, not wanting to think about a mortal Emil putting himself into harm's way. His hands curved around Emil's waist. The arrow of hair leading to his cock promised a trail of sensual delights Basile ached to explore. Dropping his fingers to the waistband of Emil's trousers, he unfastened them and shoved them down his hips.

Even standing there with his pants pooled around his ankles, Emil was a handsome man. A smattering of light brown curls covered his chest, growing thicker between his pectorals and in a line bisecting his abdomen. Veins roped around his cock, the head flushed purple. Just looking at it made Basile's mouth water, and he couldn't wait to have the American beneath him, begging for release.

He tore his lips away. Hell! What was he thinking? Shaking his head, he moved back. "No. I don't feel a thing," he lied. If his heart still beat it would have beat a mile a minute. As it was his hands shook, his entire body tingled, and his cock pounded with the need to spill itself into Emil's waiting, and Basile knew, all-too-willing body. "I think that proves it. I'm sorry, Emil. Goodbye." He spoke quickly, wanting to get the words out there and just leave. With his departure set and the wheels in place to get him home as soon as possible, he didn't want to think about resuming his relationship with Emil. He wanted to, but being tied to the United States right now wasn't a smart move. Not by a long shot.

Emil laughed. His slack-jawed grin revealed his fangs and the mouth that Basile had just thoroughly kissed. "You never did lie worth a shit." Heedless of his near-total nudity, he bent over, giving Basile a view of the long line of his back and the rounded curve of his buttocks. Unlacing his boots, he kicked them off and stepped the rest of the way out of his clothes.

"I'm not lying," Basile countered through his clenched jaw. He struggled to keep his gaze above Emil's waist. "Besides, even if things were different, it's too late. I'm returning to France."

"So you say, but you forget we have mail and vessels that cross the Atlantic now. They're working on transatlantic telegraphs if we need to speak sooner. The war will be over soon and then I can come to France, or you can resume shipping back here. Things are completely different, and I wish you'd see that," Emil said in a matter-of-fact tone. He didn't plead, didn't beg, though the raw need on his face and rampant erection testified to his sexual desire.

Such was the way of mortals. Even in the face of certain doom they held such hope and optimism. Emil hadn't yet developed the cynicism one gained after living for centuries.

"It's not that easy." Sometime during the kiss his hair had come undone from its ribbon, and Basile dragged his fingers through the strands, freeing it the rest of the way. The tie fluttered to the floor.

"Then make it that easy," Emil challenged. He reached for Basile, cupping his hands around the man's shaft, and even through the layers of clothing it throbbed to his touch.

Basile bit back a groan.

"Tonight it is that easy. I think we both need this." Emil knelt at Basile's feet and unlaced his boots. He looked up, the desire and the need in his gaze humbling the Frenchman.

He'd tried to remain dispassionate, damn it. He'd tried to put his own interests first. He couldn't. Emil's youthful optimism always wore him down. Basile removed his boots and faced Emil. Slowly, he brushed his thumb across the American's full lower lip. "We both may need this, but it's not going to change anything," he whispered.

"It doesn't have to. Not right now." Emil sealed his words with a kiss. His lips moved sensuously against Basile's, the touch so hesitant for a moment Basile feared the American would bolt away. He didn't. Instead, his hand cupped the back of Basile's head, deepening the kiss. His tongue feathered across Basile's, his other hand trailing down his arm to tangle their fingers.

Basile walked Emil back toward the bed. He lowered his former lover to the mattress, thanking the gods he'd thought to have it stuffed fresh as soon as they arrived in port. Hints of lavender still clung to the aromatic filling. On the narrow bunk, Basile braced his weight on his arms, his legs tangling with Emil's. Flesh against flesh, the bump of shaft and balls, the kind of pleasure only two men could give each other. Fingers trailed over the back, found buttocks and squeezed. And still, Basile kissed him. Sometimes not needing air was a blessing. He stroked along the underside of Emil's tongue, feeling the American's hips pump in the search for release.

A release Basile wanted to give him. Pulling his lips away, he kissed a trail over pecs and abs, down to the cock demanding attention. On his knees, hunched over in the bunk, Basile ignored the awkward position. If nothing else, it kept Emil from touching him and bringing him that much closer to the edge. He wrapped his lips around Emil's head and licked it.

The taste of salty pre-come burst on his tongue. Pure ambrosia. A groan rumbled from his chest, and he wondered how he could go so long without tasting Emil's piquant flavors. Salt and spice, the kind of musk a man could make, so different from a woman's creamy honey. Basile laved the vein throbbing on the underside of Emil's cock with his tongue, drawing a moan from the man on the bed. Cupping his balls, Basile fondled them in his hands, working them back and forth, pausing every so often to tease the sensitive skin between.

He could suck Emil's cock forever. The thought filled his mind, reminded him of all the reasons why he shouldn't shove the American away, even as he knew this one time together would be all they ever could have. Drawing Emil's shaft deeper into his throat, Basile nestled his lips at the base. Removing his mouth slowly, he nearly released Emil's cock, then he plunged forward again.

"Basile," Emil groaned, his voice ragged with need. "Oh God, I'm going to come."

Around the thick staff in his mouth, Basile grinned. Exactly how he wanted it. Give Emil a mind-blowing orgasm before he sought relief deep inside the man's body. Think about just the physical pleasures, not the emotional ones. That's all he could focus on at the moment. Anything more didn't matter.

Basile pulled his lips away. "Kneel for me."

Emil languidly rose to his knees. Turning away from Basile, he presented a glorious picture of masculine beauty. His broad shoulders and muscled back tapered to narrow hips and tight buttocks that drew Basile's gaze. Emil spread his legs, providing a good view of his balls. Basile knelt behind him, flesh against flesh, his chest pressed against Emil's back. Reaching around, he fondled Emil's balls. They were full and heavy in his hands.

Leaning forward, he kissed along the curve of Emil's shoulder. Licking the sweat from his lover's skin, Basile reveled in the crisp taste. Gentle bites raised red marks along Emil's pale flesh, working from shoulder to neck, where he nibbled on the jugular, never piercing, just hard enough to leave marks. "I want to devour you whole," Basile said with a grin. "You're like the fine pastries I used to eat before my turning. You look pale, soft, and yet there's nothing soft about you." He sank his teeth into Emil's shoulder and squeezed the base of his cock.

Emil groaned. "Fuck me."

"In good time." Basile stroked Emil's cock, the friction of flesh against flesh making the muscle leap in his palm. Working faster, increasing the pressure, he soon brought Emil to the brink of orgasm. Basile held Emil's balls in his other hand, feeling them draw tight against his body. With a ragged groan, Emil came. His seed pumped over Basile's hand, slick and perfect for what the Frenchman had in mind. Bringing his hand to his own cock, he coated it liberally, before pressing it against the tight ring of muscle.

His hand back on Emil's half-hard cock, Basile worked his body into Emil's tight sheath. How many years, how many nights had it been since he'd done this? As the heat of the American's body surrounded his cock, Basile wondered why he hadn't gone after Emil sooner.

Because at one time, very recently, Emil had been human. Basile seated himself fully inside, savoring the feeling of tight muscles around his shaft, the way Emil's cock stiffened in his hand once more. So good. So right. He rested his forehead against Emil's shoulder, eyes closed so he could simply savor the moment.

Primal urges took over. No more time for tender moments, for remembrances. His blood pounded with the need to take

Emil, hard and fast, making them both come. Beneath them, the boat rocked from side to side, the soft lapping of waves against the hull making them feel isolated from the world, or as isolated as they could get on a large gunboat. Basile pulled out, only to thrust forward again.

Basile lost himself to the heat of Emil's body, the feel of his lover's cock in his hands, his balls rolling in his other hand. A sheen of sweat erupted on Emil's skin, and Basile licked it away with each thrust. They fit together perfectly, Emil's additional couple of inches in height giving Basile unlimited access to his back. The nape of Emil's neck and the top of his spine deserved more attention. He'd loved to nip tiny love bites along the length of Emil's spine from neck to buttocks.

Basile struggled to hold onto some measure of control. He focused his attention on the minuscule sensations racing through his body. His muscles tightened, his cock swelled. Emil's sheath milked his cock, growing tighter with each thrust. Almost too much to bear, and then like a fiery explosion racing up from his balls, his cock surged forward once more. An all-too-familiar tingling started at the base of his spine, and with a hoarse yell he came.

Basile released Emil's balls to clamp his arm around the American's waist in an attempt to hold him upright. The world tilted and swayed, spots swam behind his closed eyelids. His orgasm went on and on, wave after wave of seed pulsing into Emil's body.

The American gave a strangled groan as he came once more. Basile watched, transfixed, as Emil's seed splashed against his hand. His lover's head tilted back, his eyes closed in ecstasy. The two men fell to the bed tangled together. Their sweaty bodies entwined, and all Basile could think of was damn he'd missed that. He'd missed it a lot.

It still changed nothing.

No pounding heartbeats echoed in the room, no panting breaths. They were both undead, walking corpses who traipsed among the living, if the penny dreadful writers were to be believed. Until this moment, he'd never thought of Emil in those terms. He'd always been his American lover. The one man who had gotten under his skin and pulled him from the despair the loss of his previous mortal lover had plunged him into. And in two days, he'd leave Emil for good.

Emil swung his legs over the edge of the bed. With a glance over his shoulder, his face an unreadable mask, he hurried to his clothes. He dressed in silence, not even bothering to clean up, though a pitcher of water and a basin sat secured on the top of a chest. Lines creased his forehead, his lips drawn down. It wasn't an expression Basile expected any lover to wear, not after receiving two orgasms in little more than an hour.

Basile sat on the bed. His honor demanded that he tell Emil the truth. And yet, he found he couldn't open his mouth to express the words. A case of moral lockjaw. "Are you glad you came back?" he finally asked, half-dreading Emil's answer. They'd rushed things, fell into bed too soon and now this awkwardness was the consequence.

Emil fastened his trousers and finished buttoning his shirt. He turned to face Basile, his gaze lingering. He licked his lips and scowled even harder. "If it meant things might have changed, then yeah, I'm happy. If not, well, it was a release, a way not to have to think of things for a while." He shrugged into his jacket. "Dawn's coming."

Emil's words stung like salt in an open wound. "It can't change anything," Basile said, even as his heart cried out that Emil being a vampire changed everything. Just thinking about the years of loss, the heartbreak he'd suffered, both at Emil and his prior lover's hands, had him recoiling back. Down that road lay pain, and Basile worked at all costs to avoid being hurt.

"Why not?" Emil tossed the question out between them. "You handled your business from America before. I'm sure your men wouldn't mind a chance to use this gunboat as it was designed. You captain a ship of the line. She's specifically designed for war. Why not let her live her true purpose?"

"And get her scuttled at the bottom of the Atlantic? No thank you. I have no part in your country's little war." Bolting to his feet, Basile grabbed his pants. Pulling them on, he struggled to keep his temper. "I made plans to return to France months ago. I cannot change them just because you show up and beg me to help you. The fact that you're a vampire changes nothing. I'm sorry." He moved to the windows and fastened the shutters tight against the slight glow on the horizon. "If you want to make it back safely you may wish to go now."

A knock on the door interrupted their conversation. Snatching his shirt, Basile slid it over his shoulders. He left it unbuttoned, knowing he had his First Officer and Second Officer outside to give report on the night and be ready for the day.

"This isn't done, yet," Emil said. He curled his fingers around the doorknob.

"Yes, my friend, I'm afraid it is. I have business to attend to. Be well, Emil."

"And you, Basile." With a nod, Emil opened the door and brushed past the two officers, both of whom had been with Basile many years. If they were surprised to see Basile's former lover hurrying away from his quarters, they said nothing. They were well-trained men.

"Good morning. I trust things are well setup for our meetings today?"

"Yes, sir, they are," his First Officer said. "I'd be happy to go over the plans one more time if you like."

"Thank you." Basile looked over the men's shoulders at the retreating form of Emil. Though he could recite in his sleep what should happen over the next two days, he needed the distraction. Perhaps he'd been too harsh on the young man, young vampire, he corrected, but if so, then it was for the best. If Emil were to survive centuries, he needed to learn that the world was a cruel place. He just wished he didn't have to be the vampire to teach him.

Chapter Three

Slamming the door behind him, Emil pounded his fist into the doorframe. Obscenities spewed from his mouth. He still smelled Basile on his skin, still felt his touch, his cock, his sometimes gentle and sometimes brutal lovemaking. Just thinking about it made Emil hard. He growled.

"You're in quite a mood," his commanding officer said. "I take it you don't have good news?"

Emil snarled at the older man with white-gray hair sitting in one of the two chairs in his apartment. Even this early in the morning, the official wore his uniform, his grooming impeccable as always. Coming home smelling of sweat and sex reminded Emil he'd been a frontline solider until his turning, far beneath a man of his commander's stature. Apparently his boss had let himself in.

"That would be a no, wouldn't it?" His commanding officer uncrossed his legs and leaned forward.

"It's a no. I spoke to everyone. I'm afraid they all have prior arrangements and regret to inform the United States Government that they cannot assist in our battle, but they wish us all the luck and hope that we heal our wounds soon." He spoke in a deliberate, mocking tone, mimicking the way that all the captains, including Basile, covered their own asses.

"I see," his boss said, dragging fingers through his gray hair. Though not a vampire himself, he was aware of Emil's unique talents, and they'd devised these dawn meetings to coincide with their working schedules. "Even Captain Gagnon?"

Emil nodded, his heart heavy. After what they shared, he'd expected the Frenchman to reconsider. If not assisting in the

119

blockade, then at least his decision to return to France so quickly. Though Emil had seen the pain in Basile's eyes. Emil understood all too well what leaving had cost. Pressing his lips together, he took in the room and knew it was a far cry from the luxury of Basile's ship. Two chairs and a small table which he used to take his meals, or at least he had when he was human, occupied the small room. No kitchenette, just another closet of a room that held a chest with his clothing and a narrow bed. A few yards of canvas, precious now because of the war, covered the window, blocking out the arriving sun. Emil sank into the empty chair. "Even Captain Gagnon. He's sailing for France in two days."

"That's not going to help our cause, boy. I thought you said you had connections around the dock and could convince the merchants to aid our blockade. At this rate, we'll have only a few ships patrolling the southern coast, far too few to keep out supplies those rebel bastards need." He pulled a cigar from his pocket and lit it from the lamp sitting on the table. After taking several puffs he offered it to Emil.

The vampire shook his head, politely declining as he had every night. The pungent smoke filled his nostrils, and his enhanced vampiric senses hated the stinky things. But his commanding officer liked them, and one did not tell one's commanding officer what to do. He schooled his expression. "I don't think this has anything to do with my contacts. Frankly, the war has everyone running scared." He dragged his fingers through his hair. "Recruiting from the merchants may not be the best course of action. They're concerned only with making money, not saving a nation."

His commander puffed on the cigar a few more times, looking thoughtful. "You may be right, but the merchants are all we have. I haven't been given authority to conscript the ships into service. Perhaps I can speak with the Secretary of War and see if he can grant me the authority. A very good idea."

Inwardly, Emil cringed. If the Secretary of War conscripted ships, it'd generate mistrust and ill will among the very merchants they relied upon to keep necessary supplies flowing into the union. He shook his head. "That wasn't what I meant, sir, with all due respect. We cannot just start conscripting merchant ships."

"Then I suggest you talk to Captain Gagnon and get him to see reason. With his ship of the line we could go a long way toward making the blockade work. And if he came to our cause, he'd bring several smaller merchants with him." His commanding officer rose to his feet.

"Sir, Captain Gagnon is French. I doubt he has much influence among the local merchants." Emil's stomach churned. He stood, not wanting to look up at the man who gave him orders. Truth be told, he was right. But with less than two days to convince Basile, Emil doubted he had half a chance.

"I think you'll find some way to convince him." With those words and a pointed look, the man went to the door, opened it, and strode into the hall.

Emil watched him leave, listening to the door slam behind him. Alone once more, Emil slumped into the chair. Closing his eyes, he wished he knew of a better answer to the problem. His thoughts always returned to Basile. His heart clenched, the smells on his body a harsh reminder of what they had and what he'd lost. Rising to his feet, he checked the locks on the door before staggering into the bedroom. He stripped his clothes and used the tepid water in the bottom of his basin to clean up as best he could. Falling into bed, he stared at the cracked ceiling. When the moon rose again, he'd return to Basile and make the Frenchman see reason. He had to.

~ ∞ ~

Emil sensed the last rays of sunlight dipping below the horizon when he woke. The scent of meals, most likely purchased from the tavern down the block, provided the aroma of greasy meat and cheap ale. Too many unwashed bodies clogged the air with their fetid aroma, and two doors down, the tenants' new baby wailed his dismay at being brought into such a troubled world.

Mortal problems reminded him of the world he'd left behind. A world of families and loved ones, a world where love and loss meant two totally different things. Rubbing his eyes, he sat up, aware he'd slept only in his long johns. Hunger gnawed at him like a dog with a bone. His eyes burned, and he knew if he looked in a mirror they'd glow red. Damn it, he couldn't face Basile like this. The Frenchman had made his feelings clear. Emil lumbered from the bed, feeling like Quasimodo, and splashed the last remaining water on his face. He pulled on clean clothing, realizing he'd have to pay the woman down the hall to do laundry for him again, and rubbed at his stubbled jaw. He might be the walking dead, but he still grew facial hair. He shaved, jotted a note to Basile and, announcing himself presentable, went in search of a runner.

He found a young man on the corner loitering by the tavern and paid him a few coins to run the note to Basile's ship. Emil dipped into an alley and found a homeless man, a wounded civil war soldier from the look of him, who provided enough of a meal to add a bloom to Emil's cheeks and ease the man's pain for a while. Not kill him. Emil never killed his victims, but a vampire bite created a euphoria that lasted for several hours. After procuring a bottle of the tavern's best wine, he hurried back to his apartment to wait for Basile's arrival. If Basile arrived.

Emil shook his head as he stepped inside. He bustled around the room, straightening a few days worth of newspapers and sending his clothes down the hall to be laundered. Basile had to arrive. Basile would arrive.

And he did. An hour later, a knock on Emil's apartment door startled him out of his wayward thoughts. Brushing invisible specks of lint off his shirt and waistcoat, he hurried to the door and opened it. Basile stood on the other side, dressed, impeccable as always, and looking every inch the dashing sea captain.

"I'm glad you answered my letter," Emil said as he gestured Basile to follow. He closed the door behind the Frenchman and watched as he looked around his apartment. Emil wondered what he saw. Spartan decoration, canvas hung over the windows, hardly the opulence to which Basile was accustomed. No fancy gilt knobs on his dresser or antique china basins held within a cradle of leather straps to keep them from getting broken onboard ship. The same apartment he'd had prior to enlisting with the army, and Emil knew he didn't exactly live in the lap of luxury. It was a far cry from Basile and his French chateau.

"Charming," Basile said, only a hint of mocking in his laughter. He glanced at the two chairs and the bottle of wine on the table between them. "Dinner?" He arched his eyebrow.

"It's probably not the vintages to which you're accustomed, but yes, I took the liberty of supplying dinner." Emil uncorked the bottle and poured a generous measure into each glass.

"*Bon appetit.*" Basile raised the glass to his nose and sniffed at it, before swirling the crimson liquid. He pondered it for a moment and took a small sip. "Not bad."

Relief washed through Emil. The last thing he'd wanted was for Basile to have to drink wine that might better be used as vinegar. This side of the docks, vintages could be interesting, especially after they'd passed through several hands. Emil drank, his limited palette telling him that the wine was indeed a good one. He mulled over the ways of approaching the topic with Basile.

"My superior is going to the Secretary of War to conscript merchant vessels to help with the Union blockade, unless I can convince you to sign on. The Secretary of War believes if you take our side, then other merchant vessels will follow." Emil rested his wine cup on the table between them.

"You will soon learn that mortal matters mean little to us, Emil. You haven't been a vampire very long, have you?" Basile sipped his wine and smiled indulgently.

"No, I haven't," Emil said, trying very hard not to feel like a chastised little boy. "I may be a vampire but my devotion to my country hasn't changed. Just as your devotion to France hasn't changed in all the years you've been a vampire. How can you love your country and yet, ask me to deny my own?" Needing something to do with his hands, he lifted his wineglass and drank.

Silence settled into the room. It searched out empty corners, filling it. Night created dark shadows in the corners, the sounds grew less domestic and louder as the tavern's business increased and families tucked themselves behind four paper-thin walls. The never-ending stench of the neighborhood failed to leave, and Emil wondered what Basile could be thinking. He'd always hated obvious signs of humanity. Crowded like livestock waiting for slaughter, he'd always said, though Emil suspected the gruff words hid a heart riddled with pain.

"You may be right," Basile said once his glass was empty. He refilled it from the bottle on the table. Rubbing the bridge of his nose, he stared at Emil for long moments. "I have arrangements already made though, and I cannot break them. Not even for you." He shook his head.

Emil opened his mouth, wanting, needing to say something, and yet no words came to mind. He closed his lips and pressed them together to keep from saying something stupid. So that was that. He'd tried, given it more than his best shot, and when it came down to it, tomorrow Basile would sail for France, and Emil would be left to try and find a way to blockade half of his country. "There's got to be a way. We have to do something. I can't let the Secretary of War start conscripting merchant ships."

Basile shrugged. "It is a time of war, your country will do what it deems necessary."

"Even if they deem it necessary to take *your* ship? I'm sorry, Basile. I don't believe that for one moment." Tired of toying with his wine, Emil set the glass on the table between them.

"They won't move so quickly."

"I wouldn't be sure of that." The need to do something propelled Emil to his feet. He paced the width of his small living room, his footsteps echoing.

Basile stood. He crossed the space between them. Curling his fingers over Emil's shoulders, he halted the man in his tracks. "Listen, I am a French citizen. The US government cannot claim my ship. It's against the law. Those other merchants will have to make their own decision." He sighed, as if the fight had leeched from his pores. Reaching up, he brushed a strand of hair from Emil's forehead. "I don't know why I had to run into you when I had my plans perfect. I planned to go home, to retire to my property and leave the mortal world behind." His fingers strayed along Emil's jaw. "You always did try and change my plans."

Emil's eyes fluttered closed. Standing so close to Basile, he inhaled the man's spicy scent. It would be too easy to believe that this was an earlier time, a time when all Emil had to worry about was Basile's broken heart. He smiled.

"What are you smiling about, *ma lapin*?" Basile's fingers stilled. He trailed his free hand along the sleeve of Emil's shirt.

Basile's use of the endearment shocked Emil. He stiffened against Basile's touch, battling against the hope that perhaps the vampire still harbored feelings. "You," Emil answered after long moments. "You make me smile. You blame me for ruining your plans, and yet, somehow, I wonder if you could have left Baltimore without seeing me?" His grin widened. Reaching up, he freed Basile's hair from the ribbon tying it back and threaded his fingers through the silken strands. Emil leaned forward to nuzzle Basile's neck. The vampire's scent surrounded him, penetrated his very pores, and made Emil think only of the small, rumpled bed in the other room.

"You're sure of yourself, aren't you?" Basile questioned. His lips hovered close enough that the warm breath from his words puffed across Emil's mouth.

Emil's lips parted as if to drink in the very air Basile needed to speak. "You always called me a brash American."

Basile laughed. "So I did." His laughter faded away, leaving only the two men, once lovers, wanting so very much to be lovers again, standing in the middle of Emil's living room. Through the walls, the sound of drunken laughter, a woman's shriek and a man's murmured words of seduction provided a carnal backdrop to their conversation.

Emil swallowed hard, noticing that Basile's eyes rested on his throat as it worked. The Frenchman leaned forward. His fangs scraped across already-sensitized flesh, sending shivers down Emil's spine. His cock hardened, body remembering the passion he could find from the Frenchman's touch, his bite. Emil tried to stifle his groan. He'd forgotten about Basile's bite, the euphoria the vampire could invoke with the sweetest kiss from his fangs. The pull of blood into his mouth, such an intimate act, one of total surrender. Emil's blood pounded through his veins, the need to offer such a thing to Basile nearly overwhelming. Clamping his hand on Basile's arm, he waited, hungered and hoped like hell the vampire bit him.

Basile swirled his tongue over the pulse on Emil's artery. He moved closer, his hand sliding to Emil's back, then lower so he cupped his ass and drew their bodies flush together. Their legs tangled.

Winding his arms around Basile, Emil stroked his back, the fine weave of Basile's expensive coat reminding him of their difference in station. Eyes closed, he swayed toward the Frenchman, painfully aware of the bulge in his pants. His body ached, so full it was near bursting, and still Basile languidly licked his neck as if they had all the time in the world. And perhaps, to the Frenchman, they did. After all, he'd lived for centuries, what more was a few hours?

"Basile," he breathed, resting his forehead against the Frenchman's shoulder. Emil bunched his hands in the tails of Basile's coat and struggled to try and stay in control. He wanted to slam Basile against the wall and take him, over and over again, until his pounding thrusts made Basile forget all about returning to France. Emil willed his body to behave.

"What is it that you do to me?" Basile breathed against the side of his neck. A ragged groan issued from his throat, and with a sigh he sank his fangs into Emil's neck.

Pure bliss erupted from the site. Blood pumped in Emil's veins, drawing slowly, ever so slowly, into Basile's throat, and Emil could only imagine the pleasure the vampire must be feeling. He knew, for he felt it too. Emil turned so his lips fluttered across Basile's skin. Beneath the surface, blood pooled, ripe and ready for the sucking. His fangs scraped across the skin.

Sweat. Heat. Blood. The scents and tastes combined into a heady elixir. Emil licked the pulse point, the need to savor the moment keeping him from driving his fangs in and swallowing Basile whole.

Basile hauled Emil hard enough against him to send them stumbling backwards. Sheer vampire strength kept them from tumbling over. Instead, Basile, still keeping his fangs buried in Emil's neck, lowered them to the floor. The unforgiving wood mattered little, even with no rugs to soften it. Layers of clothing protected them, prevented closer contact, and with a groan, Emil reached for Basile's frock coat.

Buttons pinged and fabric opened. With his blood flowing into Basile's body, Emil fought the belief that once again they were tied together, body and soul, blood and bone. Finally, at last, Emil sank his fangs into Basile's flesh.

The elder vampire's rich blood flowed over Emil's fangs. He groaned, his lips sealing against skin, not wanting to lose a precious drop of the fluid. Fingers stilled, the need for nakedness replaced by the hot rush of life-giving blood. Back and forth, his blood in Basile's veins, Basile's blood in his, the give and take reminiscent of the thrust and retreat of sex.

But oh, how much sweeter the exchange of blood was when accompanied by more physical pleasures. Emil lifted his hips, letting the elder vampire know the full extent of his arousal.

Basile groaned. He tangled his fingers in Emil's shorter hair, holding Emil's head still while he drank. Pulling his lips away, Basile licked the wound to seal it closed. "Now, there are other things to be enjoyed," Basile said, rearing back just enough to work on the buttons on Emil's shirt.

As soon as he'd bared Emil's chest, Basile bent his head, nuzzling the hollow of Emil's collarbone and across his clavicle. The Frenchman paid special attention to Emil's nipples, swirling his tongue around them before drawing them deep into his mouth.

Emil lost himself to sensation. Sparks darted through his blood, igniting his flesh to a fever pitch. Without the need to breathe, he simply kept his mouth closed, his entire body straining toward the kind of release only Basile could offer.

Spearing his fingers through Basile's hair, Emil held him to his breast. His chest tightened. The scarce time they had together seemed way too short. A day and a half at the most, and Basile would sail across the Atlantic. His fingers spasmed on the back of Basile's head. His other hand reached down and cupped the Frenchman's hip. Squeezing gently, Emil rocked against Basile. Enough time for foreplay. He wanted to be buried so deep inside his lover that when he left, Emil wouldn't be left behind.

Basile slid his lips from Emil's nipple. "Impatient, aren't we?"

That voice, husky and so full of promise, washed over Emil like a fresh spring rain. "Yes," he whispered. "You know I can't wait." Sliding his hand along the firm line of Basile's spine, he grabbed Basile's buttocks. "I've got to be inside you. Please."

Basile stilled. In all their years together, Emil had never asked. He'd always taken what he wanted, his vulnerability a crack in his armor. The brash young American, that's all Emil had ever been, all he'd ever wanted to be. But now, faced with Basile's leaving, he wanted more. His body demanded it, his soul cried out for it. Without waiting for an answer, he reached around and unfastened Basile's trousers, shoving them over his hips. Using his vampiric strength, Emil flipped the other man over, straddling him long enough to remove boots and clothing.

Basile lay naked. He didn't move, didn't say anything, and that alone should have told Emil something wasn't quite right. The Frenchman rested his hands behind his head and spread his legs, giving Emil a full view of his lightly furred balls. "What are you waiting for?" His thick accent made the words sound rich and decadent.

Emil dropped to his knees. The sheer perfection of Basile's body stole rational thought from his mind. A hand reached for his flank, and belatedly, Emil realized it was his hand, fingers curled to touch. Flaring his nostrils, he drew in the spicy scent that was so uniquely Basile, the sounds, the smells, even the rushing of beating mortal hearts fading away around him.

He touched Basile's thigh. Muscles jumped beneath Emil's fingers, anticipation, frustration, or a little bit of both, he wondered. Warmth indicated Basile had recently fed, and Emil flushed to know it was his blood that flowed in the vampire's veins. Strength filled every corded line of his body, the strength to withstand centuries and battles Emil could only imagine.

"Emil?" Basile's soft question hung in the air.

"Yes?"

Basile slid from beneath his touch, rising onto all fours and presenting his ass to the American. "Would you prefer me this way?" His head lowered, hair brushing aside to reveal the nape of his neck. The gentle, submissive posture seemed so at odds with the vampire Emil knew.

"Yes." He moved behind Basile, his erect cock fitting nicely in the cleft of Basile's buttocks. Leaning forward, Emil pressed his lips to that bared nape, indicating with teeth and tongue that he accepted Basile's surrender, even as he felt his own. Scraping the sensitive skin with his canines, he nipped gently.

Basile moaned. "Is this what you wanted?"

Emil's teeth stilled. His big hands held the man in place. The taste of him was intoxicating, like a human drunk on the very best wines. The valley along his spine called to Emil, a place of tastes and textures he could find nowhere else. He licked, a long swipe of his tongue like a dog, and grinned. "It's a nice beginning." From where this demanding creature came from, he didn't know, for all of a sudden his lips, his fingers, his tongue were everywhere.

He moved over Basile's body like a wave cresting against the shore. Caresses and fleeting touches led to fingers circling his cock, stroking it to full hardness, and then his other hand fondling Basile's balls. Emil fed off the sounds Basile made, the moans and whispers of encouragement that provided sexual sustenance. To think this might be their only night together, a second one when he hadn't even sought out the first.

Unable to hold back his release, Basile stiffened, his come coating Emil's fingers. The American used it to liberally coat his own cock before pressing it against Basile's anus. Emil groaned as he pushed ahead, forging inch by exquisite inch into Basile's body. The Frenchman pushed against him, his cock hardening in Emil's fingers, as if he, too, couldn't get enough. He never could. Not then, and certainly not now.

Their bodies found a rhythm that filled the room with the sound of flesh against flesh and male grunts. It wasn't about the release anymore, though that demanded he thrust harder, deeper. Fingers tightened around Basile's cock, stroking him to full-hardness and beyond, until the Frenchman's fingers curled into the floor and scored long scratches in it. Emil tried to hold off his release, tried to give Basile everything he could. But his body overrode his mind and drove rational thought away. The tight heat of Basile's body wrapped around him, tighter than any woman ever had been, and biting back his shout of triumph, Emil rode the tingling sensation starting just behind his balls. It filled him like a glass seeking water, the need to spill his seed inside of Basile. From his balls to the base of his spine, upward, outward. Each thrust coursed it through his body.

And then, head thrown back, throat corded, he came. As he pumped his seed into his lover, Emil felt another hand join his on Basile's cock. One stroke, two, and together, they both tumbled over the edge to lie in a sweaty, sated heap on the floor.

How he got onto his side, Emil didn't know. He laid there, one arm wrapped around Basile, his cock half-hard against his thigh. Spots swam in front of his vision, a testament to how hard he came, and he tried to retain the dominant, possessive mode he'd found. Basile was his. Except Emil knew that wasn't true, and instead of a union, their joining most likely said goodbye.

Chapter Four

Basile stared across the room at the man who'd taken him a little more than an hour ago. Cleaned up and dressed, they sat once more in those damnable living room chairs drinking surprisingly good wine and talking around the real issue. He finished off his glass, his fifth or sixth, and although it took a large quantity of wine to get vampires drunk, he wished he had that luxury. Because no matter how hard he tried to bar his heart from Emil, the American had snuck inside once more. Or perhaps, he'd never left.

What a mess! His agents had already taken care of the last of his cargo. Another day of leave for his men and then he'd return to France. The Americans spoke sense. If they wanted to win this war a blockade of the Southern states was the most prudent course of action. This far from home, Basile had no news of what the French government thought of such things, but he suspected they most likely supported both sides. After all, the rich agricultural crops of the South were necessary in Europe, and he knew that the British had a taste for them as well. He spun the glass in his hands, his body sated and slightly sore from the unaccustomed sexual activity.

He only postponed the inevitable. "So tell me, what do you think will happen with this war?"

Emil shrugged. "Other than too many young men will die and too many women and children left without husbands and fathers?" He set his glass down and steepled his fingers. Resting his chin on them, he closed his eyes, and Basile sensed he relived memories. "I almost died there, you know."

"No, I didn't." The thought of Emil dead, his life's blood flowing out onto the ground, clamped a vise around his heart.

"Is that how you became a vampire?" The fact that they'd fucked—no, made love—twice and he still didn't know how his partner had become a vampire was simply horribly bad manners on his part.

Emil nodded. "Yeah." His voice grew rough, and he swallowed hard. "You were gone, and I...well hell, I guess I needed to belong somewhere so when they asked for volunteers, I was right there, almost the first in line to sign up. I was assigned to an infantry company. The first battle of Bull Run saw a bullet through my heart, and if it weren't for the man who turned me, I would have died right there on the battlefield. The funny thing is I hadn't even fired a shot." He rubbed the heels of his hands across his eyes. "I didn't even get to fire my rifle before I was killed. Some soldier I turned out to be."

Basile reached across the space separating them. He rested his hand on Emil's shoulder. "There's no shame in that."

Emil looked at him, eyes red, and blinked. "The man who turned me, he has ties to the government. I know him only as the General, though I doubt that's a military rank."

"Have you seen him since?" Basile hungered for news. Vampires working within these mortals' war. It wasn't unheard of, he'd seen for himself the carrion pickers come to many such battles, drawing young men, knights, warriors, to their own personal causes. Most of the vampires tolerated them and understood that like vultures, they performed a valuable service.

"A few times," Emil said. "He made sure I had my current job, matching up my knowledge of the Baltimore docks with the Secretary of War's need for ships. Now that I've exhausted my knowledge I suppose I'll be sent to another port town, another dock, another try at convincing fat-cat merchants to help their country. Or maybe I'll just be sent back to the front lines. I doubt the rebels have enough coin to pay anyone for their services, so if it's money the merchants want, they've come to the right government."

"Money and a chance to have their ship sink to the bottom of the ocean."

Emil gaped at him. "You'd think of your purse rather than..." He shook his head. "Never mind. I guess I know the answer to that." Bolting to his feet, he paced the living room.

Short, clipped strides, his hands clasped behind his back as if he were afraid of what they would do.

Basile burst from the chair to grab Emil's arm, halting him mid-step. "That's not fair. I'd already made these arrangements before we met again. I'm sorry. There are things I have to do."

"And they don't include me or my country." Emil yanked his arm away. "You've made your feelings perfectly clear. I suppose you regret thinking with your cock and not your brain."

"No. Not at all."

He chuckled, mocking laughter that nearly broke Basile's heart. "You say that now. But if for one moment you thought your feelings for me kept you from your precious France that would change." He crossed his arms over his chest and whirled to face Basile. "Your ship leaves tomorrow. I suspect you should get back to it."

"Are you throwing me out? After all we've been through together?" In that moment, Basile regretted parting this way. The sounds of mortal lives pressed in through the thin walls, too close for comfort, and Basile hungered for his chateau with its wide-open spaces. Seclusion well away from mortals' too-impassioned lives. They lived for such a short time, everything became a crisis to them. He feared Emil hadn't been a vampire long enough to truly understand the meaning of immortal.

"Goodbye, Basile." Emil's cold voice slapped him.

"So the tables have turned, have they? Now it's your turn to throw me out." Basile laughed. "Come back with me to my ship. Let's not spend our last few hours fighting." His men had shore leave. Perhaps he should take their advice and do the same.

Emil frowned. Just then two mortals walked past his door, their boisterous, drunken laughter carrying through the apartment's walls.

Hunger gnawed at Basile. Having just fed from Emil helped, but he knew the American would need sustenance too. "Let's go get something to eat," he offered, as close to begging as he'd ever come. In just a short time, Emil had insinuated himself once more into Basile's heart, and the Frenchman didn't like it. He watched, waited, half afraid Emil might turn him down.

And if he did? Well, he'd return to his ship and sail back to France knowing whatever bonds that tied them were dissolved, just as they'd been five years ago. He was a vampire. He had centuries to get over it.

"Something to eat?" Emil spoke slowly, rolling the words around in his mouth.

Basile nodded. "On the way back to my ship."

"So what changed?" Emil asked. "The first time I saw you, you did everything but toss me into the harbor. The second time you told me in no uncertain terms to leave, then you fucked me. Are you getting soft in your old age?" He fisted his hands. Rocking back on his heels, he studied Basile, from his hair come loose from his ribbon to his wrinkled shirt, down over his trousers to his boots that still gleamed. Basile held his hands open, palms at his sides.

"You," Basile breathed. "Look, I still have to go to France. That's written in stone, but oh hell... I didn't expect to find you in Baltimore. I didn't expect that you'd be a vampire. You're here, and you are. Things have changed." He reached for Emil.

His lover looked at his outstretched hand, then up to his face, but didn't take the peace offering. "You can't say that and then leave." Squaring his shoulders, he stepped back. "You told me in no uncertain terms you're returning to France. I have a war to fight. A war I need to help my country win. We can't come together only to be torn apart." His voice grew scratchy, and Emil swallowed hard. "I won't do that again. I'm sorry."

"Oh, Emil." Basile strode forward, stopping directly in front of the American. Cupping his cheek, he ran his thumb over Emil's lower lip. Even in the low light from the lamp, Basile clearly saw Emil's brown eyes, filled with so much sorrow it twisted his gut. "We live forever. There's time for your war." Funny how he'd just had those same thoughts about himself, that he had centuries in which to get over Emil's rejection. A soft smile quirked the corner of his lips.

Emil remained silent.

Basile guessed at his mistake. Once again he'd played the role of the older, far wiser vampire. He moved closer, so close that had they been breathing their chests might have touched. "I'm sorry," he whispered. "This war is important to you. I didn't mean to diminish that. But the sentiment still holds. We're vampires. We live forever. Things will pass, but we will remain."

"Will we?" Emil whispered.

"Yes. We will," Basile confirmed, sensing the younger vampire's need to hear the reassurances that came so easily to mortals. Only this time, he knew exactly what he confirmed, and he had the power to make it so.

"Thank God," Emil breathed. Resting his head against Basile's chest, Emil wrapped both arms around him.

Basile returned the embrace, his hands flattening on Emil's back and sliding down his spine to rest just above the curve of his buttocks. How could he have forgotten how good and right it felt to hold him like this, just simply hold him. Sure, his cock pounded. From the ridge tucked against him, Emil's body had the same physical reaction. And yet, neither made a move to deepen the intimacy. Allowing his eyelids to flutter closed, he wondered if perhaps the American hadn't known what it was like to be a vampire. Maybe he did understand the true depth of being immortal. Living forever came with a price, the price of watching mortal friends and loved ones die.

"I'll go back with you to your ship," Emil said at long last. "I can't stay. As much as I might want to leave this place and go to France with you, I can't."

"I understand." Basile knew even he, who had been a vampire for so long and who tried not to become embroiled in mortal matters, did so on occasion stoop to caring about the shorter-lived inhabitants of his world. In his heart, he understood, for ten long years ago he'd fallen in love with a mortal. It had torn him up inside to leave. He feared this time it'd hurt no less.

Emil slipped from his arms. He licked his lips. "Do you think you could draw me a bath on your ship, like we used to?"

Basile grinned. His large tub, nearly big enough for two, was his pride and joy. He imported oils and soaps from the far corners of the world, though he loved his Italian castile soap the best. If he remembered correctly, so did Emil. "Of course. It would be my pleasure," he replied, knowing the double meaning wouldn't be lost.

"Then if this is to be our last night together, let's make it a memorable one." Emil opened the door with a flourish and followed Basile.

The two men said nothing as they made their way through the darkened streets to the docks. Basile's heart swelled as he looked upon the *Souverain*. He glanced at the man walking beside him, wondering what he thought of the ship that had born Basile across the Atlantic and back again dozens of times. This time, he feared he might never return to these shores, or at least not for many years. The war would make ship travel difficult in these waters, and undoubtedly Emil was painfully aware of that fact as he climbed the ladder behind him.

His men remained at their posts atop ship, a skeleton crew for the night watch. Quickly, Basile ordered the bath drawn, and his men obeyed like the fine-tuned crew they were. It should have made him proud. Instead, as he watched bucket after bucket of their precious fresh water supply be heated and poured into the tub, he thought only of how few hours lay between now and his departure. When at last the tub was filled, Basile hurried the last crewmember out of his cabin and locked the door.

He turned to Emil. "Your bath, good sir." He stifled a chuckle as he unfastened his waistcoat and slung it over the back of his chair. The buttons of his shirt followed, until he stripped out of trousers and boots to find Emil still standing there, staring at him.

Basile swished his hand through the water. Bracing his hands on the edge of the tub, he leaned over and grinned at the still-dressed Emil. "The water is the perfect temperature. Just the way you like it." Scooping up a handful of water, he flicked the droplets in Emil's direction. They splattered on the floor, missing him by a few inches.

Emil sauntered over, unfastening the buttons on his clothing. He removed each item, letting it drop to the floor.

"It'd be a shame not to enjoy this bath," Basile teased.

"Yes, it would." Emil mirrored Basile's posture on the other side of the tub. Leaning forward, they met in the middle, lips and tongues colliding in a heated, carnal kiss.

Emil groaned. Without breaking the kiss, he pushed Basile back so he could slip into the heated water. Emil sank lower.

Basile followed him, not wanting the kiss to end. With the end of his tongue, he traced the tips of Emil's fangs. He resisted the urge to rub his tongue against the point, hungering for the sweet, coppery taste of Emil's blood. Not yet. Take it slow. Take it easy. His blood pounded in his veins, his cock thick and hard between his thighs. The cool porcelain of the tub should have cooled his ardor. Instead, the naked man in the tub fueled it.

He cupped the back of Emil's head. Dropping to his knees, he massaged the muscles at the top of Emil's spine. With his other hand, he reached into the warm water, needing the slick feel of wet skin against him. A bar of soap lay on a tray not far out of reach, and he pulled his hand out of the water long enough to grab it. Immediately, suds formed on the bar, and pulling his lips away, Basile wrapped his hands around the castile soap and worked up lather. Then, he flattened his palms on Emil's chest.

Emil tipped his head back, eyelids fluttering closed. His lashes fanned against the sharp planes of his cheeks. His lips parted, body relaxed in the warm water, and Basile wondered how far the American's submission would go. The thought of bending him over the edge of the tub and taking him hard and fast came to mind, and he smiled wickedly just thinking about it. He lifted one leg over the edge of the tub and stepped into it.

Emil's eyes opened. "What are you doing?"

"What does it look like I'm doing?" Basile asked as he brought his other leg into the tub. Facing Emil, Basile lowered himself until he straddled Emil's thighs. Ignoring the needs of his body, Basile resumed soaping Emil's chest. Flattening his palms on his shoulders, he stroked down toward Emil's nipples. Swirling his fingers around the tight beads, Basile caressed up to Emil's shoulders, before starting the entire sweep over again.

Just the tactile pleasure of touching Emil aroused Basile. He ignored for a moment the erection pounding between his thighs or the stiff rod of Emil's cock pressing against him. He devoted his touch to relearning every inch of Emil's body, something he hadn't had a chance yet to do. The valley between his pectorals demanded attention, as did each ridge of his abdomen. He soaped and stroked until Emil thrust his hips against him.

"Turn around," Basile ordered.

Emil's eyes opened.

Moving toward the front of the tub, Basile watched as Emil rose onto his knees and turned the best he could in the cramped quarters. The tub wasn't quite big enough for two, but they made it work. Soon, Emil faced away from him, his knees tucked against his chest. Basile slid in behind and began his caresses once more on Emil's back.

The American leaned into his touch. Complete and total surrender. Basile couldn't look away even if his life depended on it. Emil gave a soft sigh, his muscles relaxing under Basile's caress. Each flutter of his hands brought an answering shiver deep in the American's core, until the bold sweeps of his hand from hips to shoulder and back again gave rise to a tidal wave of passion between them.

Emil gripped the side of the tub, presenting his buttocks to Basile in an unspoken invitation. Water sloshed against the sides of the ship, a counterpoint to the water in the tub. A few drops splashed over the side. Other nights, other water, times when the cabin had been soaked by their water play, came to mind, and Basile grinned. He reached for a bottle of oil. Pouring some into his palm, he stroked himself, his already hard member throbbing even more with the need to be buried inside Emil forever.

Grabbing the American's hips, he pressed his full crown against the opening to Emil's body, and if Basile hadn't missed his guess, his soul as well. As he slid into the American's body, Basile tried to go slow. Filling Emil's body felt like a hole inside of him had been filled, like two pieces of a puzzle coming together after a long absence. When his balls hung full and flush against Emil's, Basile reached around and fondled Emil's cock.

He never would be able to get enough of this. Leaning forward, he buried his face in the crook of Emil's neck, his other hand braced on the edge of the tub. Swallowing hard, resisting the lure of the pale neck pressed against his mouth, he kept from sinking his fangs into the flesh.

Emil began to move. Suspended between Basile's hand and his flesh, he rocked back and forth, one moment impaling Basile's cock deeper inside, the next retreating to get closer to his fingers. Water lapped at the edges of the tub, as if the tub were their own private vessel. Pressure built in Basile's balls, pulling them high and tight against his body.

Bodies joined. Basile closed his eyes, his entire being focused on the vampire in front of him. Each thrust caused muscles to ripple along the length of his shaft, hot and tight, a fist made perfectly for fucking. His hand tightened on the base of Emil's cock. He controlled the American's release. It would be his fingers, his lips, his rod that made his lover come, and Basile knew Emil would love every moment of it.

Just like Basile loved Emil. The floodgates around his heart opened, emotion pouring forth so quickly it nearly made him come right there. Lips opened with the need to taste clean, masculine skin, and Basile found himself mouthing Emil's neck. Squeezing his eyes closed, he tried to stem the rising tide inside him. Let him have a few moments longer. Let him make this last, something Emil could remember when he returned to his government and Basile returned to France.

No! The very thought of Emil leaving him clenched around his heart and quickened his thrusts. If only he could brand himself on Emil's heart, something to make the American follow him to hell and back, because right now, Basile knew he'd do the same. Fangs tingled and sank into flesh.

Yes! Blood, rich and warm, pumped into Basile's mouth. He swallowed greedily.

"Basile," Emil moaned. His hips pistoned faster, his need so frantic Basile tasted it in his blood.

Come for me, lover.

Though not telepathic, he swore Emil heard his unspoken order, for suddenly the American stiffened. A low, guttural cry resonated through his chest. It echoed off the cabin walls, as the vampire convulsed in Basile's arms. His rod shot wave after wave of seed over Basile's slick hand and into the cooling water in which they sat. He leaned back against Basile. "Take me," Emil growled, thrusting his ass at Basile, and impaling him even farther.

Moving the hand from Emil's semi-hard shaft to his hip, he helped Emil stand. Basile followed suit, thankful their near-identical heights made them able to do this without releasing his cock from the American's hot depths. Bending Emil over, he clamped his hands onto the edge of the tub. Basile wrapped his hands around Emil's waist, and using the new leverage he thrust, hard.

Flesh slapped against flesh. Eyes closed, blood dripping from the corner of his mouth, head thrown back in ecstasy, Basile continued his relentless pounding. *Mine. Mine. Mine.* Each thrust was met by a tiny grunt from Emil, who undoubtedly grew hard once more.

So close to release, and yet, so far away. Basile's mind churned. Love and duty warred, one moment telling him to forget about France and stay here, the next telling him to go home and stay safe. None of his thoughts mattered in the end, for a blinding flash of light behind his closed eyelids made him stiffen. Deep inside Emil, his cock twitched, and suddenly, he came. The tempest roared through him. Hot jets of come filled Emil, everything forgotten except the dizzying release of passion. He heard moans, distantly realized they were his, and then a second voice joined his as Emil came again.

Cooling water around their legs pulled his attention from the exquisite sex they'd just shared. Pressing a kiss to the base of Emil's neck, Basile slipped away. He took a moment to step from the tub, wash himself, and then grab two thick towels. He handed one to Emil as he stood, and silently both men dried, before tumbling into the bunk.

Basile lay there, the weight of Emil pressed against his side, the American's breath teasing the hairs on his chest. Hesitantly, he wrapped his arm around him and pulled him close. Everything was set. Outside the sun dared to break across the horizon, and looking at the sleeping man beside him, Basile knew he wouldn't leave until after dark. It was a new day. Valentine's Day. The day which he'd be forced to leave the man, the vampire, he never stopped loving. After living for centuries he would have thought such things would hurt less, not more, and damned himself for being a fool.

Chapter Five

Emil blinked sleep from his eyes. His senses told him the sun had barely disappeared from the horizon. His bed rocked gently from side to side. He was still on Basile's ship. The empty bed mocked him with the knowledge the Frenchman had risen. Most likely he attended to whatever duties he had on ship. He couldn't weigh anchor so long as Emil remained.

Memories rushed back, leaving him with an erection and the need to bury it inside the Frenchman. Being bathed, then being fucked in the tub played foremost in his mind. He rested his head on the pillow and debated about getting dressed and leaving. He had to report and Basile had to leave.

Emil sat. He swung his legs over the edge of the bed. Disappointed at not waking up with Basile, he stood. Gathering his clothes, he dressed and then stopped, at a loss as to what to do. He loathed the idea of appearing on deck, not knowing where Basile was or what he was doing. A perverse part of Emil wanted Basile to come and get him, to make him force Emil to leave. He frowned.

The window called. Just a few steps carried him to it where he opened the shutters and looked outside. Basile's quarters faced the open sea, dark beneath the silver light from the moon. Light glinted from the seemingly endless expanse of ocean. The water splashed against the side of the boat, the sound not unlike a lullaby. Emil glanced at the bed, debating for a moment about crawling between the crisp sheets and going to sleep. Maybe Basile would forget about him and carry him all the way back to France.

Emil snorted at his foolish notion. Something had changed between them last night when Basile stood him up in the bathtub, then proceeded to give him two releases that left him thoroughly wrung out. Even now, just thinking about the handsome Frenchman, Emil's body stirred. He pressed his hand against the glass windowpane, wondering how a ship such as this would have come by such a luxury. Obviously in battle the fragile glass would prove a liability. Except Basile's ship hadn't seen combat for many years.

Emil sighed. One time he'd entertained the notion of sailing the high seas with Basile. That had been well over five years ago. Times had changed. They had changed. Idly, Emil tongued his fangs, thinking of how much he had changed. It hadn't seemed to matter to Basile. A willing body to use while he was in port, then off he'd go, returning to France, retreating to his chateau where he'd never have to deal with the mortal world unless he wanted to. One thing Emil knew about Basile, he did not want to deal with the mortal world.

Emil fisted his hand. Bringing it to his chest, he ran the fingers of his other hand through his hair. His throat tightened. Closing his eyes, he swallowed hard, willed the anguish welling in his soul to ease. "Best get it over with," he muttered as he turned from the window.

When he opened his eyes, his gaze landed on the bed with its rumpled lavender-smelling sheets. Emil's hand fell to his side. He glanced to the middle of the room where the tub had been. Not even a droplet of water betrayed its presence. Long strides carried him to the basin. Filling it with water, he splashed his face and slicked back his hair. Still, he couldn't bring himself to go to the door.

Above him the sound of booted feet on the deck hammered home the reality. He couldn't remain on Basile's ship any longer. He needed to return, to report to his boss, and find out where the government would send him next. Boston. New York. The east coast had many harbors with many boats. Any one of them would serve the Union Army. Just because it wasn't Baltimore, didn't mean that Emil's knowledge wouldn't be useful.

Not even duty toward his country sent him to the door. Instead, he went to the wardrobe and opened it. Shirts, waistcoats, jackets, trousers, stylish clothing made from expensive fabrics hung there, waiting to be used. Grabbing a shirt, Emil brought it to his nose and inhaled deeply, thinking even here he smelled Basile.

Oh God, he still loved the Frenchman. In the harbor behind him, his country waited. On the decks above him, his lover waited. Growing up on a dock gave him nautical knowledge. He had no doubts if he stayed on Basile's ship he'd be given a job, one he'd do well. Sail away to France. Emil shook his head.

No matter how entertaining he might find the notion, he couldn't leave. Not while his government needed his services. Who knew what plans the General had for him? Who knew what would happen? As much as running away with Basile appealed to him, he couldn't. The only question remaining was, would Basile send him away or would he have to simply walk away? Pressing his lips together, he released the shirt and let it swing back into place. Emil closed the wardrobe doors. He turned on his heels, giving the room one last, fond look. Then he strode for the door.

The hallway stood empty, as did the stairs leading to the deck. He found Basile by the rail, a light breeze toying with the strands of his long, dark hair. He stared across the ocean as if he searched for something, yet feared he might not find it. Emil wondered if the object of Basile's search stood behind him. He stepped forward.

"Basile," he said, noting the moon nearly reached its zenith. If Basile intended to set sail, he needed to do it soon.

Basile didn't turn at Emil's mention of his name.

Emil stopped next to him. Curling his fingers around the rail, he glanced surreptitiously around and saw they were alone. "Happy Valentine's Day," he said with a frown.

Basile jerked. His eyes closed, his throat worked. "Happy Valentine's Day," he replied, his voice rough. "I don't suppose..."

Emil's fingers tightened at the unspoken words. That he'd like to stay here? Just as he'd made up his mind, determined to do the right thing, now Basile asked for the impossible. Sentences stopped and started in his mind, none ever making it as far as his lips. If he mentioned Basile's impending departure, Emil feared the Frenchman might see it as a hint he wanted to leave. If he mentioned his work, Basile might feel undue pressure to stay. Relaxing his grip on the rail, Emil knew he was damned if he did and damned if he didn't. He waited in the hopes that Basile's next words would clear up the confusion.

"We need to leave while the tides are favorable," Basile said, his words clearly not those he'd been about to say just a few moments ago.

Emil nodded. The high tide occurred a few hours past midnight. For Basile to steer his large ship from the harbor, the high tide guaranteed success. Glancing at the moon, he knew they had little time left. For several minutes at least, it was still Valentine's Day.

"I suppose this is it then," Emil said.

Basile nodded. "You should probably head back to your apartment. Your government needs you."

To hell with his government, Emil wanted to say. *What about you?* He released his grip on the rail and rocked back on his heels. "You're not coming back, are you?"

"No," Basile admitted. His face remained expressionless, whatever pain, or lack thereof, he felt trapped deep inside. He turned to face Emil and rested a hand on his shoulder. "It's better this way."

"Better for who?" Emil snapped back. "You, so you can return to France and live your life without having to deal with mortals, or heaven forbid, Americans? Or better for me? Cut the ties and be done with it." He stepped away.

"Emil, wait." Basile followed, their steps carrying them halfway across the deck before he stopped. "There are things we have to do in our lives. Sometimes we don't like them, but we have to do them anyway. Your service to your government is one of them."

"And your return to France is another?" Emil shrugged away from Basile's touch. "Don't patronize me. I know you want to return to your chateau and hide away from the world. You've always made it very clear you don't intend to love, or get hurt, ever again. We loved each other once and you sent me away because I was mortal. Well I'm not mortal anymore, and yet, you're still pushing me away." Emil didn't care who overheard. Trusted members of Basile's crew knew of his unique abilities as a vampire. Considering that if Basile had his way, in a few hours they'd never see each other ever again, if they realized Emil's new status, well, he didn't care.

"I love my country, just as you love yours. Don't make this harder than it has to be." Basile spoke matter-of-factly, any endearments that might have rolled off his tongue during their lovemaking gone now. Getting shot at Bull Run hurt less than the heavy pain in Emil's chest. Forever was a mighty damn long time without the one you loved.

"Why not? Or have you lived long enough to know time fades all wounds."

Basile jerked as if wounded. He stepped back.

"I thought not," Emil replied, hating the cruel twist to his words. If Basile wanted to end this, he might as well do it right. Turning on his heel, he strode to the ladder.

"Emil, wait," Basile called from behind him.

His words stopped Emil. They shouldn't have, and Emil cursed as his feet slowed and turned him back to look at Basile standing on deck. A breeze tousled his hair, and for a moment, he looked like the French lover a besotted young man had fallen in love with. Broad shoulders, narrow waist, high boots polished to a gleam visible in the moonlight, Basile looked like a handsome rake.

"The tide won't wait," Emil offered.

"I know," Basile replied. "I just..." He shook his head as if he couldn't bring himself to say whatever he wanted to say.

Emil's heart gave a silly leap anyway. "Goodbye, Basile. I hope you find the solace you crave in France." *And I hope you think about me every night and every day for the rest of your immortal life.* Emil knew he would always think of his lover, and each time it'd hurt like a hot iron in a wound.

Looking at Basile on the deck of his ship, Emil tried to get mad. He failed. Like two vessels drifting away on opposing currents, their work took them in different directions. He had to accept that, needed to accept it if he wanted to keep his sanity.

"Sir, the tides are changing," Basile's first officer called. "We need to weigh anchor now."

Basile nodded, his only acknowledgement of the words. A lengthy silence stretched between them. Basile's first officer looked from vampire to vampire, his gaze eventually landing on his employer. "Give us just a few more moments," Basile replied. His first officer nodded and hurried away to tend to other duties.

"You know you're welcome in France once the war is over," Basile offered.

"And not before?" Emil snapped. "Good thing I'm a vampire then, isn't it? That first battle killed me." Like a wounded animal, he lashed out in pain. He wanted to be alone, and yet Basile tugged at the ties between them with his words.

"Emil, don't." Basile moved closer so the entire crew wouldn't hear their words. "I'm sorry we met again like this. It's bad timing, that's all. I wish I'd known earlier you were a vampire."

"And you would have come after me because you knew then that it would be pretty damn hard to kill me, right? Now that I'm a vampire, I'm safe. You don't have to worry about tying up your emotions in some mortal who will die. That's it. Isn't it?"

Basile shook his head. "That's not it at all. Look, this isn't the time to talk about this."

His first officer hurried over. "Captain, we have to leave now."

Basile sighed. "All right. Lift anchor!"

The creaking sound of the thick ropes hauling the anchors from the bottom of the harbor sounded ominously loud to Emil's ears. He frowned. No longer weighed down, the great vessel heaved with the rise of the waves. Emil stepped forward.

"Wait," he called out. His heart in his hands, he implored Basile to hold off on his orders. A lump in his throat, Emil knew it was now or never. "I love you, Basile," he shouted to be heard over the clamor of the departing ship. "I always have."

Basile stilled. Around him the maelstrom of crewmen readied the ship to sail. One large anchor thunked into place, safely stowed inside the hull. Beneath Emil's feet, the deck trembled. The vibration worked its way up his legs, to where his heart sat like a lump in his chest. His throat convulsed as he waited for Basile's answer. After all these years apart, finally he'd found the Frenchman again, and if it took riding this ship across the Atlantic to get his answer, Emil realized with a start that he would.

A second anchor settled home. Two more to go and then the ship would float free.

"If you're going to leave, Emil, you have to go now." Basile's emotionless voice stabbed Emil like a knife.

"No, you can't mean that," Emil said. "You have to love me as much as I love you." Damn, he sounded weak, pathetic, maybe the kind of mortal who would take a rifle shot to the chest and nearly die in his first battle. Wiping his hand across his brow, he mustered the courage to remain standing and not hurry to the ladder. He wouldn't leave until he got his answer.

"That happened a long time ago, Emil. I must return to France. The tides are favorable right now. I have to go. I'm sorry." Basile turned on his heel and started to walk away.

"No!" Emil cried out. Bounding across the heaving deck, he clamped his hand onto Basile's shoulder and whirled him around. Let him be the rash mortal Basile remembered. Maybe he hadn't been a vampire so long that he'd died inside, forgotten the years of pain and misery. Mortal cares still hovered in his mind, the loss of a loved one. Years seemed like an eternity. Forever? Emil didn't even know how to contemplate such a long time. Not yet, anyway.

"Emil, you must leave," Basile implored.

The third anchor clanked home.

"Sir, we're pulling up the ladder. If you want to leave you better do it now, otherwise you're going to France with us," one of the crewmen said.

"Is that what you want? To go to France with us?" Basile asked, his emotionless mask cracking for the first time.

Emil's heart swelled. For so long he'd thought of nothing but that, but then Basile threw him away like an old newspaper. Things had changed. The war, the battle, Emil's near-death and resurrection as a vampire, all those things tilted the balance between the two men. Now, on the deck of this ship, they stood as equals.

As much as Emil wanted to throw his lot in with Basile and return to France, he couldn't. The hard-fought equality between them would end. He hadn't even packed a change of clothing.

Arriving in a foreign country penniless, homeless, not even able to speak the native language didn't sound like his idea of fun. His country needed him. More than Basile did, apparently.

"If you'd have me, I'd go to France. But not under these circumstances. If I go with you, I'm going to go as an equal. Not some stray you took under your wing. I know how that story ends." He managed a wry smile, though Basile's rejection still stung. He listened to hear the creaking of ropes, wondering if any anchors held the ship. It rocked more, afloat in the harbor.

"Ladder up, sir!" a crewman called as he hurried across deck.

"Looks like you made your decision anyway," Basile remarked.

Emil laughed. After all of this and a simple matter of timing made his decision for him. Maybe riding away on the ocean would be the best way to deal with this—no! What was he thinking? Basile obviously didn't want him. The rejection hurt far more than he expected. Going into this he knew Basile would be returning to France. A glance at the sky showed the moon past its zenith. Valentine's Day, and any delusions it might have held, were over.

"I do love you, you know. I suppose it doesn't matter now, but I never stopped loving you. When my superior told me to seek out vessels for the war effort, I knew you, and your ship, were the best. Isn't it ironic that now that I'm everything you claimed to have wanted, you don't want me. I suppose I should apologize and head back to my apartment." Emil turned for the railing.

The boat drifted slowly away from its moorings. Curling his fingers around the rail, Emil stared at the murky waters. If he wanted to return to his apartment, his job, hell, at this rate his country, he needed to jump. He glanced over his shoulder at Basile.

One word, just one word from the Frenchman would keep him here on board the ship. Anything, really, for swimming through the frigid waters of the Atlantic didn't appeal to him. At least as a vampire, he wouldn't die of hypothermia. He wondered if Basile expected him to swim for shore now.

"Anchors away," Basile's first officer called. The cry echoed along the deck as crewmembers moved into position.

Basile flinched as if shot. "It's too late for you to return to shore. You're willing to abandon everything for me?"

"Only if you love me." Emil relaxed his fingers against the railing. His heavy waistcoat would have to go, and he might need to kick off his boots, but being a vampire lent him strength he didn't have as a mortal. He had to be a good swimmer as a dock brat, and he knew he could make it back to shore. He stared at the harbor, the boats still moored there. He'd grown up there, still lived not far away. He should feel more allegiance to it, to the country that gave him a home. Instead, the vampire who had loved him at one time commanded his heart as easily as he commanded his ship.

"Go, before it's too late," Basile implored.

"Why? Why are you shoving me away? Don't you love me?" Emil said. He sounded pitiful and at that moment he didn't care. The need to have answers to his questions burned at him like a splash of sunlight on his soul.

"Emil, don't make a fool out of yourself," Basile snarled.

Emil's spine stiffened. Any feelings he might have felt lashed him in the face. Gripping the rail, he stepped onto it one foot at a time. He unfastened the buttons of his wool waistcoat. A brisk February breeze ripped through his cotton shirt. He didn't feel the cold, not when Basile's words froze him far better than the weather ever would. Emil tossed his coat onto the deck behind him.

"If you feel that way, then goodbye, Basile. I hope the world treats you kindly." Raising his arms over his head, he balanced on top of the railing for one, precarious moment. The ship, moving into deeper waters, pitched forward. Emil leapt.

He arced through the air, landing in the salt water with nary a splash. Diving underwater, he kicked his legs in long, powerful strokes. His boots filled with water. Salt stung his eyes. Rising from the water, he looked behind him.

Basile stood at the railing of his ship, Emil's coat clutched in his hands. He stared at the harbor as if searching for signs of Emil. For a long moment Emil stared at the silhouette of the ship, Basile visible on deck, then ducking his head beneath a low wave, he sliced into the water once more.

Powerful strokes of his arms carried him closer to shore. The icy water soaked his clothing. His teeth chattered. Funny how he proved his invulnerability, something Basile wanted in a lover, by leaving him. He would have barked his laughter to the night, except the need to be hidden had him angling toward a deserted corner of the wharf. He rested his hands on the wooden boards. With a mighty shove, he hauled himself from the water.

Emil stood there for a long moment. The ship loomed on the horizon, a behemoth compared to the other sailing vessels still in the harbor. Sweeping his hair back from his forehead, he unlaced his boots. He dumped water from them, before putting them back on. Wet, cold and brokenhearted, he slogged his way along the alleyways back to his apartment. A homeless person provided sustenance, warming him enough to stop his teeth from chattering.

After a winding walk through the back alleys of Baltimore, he arrived at his rooms. Not needing any lights, he staggered up the stairs. He unlocked his door, thinking how very different this was the last time he came here. No more Basile. No wine. No anticipation of anything other than a cold, lonely bed.

Emil undressed, hanging his sodden clothing over a bar in the bathroom. Drying off with a rough bit of toweling, nothing like the fine linens Basile had on board, he dressed in clean, dry clothes. Sinking into one of the chairs in the living room would only remind him of Basile's absence. At least Basile hadn't been in his bedroom. Propped against the headboard, he closed his eyes. The sounds of the mortals, though subdued with the early morning hours, still surrounded him, the lub-dub of their heartbeats audible in the neighboring apartments. He drew the crimson scent of their blood into his nostrils. His stomach rumbled.

Emil rose from the bed. His meager belongings mocked him with how easily they fit into a satchel. Settling into bed, he knew once he woke he'd go to the statehouse and request assignment elsewhere. Surely he'd have better luck in other ports, other places that wouldn't remind him of Basile and what they could have shared. Folding his arms across his chest, he closed his eyes. Basile had sent him away. No matter what happened, that alone spoke volumes.

He loved Basile. The Frenchman didn't love him. After five years some things never changed. Emil leaned over the edge of the bed. Pulling out a worn shoebox, he brought it onto the blankets. He opened the lid. Photographs and letters stared back at him, musty from disuse. Emil pulled out the top picture of him and Basile, taken by one of Baltimore's finer photographers. Looking at it, Emil searched for any signs that Basile had changed. Like the immortal vampire he was, Basile appeared ageless. His outward façade was like a stone wall, impenetrable. Just like his heart.

Emil replaced the lid on the box. He flung it across the room. It hit the wall with a muffled thud, scattering love letters and photographs all over the worn floor. Emil glanced at the lamp flickering beside the bed. How or when he'd lit it, he couldn't remember, but right now the flame provided the perfect vehicle to destroy the mementos.

Crawling off the bed, Emil gathered up the box. Holding the photograph between his thumb and forefinger, he dangled it over the flame. He wished the memories would fade just as easily. Tears stung his eyes, and with blurry vision, he watched his and Basile's past burn.

Chapter Six

Rushing to the rail, Basile leaned over it as the dark speck of Emil's form disappeared into Baltimore Harbor. He waited, his heart in his throat, for the vampire to surface and glide toward the shore with long, sure strokes. Even after he no longer saw Emil, Basile stared into the inky depths of the harbor, searching between vessels for Emil. He'd swam out of sight.

Basile closed his eyes. Slumped over the rail, he let the swaying of the deck vibrate through him, the gentle rise and fall that told him his ship headed out to sea. He struggled not to frown. This was what he wanted. Or at least he thought so before a recently turned vampire reentered his life. Dashing salt spray from his face with the back of his hand, he turned from the rail. What was done was done. Emil returned to his place, his country, and after this voyage, Basile would return to his.

Basile tried telling himself it was what he wanted. He failed. After watching Emil stand on deck, defiantly declare his love, even though Basile did everything he could to send the American away, Basile realized he had to face the facts. A part of him, a big part, wanted Emil to return to France with him. Hell, he'd nearly been ecstatic when the anchors lifted and Emil remained on board. Too bad he hadn't told the American that. Instead, he'd literally pushed him overboard, all in the name of duty.

"Sir?" His first officer strode across the deck with steady steps that only someone born and raised on a ship could have. "You're needed at the wheel."

"Very well." Basile forced himself to step away from the rail and any chance he might have at seeing Emil again. As they said, that ship had sailed. No sense in turning it around. Basile flung Emil's coat to the deck, a painful reminder of his lover's leaving.

Basile followed his first officer to the helm, relieving the man who stood at the wheel. The moment his fingers curled around the well-worn wood, something clicked into place deep inside. Returning to France meant putting the *Souverain* in dry dock, or letting someone else captain her. Neither option sounded like the right thing to do.

"The seas are getting choppy. It might be a rough ride," his first officer said.

"Very well. I can take over until close to dawn. Thank you." Turning his attention away from the man, Basile concentrated on steering the large vessel. For the most part, his ship sliced cleanly through the ocean. A stiff breeze battled the sails.

Basile forced a grin on his face. He should be happy, and yet, something gnawed at the pit of his stomach. Not hunger, for warm blood ran fresh in his veins, the bit he'd taken from a crewmember coming in off watch more than enough to satiate his hunger. Loss. Betrayal. In his mind, the sight of Emil's lithe form disappearing into the harbor repeated itself over and over again. The slight splash sounded ominously loud. The clear strokes of his arms as he swam just more evidence that normal mortal ills wouldn't befall him.

A wave buffeted the side of the ship. Cursing, Basile corrected his course, aware of the curious stares of the men nearby. As if mirroring his thoughts, the approaching storm intensified. Wind howled through the rigging. Waves crashed, some tall enough to splash over the railing and onto the deck. Out of the corner of his eye, Basile watched his first officer disappear to check on the men. Distantly, he heard the clanging of a bell. Someone must have sounded the alarm to rouse the sleeping crewmembers.

He could sail through the storm, undoubtedly making it through without incident, or he could turn around and return to port. Icy pellets dropped from the sky to clatter along the deck. The sleet hit Basile in the face, making him squint into the darkness. Clouds covered the moon. Had he been a poetic man, Basile might have compared the brewing storm to his ragged emotions. He wasn't, and right now he had a ship to guide.

The calls of his men skittering across the rapidly icing-over deck echoed around him. Basile shook his head. What the hell did he think he was doing? "Hang on, I'm heading back to port," he said with a spin of the wheel. The great ship heaved, nearly listing to one side, as it spun back to port. Several harrowing minutes passed, the ice now pelting the back of his head instead of the front, his men clinging to icy ropes and rails. Spray washed on deck, freezing on contact with the ship's cold hull.

"Came to your senses, eh?" his first officer said with a laugh. "I don't blame you. Another day or so won't hamper our return."

It wasn't the next couple of days that worried Basile. "As soon as we get back to port, call a meeting of the men."

"Very good, sir. Very good." His first officer practically beamed. "If you'll pardon my saying, but it's about time."

In spite of the sleet clinging to his hair, the treacherous footing, he laughed. "I don't suppose you could have told me this before we sailed into an ice storm." Now that the worst had passed as they returned to port, he loosened his hands on the wheel.

His first officer grinned. "No, sir. I couldn't have. I'll call a meeting of the men for tomorrow night that way you have time to do what you need to do. Am I safe in assuming we'll be in America for a while?"

Basile nodded.

"Then you'll be needing this." His first officer shoved an icy bundle of fabric at him.

Basile grabbed Emil's jacket. Sleet froze to the wool, making the jacket a wet bundle of ice crystals. Crushing the sodden fabric to his chest, he turned the wheel over to his first officer. "Thank you."

"Think nothing of it, sir. Good luck."

"I'll need it." Basile hurried across the slippery deck as fast as he could to stand at the rail as once more the *Souverain* returned to port. The anchors lowered with a heavy splash into the water, and no sooner had the ship been secured then he vaulted down the ladder.

Luckily the storm appeared to move offshore, leaving Baltimore draped in low-hanging clouds and frigid air. Basile ran. He darted through the streets, his figure noticeable only as a blur until he reached Emil's building. Emil's coat dripped water in his arms all the way up the stairs to the American's rooms. Inside, the sound of shuffling could be heard.

He wasn't too late. Emil's distinct scent still filled the rooms beyond the door, ambrosia to Basile's senses. He tried the doorknob and found it locked. He pounded on the door.

"Who is it?" Emil yelled.

"It's me. Basile," he answered, thinking no other words had scared him quite so much. He waited, weight balanced on the balls of his feet, a wet woolen coat starting to steam in his arms as it thawed, half expecting Emil to tell him to go away.

Locks clicked. The doorknob turned, hinges creaking as Emil opened the door. "I thought you'd be out to sea by now." He glanced down at the coat. "Come in. You must be frozen." Sadness hovered around the edges of Emil's voice.

"Thank you." He stepped across the threshold, wishing he'd thought to try and wring some of the moisture instead of letting the coat drip all over the floor. He held out the sodden garment to Emil.

"I'll hang this over the tub. I appreciate your bringing it back." Taking the coat, Emil carried it into the bathroom, his long strides keeping it from creating too big a puddle. Moments later he returned. "Do you have time to sit?" Emil gestured to the chairs.

"You realize if I'm to stay here you're going to have to get better furniture. Better yet, a whole new home," Basile said as he sat. He stretched his legs out before him, crossing his booted ankles. Glancing around Emil's residence, he compared it to his chateau. At this moment, he found no comparison. Home was wherever Emil was.

Emil's brow furrowed. "I thought you were returning to France. In fact, you ordered me off your ship rather than take me to France with you." He remained standing, arms crossed over his chest.

Behind him sat an open suitcase.

"You're leaving." Basile stared at the open case, the meager changes of clothing spilling out. A few books sat on one end, an empty box sat beside with the half-charred remains of letters. His letters. Pain stabbed him. So this was it. He'd been an ass and now he had eternity to suffer for his crimes.

"Yeah. I'm going to see my superiors about moving up to Boston, maybe New York. Surely I'll find a ship there that wants to join the Union Army. It'll be good to get out of Baltimore for a while."

"I see. What if I told you I'm not going to France? Would that change your mind?" Basile kept his nonchalant pose, hands resting loosely in his lap.

Emil stiffened. "Don't toy with me. Your actions spoke volumes of what you thought about your beloved France and of me. Why did you come back, Basile? Did you think stomping on my heart on Valentine's Day wasn't good enough for you?" Reaching behind him, he picked up the box. "Do you want to hear something pathetic? I love you so much I couldn't even destroy your letters. I'd planned to take them with me, these burnt bits of paper that were all I had left of you. For the love of God, don't tell me you've come back to play more of your games. I don't think I could handle it if you did."

"No games. Never any games." Basile rose to his feet. He crossed the space between them and reached for the box. Taking it from Emil's hands, he fingered through the letters. Though some were charred, others were intact, missives of love written in his flourished script and Emil's scratchy hand. "You kept them. I never knew." Gingerly, he picked up a picture, one of the first that had been taken. Holding it by the edges, he lifted it from the box. "We both look so young."

"It was only a few years ago," Emil said, though didn't reach for the mementos.

"Seems like a lifetime," Basile replied as he returned the photograph to the box. He handed them over, and Emil silently took them. He set the box back on the ground.

"I thought time moved slowly when you were a vampire as old as you." Emil strode to the chairs and sank down. "You know, I meant what I said on your ship. I do love you. I'd follow you to the ends of the Earth. My government needs me, but I think I need you more."

Emil's words freed Basile's heart like a flock of birds rising into the sky. Sending a silent prayer to a God he no longer believed in, he refused to temper the foolish grin spreading across his face. "I stood on the deck of the *Souverain*, steering her through a sudden sleet storm and I realized that home wasn't a country. It was where you are. I love you, Emil. I always have. I can only hope that you love me back."

Emil clamped his hands on Basile's shoulders. "As if it would be any other way." His eyelids fluttering closed, he slanted his lips across Basile's. The chill from the storm crept into Emil's blood, and he threaded his fingers through Basile's hair to hold the vampire against him. If he could warm him with love alone, he would. His blood pounded in his veins, hot, hungry, and between them, his cock hardened. Cupping Basile's cheek, he shivered at the touch of frozen, clammy flesh.

"Drink," Emil ordered. "You're freezing." He tilted his head.

Basile groaned. Without finesse he sank his fangs into Emil's neck.

Emil moaned at the tug of Basile's mouth against his skin. Blood roared to the site, flowing into Basile's body, and Emil hoped his cock would soon follow. He clamped onto the back of Basile's head, holding him against his neck. Beneath his touch, warmth spread from Basile's lips, across his face, through his limbs. Where he pressed against Emil, heat blossomed, until Basile no longer felt like ice in his arms.

Basile pulled his head away, licking the wound to seal it. "Thank you. For everything." Once more he touched his lips to Emil's, and this time, the American relished the warmth emanating from the vampire's body, because he knew he'd given it to him. Basile's tongue swept along the seam of Emil's lips, testing, tasting, and Emil opened to him. The thrust and parry of tongues locked both men in a heated embrace. Someone moved, Basile, maybe Emil, and suddenly, the American backed into a wall. Their hips collided, hard flesh against hard flesh.

Basile tore at his clothing. Fabric ripped. Buttons pinged onto the floor and across the room. Husky murmurs mingled with groans, and through it all, Emil felt as if he existed inside an inferno. Lust pounded through his veins and into his aching cock. Balls drawn tight, he reached for Basile's pants, and soon both men stood naked.

Basile spun him around.

Emil flattened his hands on the wall hard enough to rattle the door in its hinges. A swipe of Basile's feet widened his stance, and then yes, oh God yes, Basile's cock pressed against him. A quick lunge of his hips thrust Basile deep inside. A flare of pain bowed his back, then pleasure, nothing but carnal pleasure as Basile worked his cock deep inside. Their balls hung together, full of promise, and then, bracing his hand on Emil's waist, Basile pulled back only to pump forward again.

"I love you," Basile growled as he filled Emil once more. "I— love—you—" He punctuated each word with a thrust of his hips.

"Yes!" Emil shouted. "Fuck, yes."

Basile's thrusts slammed Emil into the wall, and he didn't care. Sometime between here and there he lost track of his body, his soul, until there was Basile. There had always been Basile. The man's brutal loving, as harsh and raw as their very relationship, brought him to the edge of release and then over.

With a hoarse shout, Emil came. His cock twitched, seed pumping from him. It splashed hot against his naked stomach. Dripped down to trickle across his balls.

Basile reached between his legs, gathering his come and smearing it across his half-hard cock. He said nothing. Didn't need to, for his pace quickened. Flesh slapped against flesh. With a harsh groan, Basile stiffened. His orgasm hit him hard and fast, his fingers tightening on Emil's waist. Inside Emil, his cock twitched, pumping out wave after wave of hot seed.

Emil groaned and rested his forehead against the wall. He let Basile fill him, mark him, his cock stirring to life once more.

Basile pressed his lips to Emil's shoulder.

The tender gesture brought a sting of tears to his eyes. These were the actions of a man well and truly in love. Slowly, Basile's cock slid free, though he made no motion to leave.

"I love you, *ma lapin*," Basile whispered.

"I love you too," Emil replied as he turned away from the wall. This time he caressed Basile's sweaty arm, tangling their fingers. He led him around the corner to the bed, and gently pushed Basile down onto his stomach. Pressing kisses on either side of his spine, Emil straddled him. "And I think it's my turn now."

"Yes, *ma lapin*, I think it is." Basile chuckled.

"What does that mean?" Emil asked in between kisses. "*Ma lapin.*"

"My rabbit. Because whenever we are together we fuck like rabbits." Basile turned to look over his shoulder. "I hope you don't mind."

"No, not at all." He swiped his tongue across the dimples at the top of Basile's buttocks and grinned when the Frenchman shivered. "I think I like that a lot." He stroked his cock, using his come and his sweat to make it nice and slick, then he braced it at Basile's opening.

The Frenchman moaned and arched his back. A single thrust sheathed him inside his lover, and Emil lay completely along Basile's body, from shoulders to toes, covering him. His cock twitched, anxious to climb toward orgasm, but Emil simply enjoyed touching Basile. His hands made long sweeps from shoulder to hips then back again. His lips sucked the base of Basile's neck, sliding the black strands of his hair aside to nibble and lick.

Then, he braced his weight on his knees and withdrew. Not the quick lovemaking Basile offered, Emil worked slowly, savoring the way Basile's muscles gripped him. They stroked him. His fangs tingled with the need to bite Basile. Not wanting to take more blood than necessary, remembering how very cold Basile had been, he sank his fangs into Basile's shoulder. He sucked, once, twice, then pulled out, sealing the wound.

Just that tiny bit of blood satisfied him. In spite of his desire to go slowly, his thrusts grew harder. The bed creaked beneath them, back and forth with their movements. Basile moaned.

Blind desire drove Emil. His goal became finding release in his lover's body. From the sounds Basile made, the Frenchman was close to coming again. Nothing mattered more than coming, and then, he stiffened. Spots flashed before his closed eyelids. The base of his spine tingled. A roaring began in his balls, pumping through his cock, erupting with long spasms of release.

159

Emil shouted. Grabbing a fistful of blanket, he struggled to stay where he was, buried deep inside Basile's body. Beneath him the Frenchman writhed, hips working frantically. With his other hand, Emil reached between them. One stroke, two, of his fingers along Basile's cock. The Frenchman came again with a hoarse shout.

Sweat slickened their bodies. Emil rolled to the side, his half-hard shaft slipping easily from his lover. On the narrow bed they cuddled, flesh against flesh. Basile tucked his head beneath Emil's chin, one arm wrapped around his hips as if he never wanted to let go.

A knock sounded on the door.

Emil stiffened. His boss. He'd completely forgotten about the man's visit. "I'll be right back," he whispered, rising from bed and tossing a blanket over Basile. It took him a moment to find a washcloth and clean up before pulling on a pair of pants. He ran his fingers through his hair, not wanting to meet his employer smelling of sex and sweat, but having little choice.

He rubbed his eyes and unfastened the locks on the door. He opened it.

"I expected you to be ready to depart," his boss said without any preamble. Stepping in, he glanced around, his frown deepening. He stood by the chair. "You're not ready to go."

"No, sir. Please sit down, sir. My plans have changed." Emil hadn't had a chance yet to think about this moment since Basile's arrival. He knew, though, what he needed to do. Basile couldn't be expected to give up his dream of returning home. Emil swallowed hard as his boss looked dubious, but sat anyway.

"You're supposed to be in Boston by tomorrow night. The arrangements have been made. Unless you've been able to convince the ships here in Baltimore to join our case." His boss wore a hat pulled down low on his face, a heavy coat against the chill night. He didn't take it off, and caked mud and slush covered his boots. He looked as close to disreputable as Emil had ever seen him. Undoubtedly the coat hid the uniform, the military medals. Those wouldn't be on display tonight.

"I think we might have better luck going to foreign countries for ships rather than relying on our own shipping fleets. Merchants aren't going to want to do anything to take them away from their money or do anything to put their ships in danger. Going to Boston, sir, would be a waste of time." Emil took the other chair.

Booted footsteps sounded in the bedroom.

Emil stiffened. He'd hoped Basile would have sense enough to remain hidden until after his boss left. After all, Basile had planned on returning to France. Probably still did, and frankly, after finally hearing Basile say he loved him, Emil knew he'd do anything to return to France with him. He meant what he said about the merchant ships. He could, and had planned, on going to Boston, but those pampered money changers knew little about running blockades. Better to seek help from navies outside their own civilian population.

"Pardon my interruption," Basile said, thickening his French accent. "I am Basile Gagnon of the ship, *Commerce de Souverain.* I believe Mr. Franks may not have all the facts. You see, I was visiting him to see if your government would be amicable to my crew and vessel helping out your cause." He gave a half-bow.

Emil forced his mouth closed.

"You weren't aware of this, Mr. Franks," his boss said.

Emil shook his head. "Apparently Captain Gagnon has made some decisions I wasn't aware of." He grinned. "But I'm sure the Union Navy would be more than thankful for his help."

"Yes, we would. Thank you."

Basile nodded. "There are some conditions for my help. Mr. Franks will accompany me, no more being errand boy for the Union Navy. And if the price is right, I should be able to convince more ships from France to join you. If those terms are acceptable to you."

The man rose to his feet. "Yes. Yes they are." He nearly tripped over himself going to Basile and shaking the Frenchman's hand. He turned and glanced at Emil. "I see you did not lie about your contacts. I shall personally handle your transfer to Captain Gagnon's ship. Do you know when you'll return to your duties?"

Emil opened his mouth, overcome by everything that had happened to really know the answer. He looked to Basile.

The Frenchman grinned. "I believe Mr. Franks will be needed indefinitely."

The government agent looked startled. "Very well then. Thank you. It was nice working with you." He pumped Emil's hand, then turned on his heel. "If you'll excuse me."

"Yes. Have a good day," Emil said.

The man touched his hat. "You too." He hurried from the apartment, slamming the door behind him. The sound of booted feet racing down the stairs echoed.

Emil turned to Basile. "You meant it? You'll join the blockade and you want me on your ship?"

Basile nodded. He reached for Emil's hand, and clasping fingers, brought it to his chest where he covered it with his other hand. "I love you, Emil. I realized that I couldn't sail to France without you. My home is where you are, and for right now, your love brings you to these shores. Someday I'll return to my chateau, but when I do, we'll visit it together." He lifted Emil's hand to his lips and pressed a kiss to the palm.

"I love my country," Emil said. "But I love you more."

"I know," Basile replied, and he sealed his bargain with a kiss.

About the Author

Mary credits freshman American History and her grandmother's love of *Gone with the Wind* for inspiring her interest in the civil war. Visiting Wilson's Creek near Springfield, Missouri, cemented her love of this time period, and she's thrilled to be able to bring this era to life for readers.

To learn more about Mary Winter, please visit www.marywinter.com. Send an email to mary@marywinter.com or join her Yahoo! group to join in the fun with other readers as well as Mary!

http://groups.yahoo.com/group/marywinterchat.

Sign up for her newsletter by sending a blank email to newsletter-subscribe@marywinter.com.

Hot Ticket

K. A. Mitchell

Dedication

For both my Kathryns.
Thanks to MERWA for helping me get a handle on Elliot.

Chapter One

Cade squinted at the travel alarm clock on the coffee table. Years of familiarity didn't do shit to ease the jolt of panic and the sinking sensation he got from being late. Again. He rolled off the couch and bounced off the walls on his way to the shower. It was probably a really stupid waste of time to shower before going to pick through garbage, but he couldn't face even the world of community service without one.

Breakfast though, that he would skip. The guy who stocked the bar at his work told him the smell would be the worst part, so he pulled on a hooded sweatshirt he could yank up over his nose if it got too bad. He jotted down a note for Steve since he'd forgotten to tell him where he had to be at this ridiculous hour and left the apartment only ten minutes behind. If his twenty-year-old car would start and if he didn't hit every light, he could still make it with a few minutes to spare.

Getting old Bucky to start was going to be the bigger *if,* he realized as a blast of bitter Vermont January tore through his nostrils and down his throat, freezing every cilia in his lungs. At least it was too damned cold to snow. Bucky and his electrical system didn't think much of the weather either. The old Plymouth still had heart, but not when it was five below. After a few teasing rumbles, Bucky shuddered and quit.

Cade cursed and shoved in his earbuds, cuing up his highly appropriate playlist "Mike is a Cheating Asshole". He checked the time and cursed again, sprinting toward the bus stop, his lungs scraping and tearing as they fought off the cold. With a last burst of energy, he managed a dead heat with the bus at the corner.

The bus driver was apparently sympathetic to freezing waiters running up predawn streets with court orders to work sanitation due to cheating bastard ex-lovers bent on petty revenge, because the driver let the tie go to the runner and waited while Cade caught his breath before climbing on.

He was only seven minutes late for orientation. If the bored-looking man at the front of the room had anything useful to explain about sorting recyclables, Cade couldn't hear him. He needed the distraction of both the music blaring in his headphones and the sweatshirt over his nose to keep from gagging on the smell. And they weren't even in the room with the trash.

Cade had been a waiter most of his adult life, so he'd thought himself immune to being grossed out, but he was wrong. Just about every other person in the room had a shirt over his nose. Cade had no idea how he was going to survive thirty hours of this. But then he thought of Mike's smug smile in the courtroom and ground his teeth together. Not only was he going to get through this, he was going to fucking enjoy it. Though possibly not as much as the sound of the windshield of Mike's BMW shattering when he'd put Mike's nine iron through it.

The stench in the room that actually held the trash was about a hundred times worse than the orientation room, but after the first hour, Cade could breathe without the cloth over his nose. The sorting was getting easier, too, falling into the rhythm of the tracks in his ears. His eyes picked out a familiar-looking envelope, the kind that concert tickets from Ticketstat! always came in. He grabbed at the envelope, the weight and stiffness of something inside obvious despite his gloves. Instantly, there was another gloved hand on the envelope.

He followed the gloved hand up to a pair of dark blue eyes under chocolate brown hair cut and arranged too perfectly to be found on a straight guy, please God. Because his lips were full in contrast to a solid, diamond-edged jaw, and it would be a crying shame if he didn't bat for Cade's team even if he was a little younger and prettier than Cade could picture in his bed.

Cade almost forgot the envelope between them until he felt it sliding free. He renewed his slimy grip on it.

"I think I had it first." He tugged one of his earbuds free and flashed the guy the smile that got him all the best tips at La Pomme D'Orée.

Thick dark brows arched. "But it's on my side."

Cade smiled again and twisted his wrist until he had sole possession of the envelope. "Why don't we see what the tickets are for?" He wiped a hand down the thigh of the baggy grey coveralls they'd been given and pinched a corner of one of the tickets, sliding it out enough so that both of them could read it.

"Academy of St. Martin in the Fields." The other man breathed the words like a prayer. "That concert sold out almost immediately."

Cade whistled. "Probably because all the state legislators snatched up the tickets." Cade slid the ticket back into the envelope and tucked it inside his coverall.

"Wait. Why do the tickets belong to you?" The indignant entitlement reminded Cade of every other privileged bastard he knew.

"You want to turn them in?"

"No, but—" The guy was cute when he sputtered, a flush darkening cheeks tanned golden brown. No shit he thought the world belonged to him. How else would he be that tan in Vermont in January?

"Look. There are two. We'll split them, okay?"

"You can't possibly be interested in classical music."

Cade felt a flush of anger. "And you know this about me because I'm picking trash on community service since I got busted for something? I hate to break it to you, but you're up to your balls in shit yourself no matter how fucking rich you are."

Cade watched the swallow bob down along the tan skin of the guy's throat. The guy might be a bit of an ass but damn, where had something this pretty been hiding in such a tiny little town?

"I just meant—" He pointed at Cade's earphones.

"Oh." Cade had been cycling through his heavy-metal collection, and it was obviously bleeding through even the noise of the sorting. They were both guilty of making snap judgments, but he didn't think the other guy deserved an apology.

He felt eyes on them, knew they were about to get chewed out for standing around, and Cade wasn't spending one minute longer than his thirty hours doing this. "Look, why don't we discuss this when we get out of here?" He tossed three water bottles into the plastics bin behind him and reached for a can of dog food, hoping his sudden display of industriousness would keep whoever was watching them happy.

He got a clenched-jaw nod from the other guy and kept sorting.

This was the worst thing that had ever happened to him. The worst thing that could ever happen to him. Elliot spent a lot of time ensuring he didn't make mistakes. And now he had an arrest record and would spend the next three Saturdays digging through trash because he'd tried to buy his sister a nice Christmas present. The one positive thing that might come out of this—those tickets he knew he'd seen first—he'd somehow lost to a man who found it necessary to pierce fifteen holes in his head. It was completely overdone, since the man's smile was certainly bright enough to attract attention all on its own.

Elliot's back was aching by the time the five-hour shift was over. He was stretching the ache out when he realized the pierced guy was disappearing with *his* concert tickets.

"Wait." Elliot hurried after him.

The other man peeled off his gloves and looked up. He was shorter than Elliot, with eyes the warm light brown of whiskey, almost the exact same shade as the hair gelled and spiked on his head.

"Oh yeah. Look, man, I need to go home and shower and possibly burn these clothes. Here." He held out one of the tickets. "Guess I'll see you there."

"I thought we were going to talk about it."

"About?"

Elliot needed both of those tickets. As soon as he'd heard about the concert, that the Academy of St. Martin in the Fields was coming here, he'd had the most perfect plan. It was finally what he needed to get up enough nerve to ask James out, but while Elliot made arrangements in his head, the tickets had sold out almost as soon as they'd gone on sale. The man with the pierced eyebrow and fourteen more posts dotting the curves of his ears could not possibly be serious about spending an evening listening to Haydn and Boyce.

"I just thought maybe—"

"I'd give you the other ticket?"

"I could pay you."

"Really? Because the face price is eighty-five dollars and considering it's sold out I could probably do pretty well on the open market."

Elliot closed his eyes. "How much?"

"I don't want to sell it."

The guy was probably just holding out for more money. "Can't we discuss this? I mean—"

The other man shifted impatiently, pulling off the coverall and dropping it in the bin. "Man, I wasn't kidding about that shower. Hey, you know Café Heaven on School Street?"

"Yes."

"I'll meet you there in an hour and a half, okay?"

ॐ

The guy with the piercings was late, late enough for Elliot to get halfway through a cup of cappuccino and to start thinking that he'd been taken for a ride. Pierced guy hadn't wanted to give up the ticket, so he had just brushed Elliot off without ever intending to meet him here. If he didn't stop being so stupidly trusting of people, he was going to end up in worse trouble than he already was.

He should have suggested they meet at La Patisserie. That way he could have watched James if he was working, maybe talked with him about the classical music playing in the bakery. If Elliot couldn't get the guy to give up the other ticket, maybe he could give his own ticket to James. That would be a terrific first date. "I'll just wait out here. Have fun."

No, the guy must simply want more money. Elliot had been prepared to spend two hundred dollars on the tickets, so he could offer that much. If the guy showed.

Then he did. The door banged open and the cold shot all the way over to Elliot's table in the corner. The barista waved a hand in greeting as the man who had *his* ticket made his way to the counter. He was wearing a battered green army jacket that barely covered the top of his hips. It was only reasonable that Elliot should study him if he was going to figure out what approach would get him what he wanted. The fact that the perfect curve of the guy's ass was obvious even under his jacket was just a bonus.

The guy greeted the barista with a kiss. A nice ass, pierced ears and affectionate kisses on male baristas didn't necessarily mean anything. Elliot had been spectacularly mistaken before— the last time he'd been dumb enough to trust his instincts—so he wouldn't assume the other man was gay unless the guy said something. But if he was, that would have to be a plus. He'd understand Elliot's designs on James and that ticket.

"Sorry I'm late," the man said as he slid into the chair across from Elliot, but he didn't sound at all sorry. "I'm Cade McKeun." He held out his hand.

Elliot shook the offered hand, startled by the rush of heat until he realized it was the hand that had been cradling Cade's mug of inky black coffee. "Elliot Graham." And as he always did, he added, "Please spare me the *E.T.* imitations. I've heard them all."

Cade grinned. "So, Elliot, how did you fuck up enough to end up on the wrong side of trash collection?"

It wasn't as if Elliot didn't use that sort of language in justifiable situations, but Cade seemed to brandish crude language like an extension of his outrageous jewelry. Elliot's stepfather always said that people who cursed extensively lacked imagination.

"I was trying to buy a Christmas present for my sister."

"Sounds innocent enough."

"The present turned out to be stolen." And like an idiot, he'd paid for the Coach bag with a check. Helen at work had told him her brother-in-law could get him a good deal. Elliot just had no idea how good the deal was. At least he'd been arrested before he'd given the bag to his sister so no one in his family was aware of his disgrace. His parents didn't read the Montpelier paper.

"Fourth-degree possession of stolen property," Elliot clarified. It felt good to actually say it to someone who couldn't judge him. After all, Cade could hardly be critical when he must have done something similarly stupid. "What about you?"

Cade took a sip of his coffee, long fingers wrapping around the porcelain mug in a way that made the warmth Elliot had felt in his hand jump into his stomach.

"Vandalism." Cade's smile suggested he wasn't any sorrier about the vandalism than he had been about keeping Elliot waiting.

"Really?"

"Oh yeah."

Elliot tried to imagine this smiling man spray painting a building or slashing tires. He waited, but Cade offered no further explanation. Did Cade do that kind of thing often? In the sanitation building, Elliot had thought Cade was about his age, but now, seeing his hands and face under the golden light of the coffee shop, Elliot realized Cade was older, way too old to be entertained by Halloween-style pranks.

Cade watched him, amusement making his light brown eyes even warmer.

"What?" Elliot asked.

"You look like you just figured out you're handcuffed to an axe murderer." Cade smiled again and Elliot felt that warmth tug at him, pulling tight and deep. *James,* he reminded himself. James, who was attending the New England Culinary Institute and did not commit unrepentant acts of vandalism and wear fifteen—Cade flicked his tongue forward as he drank from his mug, revealing yet another piercing—sixteen pieces of metal in his head.

The man's lips curved in a satisfied smile. "It was a personal thing. Between me and my ex-boyfriend."

The confirmation that Cade was gay acted like an accelerant on that heat in Elliot's belly. It sizzled along his nerves, turning his skin hot and sensitive under his sweater. The information gave Elliot's brain permission to replay the way Cade's ass had looked when he leaned over the counter to kiss the barista, that worn jacket riding up far enough to show how tightly fitted the jeans were over his round ass. Elliot's fingers twitched at the idea of running his hand over it. He gave himself a mental shake. James. The ticket. Elliot had plans, and they didn't involve a detour to find out how that ball sitting on Cade's tongue would feel if they kissed. If Cade licked his skin.

Cade's look held something other than amusement now, and his eyes seemed darker. As if he could tell where Elliot's thoughts were, Cade pushed the barbell piercing his tongue out between his teeth and let it flick back with a click. Elliot licked the foam off his own lips, though he couldn't remember the last time he'd taken a sip of his cappuccino.

Cade's gaze followed the movement of Elliot's tongue. Was it his imagination or had Cade leaned closer? The tug Elliot felt inside ran right down into his dick and he fought against the need to pull at his jeans. So they were attracted to each other. God knew why. There was just something about Cade McKeun. Something about the appraising look in his eyes that made Elliot want to know what shade of brown those eyes would be if Elliot's hand were on Cade's dick.

Elliot had to get things back on track. "Umm, about that ticket. I'd be willing to give you two hundred for it."

Cade's eyes widened. "Wow. That's definitely something to think about."

"Why do you want it?"

"I love live music, and you gotta admit, that kind of quality performance is pretty rare around here."

"But Haydn and—"

"William Boyce? Little known eighteenth-century composer? I have all his sonatas right here." Cade placed an expensive-looking MP3 player on the table and spun the wheel. "See?" He turned it to show the display.

"You could have just put those pieces on there now."

Cade laughed. "So I could drive up the price? Do I look like a ticket-scalping con man to you?"

"No." He didn't know what to make of Cade. Elliot would have sworn an hour ago that he would never find a tongue ring anything but repulsive, but now he couldn't stop thinking about how that ball would feel on his skin, rolling over his—*for the love of God, Elliot, stop thinking with your little head.*

Elliot fidgeted with the sugar packets he'd brought to the table. "Want some?"

"Of that crap? Hell no."

"I wish I could drink coffee black."

"You really ought to get off the milk. They put so many hormones in it you'll be growing tits."

"Really?"

"Oh yeah. The government doesn't care what crap we're fed. They just want us docile."

First piercings, now Elliot found paranoia cute? It had been a long winter. Or maybe he just needed to get laid. "You have evidence of this?"

"Have you been paying any attention for the last ten years—oh." Cade's smile took on a cynical twist. "Ten years ago you were still playing in a sandbox."

Anger rather than embarrassment forced heat to Elliot's cheeks. "So do you want the two hundred or not?" He wasn't about to get into some kind of contest with someone who thought he knew everything because he'd been on the planet longer.

"You have the money with you?"

"No." And he certainly wasn't going to be stupid enough to pay with a check again. He took a deep sip from his mug.

"Look, kid, I'll give you the ticket."

Elliot choked on the hot liquid in his throat, finally managing to croak, "What?"

"All you gotta do is meet me Thursday at five thirty at Verde Loco."

"You're going to just give me the other ticket?"

"If you show."

"I just have to show up?"

"Mostly." Cade leaned over and wiped at Elliot's lips with a napkin. His thumb brushed the corner of Elliot's mouth. With a wink, Cade popped the thumb in his own mouth and made a show of licking it clean.

"I—I thought milk was dangerous."

"Sometimes the risk is worth it."

Chapter Two

Cade watched Elliot pace in front of the restaurant. The wind had picked up, sending the ends of Elliot's long wool coat flapping around his legs. Why the hell didn't Elliot just come in? He'd been out there since twenty after five. Could Cade have freaked the kid out so much that he had to summon up courage in a ten-degree windchill in order to face him?

As Cade studied Elliot, the kid turned his collar up around his iron-hard jaw before looking in one direction and then the other. When Elliot shook his head as if in disgust, Cade knew. Convinced Cade would be late again, Elliot was waiting outside for him. Cade ought to go out to collect his date, but he wondered how long the kid's righteous indignation would keep him warm.

Why had Cade demanded a second meeting? He'd definitely been wrong about Elliot at first glance. The kid wasn't one of those privileged types who got under Cade's skin, he was just wrapped a little tight. Probably because he was so young. Elliot needed some shaking up.

Cade liked Elliot's no-bullshit style, and it was fun to watch the kid react to some of the outrageous things Cade said, but he had to be honest with himself. More than a bit of his willingness to part with that ticket was the fact that Elliot was adorable as fuck.

Cade would miss the chance to hear the Academy and Boyce—the sonata in D minor was perfect for moping around on a rainy day—but he wanted to see what Elliot looked like when he smiled. He didn't meet many new people in Montpelier and missing the concert would be worth it if Elliot was as interesting a person as Cade thought he might be.

He pushed away from the table and went out to collect Elliot.

"You gonna freeze your balls off or you want some dinner?"

Elliot spun around, lips pursed in that cute sputter. "When did you get here?"

"'Bout ten minutes ago. Let's go, man. I'm not standing out here all night." His table was gone, but there were a few empty stools at the counter lining the window. Cade steered them to a vacant pair. "I'm having one of their Everything Burritos. What can I get you?"

"Just the ticket, thanks." Elliot didn't bother to claim one of the stools.

"Just like that? You're not having dinner?"

"Cade—I don't think—" Elliot appeared to be having some kind of internal dialogue. The lids came down halfway over those dark blue eyes and then he looked straight at Cade, full dark lips twitching. "Why not? I'll have the same thing."

"Jalapenos and all?"

"Bring it," Elliot said with assurance.

"You got it."

Elliot had taken off his overcoat by the time Cade came back with the food, two mammoth burritos wrapped in foil. With the coat across his lap, the breadth of Elliot's shoulders under the blue dress shirt was impressive. He was wearing a tie, Cade noticed as he swung onto the stool. No suit jacket, though, so Elliot probably didn't work at the capitol.

"Here you go." Cade slid the plate between them and carefully placed the three bottles he'd been carrying on the counter—soda, bottled iced tea and bottled water. "Take your pick."

Elliot picked up the water. "Don't you know this is just bottled tap water from New Jersey?"

Cade had the distinct feeling Elliot was making fun of him, and he liked it. Not many people tried.

"This has never even sat next to a tea leaf." Cade tapped the glass of the iced-tea bottle.

"Flip you for the soda." And there was Elliot's laugh. Deep and warm, it poured into Cade like syrup, a heavy, sweet pull low down inside him.

As it turned out, Elliot went through the soda and the water and the fruity iced tea, and was still fanning his mouth with his hand, tongue brushing his bottom lip.

"Hang on a sec." Cade got up and grabbed a sugar packet. "Pour this wherever it burns."

Elliot looked at Cade with doubt furrowing his brow, but the pain won out. Gaze narrowed, the kid dumped the sugar on his tongue, and then his eyes widened in relief. "It worked."

"Always does. Sugar blocks the receptors for the capsaicin in peppers."

Elliot moved his tongue between his lips.

"Pepper doesn't cause any actual burns, it just feels like it does."

"How do you know all this?"

"Chemistry."

"You're a chemist?" Elliot sounded interested rather than incredulous, and Cade wished he had a better answer.

"No. But I took organic chem in college."

"Where did you go?"

Cade wanted to wince. He hadn't been cut out for an academic life, but he really didn't want to hear the wasted-potential speech from Elliot. "MIT."

Elliot's lips looked like they were about to spit out a million questions. Cade avoided the Q&A session and knocked an item off his to-do list when he leaned over and kissed him. It was quick and hard, but long enough for Cade to know he needed to try it again.

Elliot blushed, the color burning high on his bronze cheeks. Freckles dotted his skin, spreading out from his nose, speckling the corners of his eyes.

Elliot's hand came up to rest on Cade's sleeve, as if to push him away if Cade gave in to the urge to taste those freckles. "What's this?" He fingered the patch on Cade's sleeve.

"Stone Temple Pilots. I followed them on tour in '93."

Elliot released his sleeve. "I've been out of Vermont twice."

"It's a nice place to hang," Cade said, smiling. "I always end up coming back here. Though after a few more winters I think I'll be ready to move to Hawaii."

"I just got back from Florida."

That explained the tan. Elliot talked about the job he'd just taken at a travel agency and how he was looking forward to more trips to look into arrangements. Cade didn't understand how someone could get his jollies planning trips for other people while he stayed put in Montpelier, but it worked for Elliot. Excitement turned his eyes a darker blue, gave his face an animation that had Cade wanting to pin Elliot up against the counter and lick the sweet spice right out of his mouth.

Cade took the ticket out of his jacket and placed it on the counter. "The concert's on Valentine's Day. Did you need this ticket for someone special?" He really hoped Elliot had been planning on taking his mom.

Elliot's fingers brushed Cade's where they rested on the ticket. It was too light a touch. Cade shouldn't have been able to feel that all the way in his gut.

"I'm not sure." Elliot didn't take the ticket.

Cade slid it closer, but kept his hand on it. "Hey, I'm going to a concert tonight. Wanna come with me?"

"What concert?"

"Lizzie Borden's Sofa. In Middlebury."

"That's an hour and a half away."

"Yeah. I've got to head out soon if I'm going to make it."

"Are they like Stone Temple Pilots?" Elliot's eyes narrowed in suspicion, like they had as he'd tried Cade's sugar solution.

"Not exactly."

Elliot sprinkled a little more sugar in his mouth. "Am I going to regret it as much as the jalapenos?"

Cade thought of Elliot in his yellow and blue striped tie bouncing in a mosh pit. "Possibly. It's not a trip to Florida, but I can guarantee that you won't be bored."

"I have to work tomorrow."

"So do I." Cade lifted his hand off the ticket.

Elliot looked at him for a while before making up his mind. The tension ramped up Cade's pulse, and he was tapping his toes in his boots.

"Okay." Elliot stood and shrugged on his coat. With a last look at Cade, Elliot slipped the ticket into his breast pocket.

"Great. I'll drive."

"I could—"

"Drive your gas-guzzling SUV that constantly reminds everyone of your masculinity?"

"At least I don't have to wear every piece of jewelry I own at the same time to establish my nonconformity. And four-wheel drive is only sensible in this kind of weather."

Cade gave a half smile at Elliot's hit. "It's not snowing now, and trust me, you'll be glad you left your car at home."

℘

Elliot found himself longing for the security of his Highlander when Cade's little shoebox of a car seemed to cough and hesitate at the peak of Stark Mountain. He looked at the mountain road and barely resisted checking his cell phone for signal strength. Cade's gloved hand hovered over the gear stick, and then they were over the crest and following the switchbacks down into the next valley.

But Elliot was glad they'd brought Cade's car when they bounced into the graveled lot of something-aphoria. The lights kept buzzing out so he couldn't read the whole sign. Calling whatever-aphoria a dive would be giving it too much credit. Even the cars in the lot looked like they'd be more at home doing community service—or sitting outside the county jail.

The first breath of air inside made Elliot wish *he* were back doing community service. The trash had smelled better. Beer, sweat, smoke and God, was that piss? The sound assaulting his ears could hardly be called music, nothing but screams and disorganized riffs. And the mass of people—shouting, moving, pushing toward them and away.

"Well?" Cade managed to make himself heard by screaming in Elliot's ear. His yell had a deep rough edge that vibrated down Elliot's neck.

"The people terrify me. And the music hurts my ears." Which was his polite way of saying he felt like he was about to be mauled by Rottweilers. That's what the crowd reminded him of. Guard dogs leaping at the ends of their leashes, barely restrained violence.

"That's because you're not really into it yet." Cade nudged him forward until the crowd swallowed them in.

Bodies jarred against him until he was nearly off his feet, but Cade stayed next to him, mostly because Elliot had a death grip on one of the patches on his jacket. The black T-shirt and flannel Cade had forced Elliot to change into ensured that he didn't stick out as much as he would have in his shirt and tie.

The incoherent rant from the lead singer stopped for a few bars, and Elliot caught a thread of melody, harsher and more disjointed than anything he would choose to listen to, but the energy underneath it was undeniable—or maybe it was because Cade swayed with him at that moment, his back resting against Elliot's chest. Someone shoved them from behind, sending his hips slamming into Cade's ass. Elliot could just imagine the twist of a smile on Cade's lips as he ground his ass back against Elliot's cock. Then they were shoved in another direction, and Elliot clung to the patch so hard he thought he'd tear it free.

გა

Cade kept an eye on Elliot as they made their way back over the mountains. The impulse to drag Elliot along hadn't been a complete waste, though part of him wondered if he'd been trying to push Elliot into running in the other direction. Cade was waiting for one of the kid's scathing remarks as they started the first climb through the state park. Elliot had seemed about to speak a dozen times as they left Metaphoria, but just kept licking his lips and falling into silence.

"That was interesting," he said finally.

Cade gave a half smile. "Interesting?"

181

"It's clear that some of the fans simply derive a thrill from doing something that could be considered rebellious."

"But?"

"I can also understand the appeal of releasing energy that way, almost feeding off the violence of the music and the—was that what they call moshing?"

Cade nodded.

Elliot rubbed at his ears. "But I might appreciate the experience more if my head would stop ringing."

Cade laughed. So not a total disaster. Had he wanted it to be?

A shudder ran through Bucky's frame. "Fuck." He dropped into a lower gear. They made it over the top and were on the downslope when the car bucked again and died. Cade popped it into neutral and peered into the black, looking for a place to pull off. The headlights had died along with the car. Elliot sucked in his breath in the silence, but he said nothing to distract Cade from trying to navigate in the darkness.

His gaze picked out a darker patch, no trees, no starlight reflecting off the pines, recognized it as the pull-off for a hiking trail and guided the car into it. At least the brakes still worked.

As the crunch of gravel and snow under the tires faded into the night, Cade looked through the windshield at the black trees and waited for Elliot to explode. Fuck, Cade knew he would have.

"Out of gas?" Elliot's tone was mild.

"I wish it were that simple." Cade waited a couple of minutes, and then turned the key. Bucky didn't even cough.

"It's a good thing we didn't bring my gas-guzzling SUV. I'd hate to have nothing but proof of my masculinity to transport us back home."

Cade couldn't help laughing. He pulled his cell out of his jacket and was completely unsurprised when the display told him he had no signal. He held it up to show Elliot.

With his first show of exasperation, Elliot fished out his own phone. They looked at each other until the lights from their phone displays faded.

"So?" Elliot said at last.

"I could pretend to check under the hood, but I already know what's wrong and I can't fix it. The electrical system is totally screwed up on this car. Sometimes it's just the fuel pump and I can start it again after a few hours. It's never done it after it's been working for a while though."

Elliot checked the display of his phone again. "I have to be at work in six hours."

"Well, the people who work at the ski resort should be coming by around six or seven—or the car may decide to start working again before then."

The tension coming off Elliot should have been enough to spark the car back to life, but he only said, "I can safely say that this is far worse than the jalapeños."

Cade tried the ignition again. Their breaths were already visible in the car, despite the fact that he'd had the heat blasting right until the car died.

"There's a blanket in the back." He set the emergency brake and put the car back into first gear.

Elliot looked over his shoulder into the backseat before turning to face Cade. His eyes had adjusted to the dark now, and the expression on Elliot's face was easy to read.

Elliot arched one dark brow. "This isn't an elaborate plan to get in my pants, is it?"

"Elliot, man, I'm not gonna deny that I would absolutely love to find out what's in your pants, but in about five minutes I'm gonna be too goddamned cold to do anything about it." Cade turned his whole body in the seat. "And I was kind of hoping I wouldn't need a plan."

He counted Elliot's breaths on puffs of steam. Cade already knew Elliot didn't like to do or say anything without thinking it through eight different ways. On the third breath, Elliot's hand landed on Cade's thigh. Even through his cargo pants and Elliot's glove, Cade could feel the heat of the kid's skin. Cade leaned forward to meet his kiss, their lips warming as they brushed together.

It was dry at first, then Elliot's tongue slipped into Cade's mouth, and he opened to the tingling heat with a groan. Elliot's hands came up to grab Cade's face, holding him still to take a long, slow taste of his mouth.

Arousal hit his stomach like a shot of whiskey, a bomb of warmth that flooded his thighs, and by the time he'd licked into Elliot's mouth, Cade was already shifting his hips around in the seat to try to ease the press of his dick in suddenly far-too-tight pants. For someone who looked like he needed lessons in cutting loose enough to be ten minutes late for work, Elliot was a damned good kisser. Cade rested his own hands on Elliot's neck and let him wind their bodies up tighter.

When lack of oxygen became as much an issue as the lack of blood flow anywhere but his throbbing dick, Cade pulled back. Elliot's hands still cupped Cade's face as their breaths echoed in the little car.

"Do you always smile when you kiss?" Elliot asked.

"If I'm having fun."

Elliot leaned back in, lips, tongue, teeth tugging on Cade's lower lip, and Cade twisted his neck to get deeper, to open his mouth farther. He wanted to climb over the gear stick and straddle Elliot, get his hands on those wide shoulders, grind their cocks together. He needed the hard press of skin, but it was zero fucking degrees and he'd be lucky if he could stand to have his gloves off long enough to touch the kid.

Elliot seemed to have the same idea because he shifted closer and then grunted "Ow" as some part of him connected with the gear stick.

"Backseat. C'mon."

Elliot looked around the headrest and arched his brow again. "Do you know how much room there would be in my SUV?"

"If we were in your SUV, you'd already be dropping me off." Cade slid a hand up Elliot's inseam. "Not getting off."

"You got crackers to go with a line that cheesy?" But Elliot's breath hitched as Cade's fingers dipped down next to his balls.

"C'mon." Cade jerked his head at the backseat.

Elliot put his hand on the door handle.

"Don't. It'll let in too much cold air."

Elliot twisted back around and looked at Cade. "You first."

"All right." Cade tugged his seat up and wiggled over and between the seats. To his profound disappointment, Elliot didn't take advantage of Cade's ass-up position to do any groping. He bit his lips against a sigh. Neither he nor his dick was in the mood for gentlemanly behavior. Elliot hadn't seemed at all shy when he'd had his tongue down Cade's throat.

Elliot followed, landing half on Cade, heavy wool coat blanketing them both. Cade decided that if he was going to keep his dick happy he was going to have to move things along. He peeled off one of his gloves, threaded his fingers through Elliot's short soft hair and jerked him up for a long, hard kiss.

"That's, that's, your tongue ring is—" Elliot panted.

Now that they were on the right page again with the panting and Elliot's hands rubbing on Cade's chest, he didn't mind slowing down a bit. "Wait until you feel it everywhere else." He licked along that knife-edged jaw, scraping along stubble until he could flick Elliot's earlobe, run the ball over the soft space behind his ear. Elliot's hands tightened on his shirt.

"Let's use the coats as blankets," Cade suggested. He had the feeling that spunk and wool made for a hellish stain combo.

He helped Elliot slide the coat off his shoulders.

"What about yours?" Elliot leaned away from him.

"Yeah." Cade pushed up and wrestled free of the sleeves, tucking his gloves in the pockets. When he pressed back, he had to clench his teeth to keep them from chattering. Without Elliot against him and his jacket for insulation, the frozen plastic of the seat stabbed right into his bones. He pulled Elliot back down on top of him, grabbing at the blanket and yanking it and their coats over the top of them.

They were both half off the seat, but Cade didn't care as long as Elliot was sharing his body heat. Cade was so cold he forgot his ulterior motive for dragging them into the backseat until he felt Elliot's hard-on rubbing against him. Cade opened his legs wider, pressing Elliot's hips with his thighs, his body flushing with heat. Elliot kissed him again, a hot, slow rub of their tongues with a wet suggestion that Cade was definitely interested in following up.

Elliot's groan vibrated against Cade's mouth, and he arched up into that warm body, worming his hand between them until he could palm Elliot's dick through his jeans. Shit. He hoped to hell Elliot knew what to do with what he was packing because the weight and length made an impression even through the denim.

Elliot's hand tugged hard in Cade's hair, an aggression he was only too happy to go along with. He tipped his head back and let Elliot mouth the side of his neck.

"Yeah, fuck." The words had barely left Cade's lips before Elliot froze.

Cade waited in confusion as Elliot released his hair and pushed away. The kid's face had gone wary.

"Elliot?"

Chapter Three

Elliot couldn't believe the way he'd been acting since Cade had turned to face him. Grabbing the man's head, pulling his hair, slamming him up against the back door—God, Cade would think he was a sex-starved freak.

"Elliot? You all right, man?" Cade was still smiling, lips wet from Elliot's mouth.

Oh he was all right—he could even think now that Cade had stopped rubbing Elliot's cock. Think about being on the verge of having sex with someone he'd just met, think about how he seemed to have completely forgotten all those carefully constructed James plans. Actually, Cade moaning *fuck* as his legs opened around Elliot's hips had just about deprived him of any memory of James.

This wasn't supposed to happen with Cade—Cade, who was so determined to be different that he had to drag them up here in his crappy little car and get them stuck freezing to death on a mountain in January.

"Elliot." Cade's thumb stroked the edge of Elliot's jaw. "Have you—is this your first time with a guy?"

"No." It wasn't. It wasn't as if he had the kind of experience he was sure Cade had, but it definitely wasn't his first time.

"It's okay. I mean, I don't care." Cade sat up and leaned into Elliot, both hands now stroking the sides of his face. "It's not that complicated. You've got a dick—you know what feels good."

Cade was pushing Elliot back against the seat, and that would be an end to the amazing sensation of knowing Cade was letting Elliot do what he wanted.

"I said it's not my first time." Elliot shoved Cade back against the door.

Cade's legs dropped wide again, his thumb rubbing Elliot's lips. "Knock yourself out, kid."

Elliot wasn't even sure if he liked Cade. He fascinated Elliot but scared him a little too. Every time Cade looked at him, Elliot's stomach made a leap as if he were jumping off the top of the falls into Dunham Brook.

"Elliot. We could just share body heat. I promise to keep my hands to myself."

"I don't." He may have only jumped once, stupid on beer and cinnamon schnapps, but once the choking fear had subsided, the free fall had been fun.

He ran his hands under the loose flannel shirt Cade wore over his T-shirt, finding hard muscle under the cotton. When Elliot stroked over Cade's ribs, the muscles under Elliot's fingers jumped and Cade jerked away.

"Ticklish," Cade admitted.

The crack in Cade's cool demeanor made Elliot feel a little less hesitant. He stroked harder. "Where else?"

"Gonna have to find out on your own."

The challenge in Cade's voice sent another pump of blood to Elliot's cock. "I can handle that."

Elliot shoved up the hem of Cade's shirt, thumbs sliding across the skin just above the waistband of those outrageous plaid pants. Cade shivered.

"There too?"

"Yeah."

Elliot undid the top button of Cade's pants.

"Definitely there." Cade's voice was quiet, but with a rough edge that teased Elliot's ears like a brush of lips and stubble.

His fingers slid through the soft hair below Cade's navel, and Elliot swore Cade vibrated against him—or maybe the guy was just cold. Elliot found the tab on the zipper, the sound of metal purring loud in the car.

His palm connected with a damp patch of cotton as Cade's dick jumped to meet his hand. The sound from Cade now was deeper than his usual tenor, his harsh breath loud in Elliot's ear. Knowing it wasn't the cold that got Cade to jerk and moan made Elliot's toes curl in his boots. He reached into Cade's boxers and found the hard satin of his cock. Elliot wished he could see it, could watch the dark flush of blood, the drops of precome on the head, but he let his fingers tell him all they could. Heavy, a gentle curve toward Cade's stomach and the thick vein on the underside pulsing fast. Cade's teeth flashed in a grin as Elliot tightened his grip and jacked him slowly.

He watched Cade's face for clues and got nothing but that wide smile. "What do you like?"

"It's more fun if you figure it out on your own, don't you think?"

Elliot twisted his grip, and Cade's teeth sank into his lower lip, lids dropping shut over his glittering eyes. When he pressed a thumb into Cade's slit, Cade rocked up into his fist. But when Elliot rubbed hard under the head, Cade spat out a string of soft, encouraging curses.

Cade had one bent leg on the floor, the other cocked against the back of the seat. The blanket and coats had dropped around Elliot's thighs, but he wasn't feeling the cold anymore. He pushed himself off the seat until he was hunched in an awkward crouch in the foot well, Cade's dick bobbing next to his mouth.

"Elliot, man, you—ah fuck."

Elliot sealed his mouth around the head and licked, tasting Cade. Salt and musk and something like wood smoke rolled over Elliot's tongue with the weight of Cade's cock. Cade's body was shuddering, the muscles bunching under Elliot's hand where it rested on Cade's thigh. Elliot wanted to think Cade was fighting the urge to drive up into Elliot's mouth, that he was bringing Cade to the brink of losing control. Cade seemed so unreachable, so sure of his way of looking at the world, the idea that Elliot could make this man fall apart with his mouth and hands swelled his own cock to almost the point of pain.

His tongue worked the knot of nerves under the head while his hand tugged fast and hard on the shaft.

He hadn't thought Cade's vocabulary could become more fragmented, but the sounds he was making were barely recognizable as words—even obscene ones. Elliot didn't have a lot of practice, though based on his limited experience he was reasonably sure he knew what felt good, and porn videos were nothing if not instructive, but no one had ever responded the way Cade was.

The way Cade was reacting to Elliot's mouth on his cock was dizzying. Elliot felt like just rubbing himself through his jeans might be enough to finish him if Cade kept moaning like that. Hoarse whispers, begging and then the sound of his name, Cade's hands urgent on Elliot's head, pulling his hair hard enough to sting.

"Elliot—fuck—I'm—Jesus fuck—Elliot—don't—I'm coming—ah..."

Elliot just sucked harder and sped up his hand. He wasn't going to give up on this now, even if it meant a bitter mouthful.

The *ah* ended in a long, deep whine, and Cade curled up into him, hips jerking as he shot come straight to the back of Elliot's throat, one spurt after another until Elliot finally had to pull off to catch his breath and swallow.

Elliot stroked Cade until his breathing slowed, thumb rubbing against the softening skin of the head of Cade's dick. At last, Cade twisted out of Elliot's grip, and pulled him up with surprising strength for someone whose muscles should have been profoundly relaxed.

"Goddamnit, Elliot, why didn't you pull off?"

He couldn't imagine why his swallowing had Cade so annoyed. Elliot shrugged.

"You don't know fuck about me. Did it even occur to you that I could be positive?"

It actually hadn't. As alarm turned his neck muscles to coils of rusty wire, he heard himself say calmly, "Are you?"

"Not that I know of but—"

"Then what are we talking about? You were already—when I started you were—" God, sex was fun but it wasn't exactly an easy topic to discuss.

"At a better time we're going to have a long conversation about viral load and risk factors." Cade shook his head, leaving Elliot feeling about fifteen years old.

"We've got nothing but time at the moment."

"I'd think you'd have something else in mind *at the moment.*" Cade's hand was sliding up Elliot's thigh again.

"And what about risk factors?"

"So tell me. Other than blow jobs, have you ever had unprotected sex?"

"No." Other than blow jobs, he hadn't had sex, but he wasn't telling Cade that.

"How many lovers?"

Oh crap, Elliot should have kept his mouth shut. And somehow he knew Cade already knew the answer.

"Three." More like two and a half, but Elliot wasn't telling Cade about Josh either.

Cade nodded.

"What?" Elliot hated the idea that he was that predictable, as if predictability was suddenly something to be ashamed of.

"Low risk. So? You wanna talk some more or you want to find out why I got my tongue pierced?"

Cade's words probably wouldn't be considered sexy even by a lax judge, but the sensory image they provoked made Elliot's breath tangle in his throat until he had to cough. He was achingly hard again.

"Was that a yes?"

Elliot was too short of breath to do anything but nod.

"Lean back."

Elliot leaned back on his knees and pressed into the opposite corner of the car. Cade shifted to the side so Elliot could stretch out his legs.

"Perfect." Cade kissed him, the ball on his tongue rubbing and tingling in Elliot's mouth.

The taste of come faded into the taste of Cade, the unpredictable press of the metal at sensitive points in Elliot's mouth cranked his pulse rate over a hundred and his spine arched and drove the back of his skull into the doorframe. Then Cade's hand was there to cushion Elliot's head, warm fingers stroking behind his ear. Cade drew his tongue up the side of Elliot's neck, the extra tickle of the ball almost enough of a distraction that Cade's other hand had already unfastened Elliot's jeans before he noticed. Cade's palm working Elliot's cock through his briefs wasn't something Elliot could miss though, even with Cade back to kissing him.

The first shock of skin to skin resonated through Elliot until his nerves were on fire.

"Elliot, fuck." Cade's voice was as breathy as it had been when Elliot had had his hand on Cade's dick. "I can't wait, man. Your cock feels so good."

Not waiting was just fine with Elliot. Cade's hand knew what to do with Elliot's dick better than he did, and every touch of that piercing on his skin just made him desperate to find out what it was going to feel like on his cock.

Cade slipped down his body with a grace Elliot would have expected from someone much smaller, folded himself in the space between Elliot's legs and lapped at the head of his cock.

That first wet touch, Cade's mouth so hot in that cold air, forced Elliot's eyes closed and dragged a groan from his lips.

"Here." Cade hauled the blanket up over his head.

Elliot looked down at Cade, watched the shine in his eyes as he licked up the side of Elliot's dick.

"Things are gonna get wet, and I don't want anything getting cold." Cade dropped the edge of the blanket in the middle of Elliot's chest, leaving him feeling almost alone, like some kind of invisible force was pulling his cock into all that slick heat, and then he heard Cade groan around him, the humming rolling deep inside him.

Cade licked up the length of him again before flicking around the head, the ball catching just under the crown of Elliot's dick. Elliot hadn't had that many blow jobs and he'd considered all of them a memorable experience, but he was pretty damned sure he wanted all of them to be from someone with a tongue piercing from now on. The ball dipped into his slit, a blinding wave of pleasure that drove his hips forward.

Cade didn't pull off or push Elliot back down, just slid deeper on him, tongue flicking, the softness at the back of Cade's throat caressing him. Then Cade swallowed around him. Elliot's hand squeezed the door handle until he heard the plastic crack. His dick swelled again, his balls tightening against his body. Cade backed off.

His voice was muffled but intelligible. "Not yet, kid, I'm not nearly done."

He kissed his way down to Elliot's balls, sucking on them through the cotton before pulling Elliot's briefs to the side, then Cade's tongue dragged around the sac.

When his tongue pressed lower, Elliot jerked, then that wet mouth was back on his balls. His hips were in constant motion, rocking into Cade's hands as rough thumbs pressed circles into Elliot's hipbones.

Cade kissed the head of Elliot's cock again, rolled the ball into his slit before swallowing around him with a wet gulp that Elliot could hear even through the blanket. It sounded obscene and so hot that his hand crunched the plastic again.

As Cade's lips slid down Elliot's shaft, a tingle burned through his balls. Cade took him deeper and deeper before riding up and down in a quick bob that Elliot was pretty sure was the best thing that ever happened to him. In fact, having his cock in Cade's mouth for the rest of Elliot's life seemed like a pretty good plan. He was going to have to work on how to make that happen as soon as he could think straight.

Elliot arched his spine. Cade dragged the ball of his piercing around Elliot's rim before pulling off again, and now Elliot knew why people were driven to curse.

"Goddamnit. Don't—please."

Cade dropped a hard kiss on the skin just above Elliot's cock, teeth tugging at the hair, and the ache receded a little.

"Please don't do that again."

"This?" Cade licked and sucked against the bone, the pressure easing Elliot back from the edge.

"No. You know."

"What?"

Elliot might not be able to see it, but he knew Cade was grinning under that blanket. His tongue started teasing again, and Elliot felt himself sliding back into a place where words were pretty hard to form.

"Stop. Cade, please let me come."

And he did. God, he did. Cade dove back down on him, a hard deep suck, his hand on the root of Elliot's cock, lips sliding to meet his fingers as they dragged up. Elliot swore Cade was fucking him with his mouth, his tongue, even though Elliot was the one who couldn't seem to stop slamming his hips up into that wet pressure. The build this time felt bigger, drawing up from so deep inside him he could feel his muscles shake.

He was barely able to gasp out a warning, but Cade didn't let up with his mouth and tongue, and this time when that point of pressure dipped into Elliot's slit, the heat rushed through his balls and he exploded over the edge, coming longer and harder than he ever had in his life. Cade seemed to know just when Elliot couldn't take any more and eased off his cock with gentle licks and kisses.

The post-orgasmic haze parted enough for him to feel Cade tucking him back into his pants, crawling back up to drop a kiss on the side of his neck.

"Think you might be wearing the imprint of the door on your skull for a while, man." Cade gently pulled Elliot a little lower on the seat. Elliot straightened out his neck with an audible crack. "You were so quiet there I thought maybe I was doing something wrong."

Elliot was pretty sure he'd lost a few brain cells when he came, and he certainly wasn't up to verbal sparring with Cade, but he knew he was being teased. "Liar."

"Yeah, well then you mentioned the part about living in my mouth forever so I figured I was on the right track."

Elliot could feel the blush in his cheeks, though he was surprised his circulation was up for it. He was pretty sure nothing was going to be up for anything for a quite a while. He really hadn't thought he'd said that aloud.

"It seemed like a good idea at the time," he admitted.

Cade laughed against Elliot's chest and dragged the blanket up over both of them. "And now?"

Elliot thought of the way that ball dipped into his slit, tugged at the rim of his cock. "It still holds some appeal."

"You do a pretty good job yourself, kid."

Now he knew Cade was definitely lying. Elliot was probably down at the bottom of a considerable list.

"Seriously. You're fucking intense about it, man. It's really hot."

Intense? Intense was good. And Cade had certainly seemed to be enjoying himself.

Cade's thumb brushed across Elliot's lips. "So, that's quite an impressive cock you got there. It good at any other tricks?"

Elliot's mind shorted out for a few seconds. It sounded like Cade was talking about fucking—with penetration—specifically, about Elliot penetrating Cade. The idea of being inside him, of having Cade arch into him, that soft, hoarse voice begging as Elliot drove his cock into Cade's ass—it was like Elliot's brain had stumbled onto a free-porn link, and he couldn't shut it down. He didn't want to.

"Elliot? You freaking out again, man?"

"I'm not freaking out." Which was a surprise. He hadn't expected to end up doing any of this when he got out of bed this morning, and if nothing else, he really ought to be angry with Cade for insisting they take his car and getting them stuck up here.

Maybe Cade talking to him was stalling it, or maybe he wasn't going to freak out, because that porn video was still playing in his head and Elliot could feel his dick, still sticky and damp from Cade's mouth, stir in his jeans.

"Well, don't fall asleep either. It's too dangerous. I'll try to start the car again in a bit. You warm enough?" Cade pulled Elliot's coat on top of the blanket and handed him his own jacket. "Here. I know your neck's gotta be killing you."

Elliot tucked Cade's jacket behind his head and everything got a lot more comfortable. Cade was a warm weight against his chest. Elliot's head was cushioned from the cold glass. If his dick could remember that he'd come hard enough to stop his heart and forget about Cade's hand resting just below his waist, he'd be perfectly content.

"So, were you born in Montpelier?" Cade's words broke into the warm place where Elliot had been drifting.

"Hmm?"

"We can't fall asleep, man."

"Oh. No. Bennington." Elliot really didn't want to talk about his childhood. The fact that his dad's failures had dragged them through every town in Vermont big enough to have a crossroads, then Elise in the hospital, Dad dying. It always sounded like some kind of lame ploy for sympathy. Besides, he had a feeling Cade had a much more interesting life story.

"How was Florida?" Cade must have read Elliot's reluctance in his answer.

"Nice. Warm. Not hot. But warm. And sunny." The memory of the sun soaking into his bones and the lush green smell made him even drowsier.

"Did you go to Disney World?"

"No, Fort Lauderdale. Tell me about following a band around."

Cade was good at telling stories, making incidents that probably had been ordeals at the time seem funny. His voice was soft, but the way he was laying on Elliot made it rumble against his chest, so he could feel it as much as he could hear it.

"Elliot."

He was cold, and Cade was snapping a finger against his cheek. He jerked awake.

"I'm going to try to start the car. Don't fall asleep again. Move around a little." Cade climbed over the seats.

Elliot shook himself awake and fumbled for his cell phone. It was almost five. They'd been there almost three hours.

Cade was talking again, a low whisper.

Elliot pulled on his coat and leaned forward over the seat. "Are you talking to the car?"

"Yep." Cade didn't sound at all embarrassed.

"You do know it's just a machine, right?"

"And you're just a bio-chemical-electrical machine yourself. Ready, Bucky?"

Elliot held his breath as Cade turned the ignition. The car flared to life.

"If you're coming up front, hurry up. We're moving." Cade blasted the heat, and Elliot flung open the door and hurried to the front seat. "See, I'll have you back in plenty of time for work," Cade said as he pulled onto the highway.

"If we make it back over the mountain." Instead of being warmed by the burst of activity, Elliot was shivering. "Are you going to be late for work?"

"Nope. I don't have to be there until four thirty."

"But it's almost five— That was a dirty trick."

"What?"

"You made it sound like you had to be at work in the morning. You'll get to sleep all day."

Cade's teeth were bright in the light from the dashboard. "But didn't you like your adventure? You can go back to your regularly scheduled life, no harm no foul."

Elliot's brain looped back through his new favorite porn video. The way Cade had talked, Elliot'd had the impression that they'd see each other again. Of course, they'd see each other. It was almost impossible not to run into each other in a town the size of Montpelier, and they'd both be doing community service again on Saturday, but didn't Cade want...

Cade wasn't Josh, and there certainly wasn't any doubt about Cade's sexuality, but Elliot still couldn't bring himself to say anything, to take that risk.

He tried to find something to say that wouldn't expose him to another spectacular humiliation brought on by assumptions. "Where do you work?"

"I'm a waiter at La Pomme D'Orée."

That left him stunned all the way down Stark Mountain. Cade had gone to MIT and he worked as a waiter? There wasn't any way to ask him about it that wouldn't sound critical, so Elliot just watched the road, looking for the flash of eyes on the roadside that might give warning of a deer about to leap in front of them.

As the silence stretched on, Cade spun the volume up on the radio. They didn't talk again until a quick good night at Elliot's apartment.

Chapter Four

Work was slow. Even for five thirty on a Friday in January it was slow. The legislature must be running late. All Cade had was a sweet little old couple celebrating an anniversary that had to be way past gold and heading on to diamond and another couple that would be lucky to see ten years the way they couldn't seem to order without glaring at each other. The two other tables were split between Diane and Rick. When he went to collect Ms. Cranky's appletini and Mr. Cranky's vodka tonic, Cade found the bar empty of life except for a seriously bored Henry behind the bar turning each bottle to perfect alignment.

Jeanette signaled from her hostess stand while Cade was keeping an eye on the venerable lovebirds.

"Someone at the bar asked for you."

It couldn't be Mike. Jeanette wouldn't be smiling like that if it were Mike, but her words still churned acid in his stomach. Mike had taken some kind of fucked-up delight in dropping in the first few months after they broke up; and although Cade's coworkers and manager tried to shield him, Mike was a legislative aide and La Pomme D'Orée made its money on being the place for lobbyists to take legislators.

Cade recognized his visitor right away, and the panic faded into a ball of warmth. Elliot. Cade had done more than enough pushing yesterday, and he wasn't sure how the kid would respond. He'd been hoping to see the kid again—outside of trash sorting. Though considering what Elliot had between his legs, Cade ought to stop calling him kid. But Cade needed the reminder. Despite Elliot's serious demeanor and whatever part of his early twenties he may have checked off on the calendar, Elliot was still a kid, taking a walk on the wild side.

Before Elliot could turn around, Cade ducked back out of the bar and asked Rick to keep an eye on the sweet old couple. He came from behind Elliot, through the customer entrance, just wanting to look at him for another minute. The kid had some kind of mixed drink in front of him that looked like it hadn't even been sipped. Henry definitely would have ID'd him.

It wasn't just that Elliot had adorable working for him—and he sure as hell had that. And it wasn't just that Cade was dying to find out how Elliot's devastatingly intense focus and attention to detail during a blow job would translate to fucking in a more accommodating space—though Cade's imagination on that subject had given him a nice long session with his hand in the shower this afternoon. It was Elliot. His intensity, self-control, even his dry wit, all of that seemed to be covering a core of restless passion Cade was dying to tap into.

"Hey, man." He slipped into the space between Elliot's chair and the one next to him. Cade gave Henry a nod to let the bartender know not to charge Elliot before taking a proprietary sip of the kid's drink. "A Manhattan?"

Elliot nodded.

Cade shouldn't. He really planned to back off, but something in him wouldn't rest until he'd gotten another glimpse of the guy Elliot hid inside. Cade plucked the cherry out of the drink and sucked it between his lips before rolling it over his tongue and into his throat. Elliot's pupils widened.

"Henry'll get you another one."

"Your—ah—piercings?"

"I can't wear 'em all at work. Just something small." He patted the diamond studs in his lowest holes.

"And you put up with that?"

"I'd put up with a lot more for the tips I make here." Cade heard the door open, deep voices, the usual Friday night batch of state senators. They'd be in here for drinks before moving on to the dining room. As much as his manager loved him, Cade didn't think the love extended enough to allow him time to flirt in the bar when he was supposed to be working. "Come with me for a second?"

"Okay." Elliot stepped off the tall swiveling chair, and Cade led him through the back into the linen storage and shut the door behind them, leaning against it. Diane would just love to stumble in here "accidentally". "You look so different."

Cade looked down at his black pants and white shirt. He supposed it was a bit of a change from the yellow and green plaid cargo pants he'd had on last night. "You like it?"

Elliot shrugged. Cade supposed the kid had been raised on the second golden rule—if you can't say something nice, say nothing at all.

"Tell you what. Sometime I'll let you ransack my closet and play dress up like I did to you last night and you can see what you like best."

The sputter was back, and Cade couldn't help taking the step forward that would get his mouth in contact with Elliot's. He tasted like bourbon and bitter vermouth, and Cade wanted it all to go away until Elliot tasted like he did in the car last night. Until all Cade could taste was them together, hot and eager.

Elliot stepped into Cade and pushed him back against the door, hands tugging at Cade's hips until they were sharing space. Now Cade hated his boring clothes just because they were on and keeping him from the rigid heat pressing into him.

He got one hand on Elliot's jaw and used the other on Elliot's ass to drive him closer, until they were both hard and panting, cocks sliding past each other through the barriers.

Elliot lifted his head. "What time do you get off work?"

"I probably won't be home until two."

Elliot groaned in frustration and rocked his hips harder.

"Man, I would love to see you enjoying a little public sex, but I really like my job."

His words acted like an ice bath. Elliot stepped away, eyes lowered, face flushed. "Sorry. I don't usually—God, Cade, I'm so sorry."

"It's okay." He rubbed his thumb over Elliot's sputtering lips and hooked the other hand in his belt loop. "I've got a few minutes. Just not long enough to do you right."

Elliot was still looking away.

"Listen," Cade went on. "I want to take this further, I do, but I've got something you need to hear first."

Elliot's eyes met Cade's then, and the fear he saw there made his gut ache.

"This isn't some kind of pity request or whatever, but if we're gonna fuck and damn do I want to, you should know this."

Elliot didn't look particularly reassured.

"I was with somebody for a while—a long time—" Civil union, their families at the county clerk's office, Mike so heart-stoppingly gorgeous in his suit, God, he'd loved that bastard, "—and we weren't using condoms anymore, and then—" The flood in the basement at La Pomme, coming home, Mike fucking some twink in their bed, finding out Cade had been oblivious to the fact that Mike's dick had been in more twink asses than Cade had thought there were in the entire state of Vermont. He swallowed back the pain of betrayal and went on, "—I found out he'd been cheating on me—and he hadn't been safe about it. I got tested, and I was clean, but I can't really be one hundred percent sure until I get another test next month. We should be okay if you use a rubber, but I thought you should know."

Elliot's face relaxed and then tightened again. "Is this the vandalism ex?"

"Yeah. I kind of took my feelings out on his car. Still not sorry about it. Asshole had it coming." Cade lifted his head and waited for that to be the last straw for Elliot.

"Couldn't you have paid the damages?"

"I could have, but the fucker wanted an apology. In court. I said he could go to hell. I'm lucky I didn't go to jail for contempt. Maybe the judge had a messy breakup in her past."

Cade didn't know what he expected, but it wasn't a warm burst of laughter from Elliot. "What did he say then?"

"Hoped I liked community service. Hoped I'd get recycling because I'd been nothing but a waste of his time. I should have fucked up his tires too."

Elliot smiled, his brows rising up to his hairline. "He sounds like a piece of work."

"Whatever. I don't really feel like dragging him into everything, but until I get that six-month test—I just can't be a dick about it. I wanted to be straight with you." Cade was over the bastard. If Mike would just stop popping up from time to time, and Cade could get that test back with a nice negative on it, Mike would be out of Cade's head for good.

"Thanks. I know it sounds kind of dumb, but I really appreciate it."

There was a story there, maybe a key to whatever kept Elliot wound so tight, but Cade had to get back to work, and Elliot didn't look to be sharing at the moment.

"I'm sorry, man, but I've really—"

"I know." Elliot's eyes were dark as he leaned in and kissed him. "Guess I'll see you tomorrow."

&

The trash center still smelled worse than anything Elliot could imagine. His back ached after the first two hours, and the bitter humiliation of being punished still left him as queasy as the smell, but he was almost having fun. Cade wasn't wearing his earphones, and they talked over the noise of the clanking and thunking and machinery crushing.

Cade told stories about his family, how his parents had been living on a commune when he was born—though now they preferred to call it an experiment in eco-friendly habitation—and how his younger brother was the black sheep of the family because he had gone into, horror of horrors, the world of New York City finance and been married in a church.

When Cade asked if Elliot was as good at organizing trips as he was at organizing trash, Elliot considered explaining that he had always been the one to make sure all their stuff made it into the van when Dad came home and said they were moving. But the conversation had been so light, and Cade's family stories so funny, Elliot just talked about his stepfather. How he'd been the main reason Elliot had gone to college, and then Elliot gave an imitation of how his stepfather would lecture if he found out about Elliot's arrest record. Elliot was relieved when the conversation drifted back to some of Cade's adventures in getting to concerts hundreds of miles away from where he was when he decided to go.

They walked out together, stripping off the coveralls and gloves. Cade stretched his back and yawned. "I've got to be back to work in four hours. Guess I'd better head home for a shower."

"Uhm—"

Cade lowered his arms and waited, his head tilted.

Coffee? No, they'd done that. *Just tell him what you want, Elliot. He wants it too.* "You could shower at my place, it's actually closer to the restaurant than yours. Or I could bring you back here for your car—"

"Bucky wouldn't start again this morning. I'm going to have to do something about him eventually."

"I could drive you to the restaurant if you wanted—after—"

Cade's grin made Elliot's blood rush downhill. "After what, Elliot?"

Elliot really couldn't find the words. Not with Cade standing so close, so cocky, sensuality pouring off him in pulse-pounding waves.

Cade closed the gap to inches. "After you fuck me? That is where we're headed, right? 'Cause I got about three hours of sleep last night and if I don't have a better offer I'm taking a nap."

Elliot swallowed and nodded. If he was going to do it, he really ought to be able to say it. "I want to have sex with you."

"Where'd you park, man?"

∞

They stopped at Cade's so he could run in to grab his work clothes, and then they were at Elliot's building. The apartment was tiny but there was off-street parking in the back and that made the rent worth it. And he was close enough to walk to work in the summer. Thinking about his apartment and parking and walking to work wasn't doing much to calm the nervousness that made his legs feel as weak as the shocks in Cade's ancient car.

Elliot was going to lose his virginity in the next few hours, and every other thought he tried to use to stop obsessing over that fact was getting shoved to the side. They'd climbed the second flight of stairs and were in the hall when Cade spoke. He made an exaggerated sniff of his clothes and rolled his eyes. "Bathroom?"

Elliot pointed to the door next to the kitchen.

Cade dropped his bag, his coat and shirts on the floor on his way, looking back over his shoulder as he tugged the last layer over his head. "You comin' or what?"

Elliot dropped his own shirt and looked down at his chest. He should have been working out more this winter. The shoulders and back he'd glimpsed before Cade disappeared into the bathroom had been ropey with muscles. Elliot wasn't all soft, but he didn't have the kind of definition he got when he was hiking almost every weekend in the summer.

He pushed open the door. Cade was already in the shower, his ripped-up jeans tossed over the back of the toilet. Hooking his thumbs under his waistband, Elliot hesitated. Cade was on the other side of the heavy blue shower curtain Elliot's mother had chosen. Wet, naked, waiting for him. He was going to think Elliot had changed his mind if he didn't get in there.

He wished he had some kind of an instruction manual. Porn covered the mechanics, but didn't spend a lot of time on the preliminaries. Was there something he was supposed to do first? There was the one video where the top had blown the bottom in the shower before fucking him. Elliot thought he'd like to try that.

Glad to have some kind of plan fixed in his head, Elliot unfastened his jeans and slid them and his briefs off, tossing them on top of Cade's. He pulled a couple towels from the cabinet over the toilet and put them on the seat. There wasn't much else he could do before climbing in.

He yanked open the curtain before he changed his mind. Cade grinned and shifted to one side to share the spray. "Thought you'd never make it. I did mention I had a time crunch, right?"

Elliot was saved from answering by the sluice of water over his face.

"Jesus fucking Christ, man, you're big everywhere, aren't you?"

Knowing what was about to happen had him half-hard since they had left the sanitation center. With Cade's eyes deepening from their usual light brown as his gaze traveled over Elliot's body, he felt his cock twitch and fill.

"Every inch of you is hot, but shit." Cade's soapy fingers reached for Elliot. "You really got a prize when they were handing out the cocks, hmm?"

He hadn't exactly seen enough to make a broad comparison, but he knew he was thicker than average. Cade stroked, long slow pulls that were making Elliot forget about everything but that hand on his cock. Cade seemed to have a way of disrupting every plan Elliot had, but since giving in so far had led to the best orgasm of his life, he wasn't about to start complaining.

Elliot watched those long fingers tug his dick fully hard, then traced his own back up Cade's strong forearm to his biceps and squeezed him there, measuring the strength.

"Those trays are fucking heavy," Cade said.

Elliot trailed his hand across Cade's chest, fingers lingering on the bar piercing his right nipple. Cade's breath quickened as he arched closer. Elliot gave a tug. Cade's teeth sank into his lip.

"It doesn't hurt?"

"No." A snort of laughter came out of Cade's nose. "At least not anymore."

Elliot looked down at his own flat nipples. "They don't do much for me."

Cade leaned in and lapped over one, the ball on his tongue tugging before he used his teeth. It still wasn't as much fun as the hand working Elliot's cock, but the pressure tingled a little.

Elliot continued exploring. Those hard pecs and that flat stomach didn't just come from carrying trays of food.

"Yoga," Cade said as if answering Elliot's unspoken question.

Elliot sputtered, and Cade pulled his hand away. The idea of the always-wired Cade settling down enough to chant while sitting cross-legged on the floor was unbelievable.

Cade's eyebrow ring shot up as he gave Elliot a questioning look.

He tried not to laugh. "It doesn't seem your speed."

"It's good exercise, but I really need to work on my control." Cade's hands rubbed Elliot's hips and slipped down to his thighs. "Turn around."

"Huh?" That was definitely not part of the plan.

"I'm going to wash your back. And then, you can wash mine."

Until meeting Cade, Elliot had never realized you could hear someone grin. Cade's was always bright, promising fun if Elliot would just take that running jump.

Elliot turned. Cade did more than wash Elliot's back, strong fingers worked the ache out of muscles stiff from the work this morning, muscles made even tenser as Elliot anticipated what they were going to do. Cade's hands ran up Elliot's neck into his scalp, soothing away the fear that he was somehow going to mess things up, that Cade would laugh and make Elliot feel stupid.

He froze when Cade's hands got to his butt, but all Cade offered was more caressing strokes of his soapy hands. They felt amazing on Elliot's thighs, stroking down hard, teasingly light on the way back up. He'd never realized that someone rubbing his thighs could make his dick feel that good.

Cade's hands slipped around Elliot's waist, soaping his chest and then his belly, following the trail of hair but stopping before landing on his cock.

"Rinse."

Elliot turned slowly under the spray until he was facing Cade. Cade handed off the soap and spun around, bracing his hands against the far tiles. Elliot stared for a few moments. A Celtic cross stretched between Cade's shoulder blades and down his spine, intricate knot work in blue-black ink. Elliot rubbed along the outline. Another tattoo, a scrolling line, decorated the dip just above Cade's ass.

Elliot licked the top bar of the cross, above where he'd rubbed in the soap. The skin was smooth under the decoration until he came to the overlapping lines in the center. He leaned back and rubbed a thick lather on his hands.

His soap smelled different on Cade's skin, spicier, more of the eye-opening scent promised in commercials. Elliot tried to imitate the way Cade's hands had worked on his stiff back, seeking out the muscles under the skin. His thumbs dipped into the V of Cade's spine and stroked all the way down.

Cade's ass tipped toward Elliot, the tattoo and the motion inviting his touch.

Now? Was he supposed to start now? They never showed people leaving to go put on a condom in porn. He supposed it was an interruption you just got used to. He trailed his hand over Cade's butt, fingers tingling, edging toward the crease. Cade made one of those deep, rough sounds Elliot remembered from the car and arched his back.

Elliot didn't know what to do next. Cade did. And everything would get a whole lot simpler if Elliot would just admit he'd never done this before. Cade had been honest so far. It wasn't going to be like the mistake with Josh, who evidently had decided that coming with Elliot's mouth on his cock didn't make him gay. Elliot pushed away the memory of Josh's snarl. *I'm not a fucking fag, asshole.*

"Cade."

"Mmmm?"

Cade shifted and Elliot's fingers slid into that tempting crease. He jerked his hand back.

"I've—I've never done this before."

Chapter Five

Cade looked over his shoulder. He was smiling, but not laughing. "I wondered about that. It's all right. Once you get going, biology kind of takes over."

It was the getting-going part that was causing Elliot so much trouble. Now that he had explained the problem, he was hoping Cade would come up with a solution. Cade turned all the way around and kissed him.

"Don't go all deer-in-the-headlights on me, man. It's really not that complicated." Cade pressed him back against the tiles, his mouth as hot as the tiles were cold, tongue stroking, driving between Elliot's lips, that ball and bar teasing, tingling. Elliot wrapped an arm around Cade, pulled him tight until the hard press of Cade's cock rubbed against his own.

Cade took the soap from Elliot's hand and brought it down between them, soaping their cocks until the rough grind and tug turned slick. Grabbing Elliot's hand, Cade layered it with his own until they had a perfect channel for their cocks to slide through. Never stopping the kiss, Cade rocked his hips until Elliot caught the rhythm. One up, the other down, rims flicking against each other so that they were passing a moan back and forth in the kiss.

Cade's hips jerked faster, and Elliot matched him. He couldn't breathe anymore and had to pull his mouth away, gasping.

"Just like that. Easy as breathing," Cade whispered.

Elliot wouldn't go that far, because breathing wasn't particularly easy at the moment either. He was afraid the hot water would run out and then he was afraid it wouldn't because his body was already climbing toward orgasm. Even his scalp was on fire and his balls felt like they were packed with dynamite.

"Cade—I have to—stop."

"It's all right."

"No." It wasn't. He was going to come like this if they didn't stop, and coming from a hand job was definitely not part of the plan. But he couldn't stop rocking, couldn't move his hand off their cocks any more than he could cut off his own finger.

"Trust me, kid." Cade slammed Elliot back against the tiles, kissing him again, eating at his mouth, and he couldn't hang on much longer.

"I'm—"

"Yeah, go on."

Elliot let it go. His spine seized and his cock pulsed, and then his soul was pumping out through his dick, long and hard, everything liquid, hot, slippery, inside and out. The contractions kept shaking through him, and he dropped his head on Cade's shoulder, sucking and gasping.

Cade slammed against Elliot again, that harsh whine ringing through the tiny room as Cade jerked and splashed thick spurts across their stomachs.

Elliot didn't know how long they stood there, leaning into each other as their breathing slowed, but the loss of hot water galvanized them into moving.

As Cade toweled his back, Elliot saw the dark red bruise on his collarbone. "Cade—God, I'm so sorry. I didn't mean—"

"No problem. I went a little hard on your mouth too." Cade pressing his fingers against Elliot's lips made him aware of how hot and swollen they felt.

Cade scrubbed at his hair, and glanced in the mirror, twisting the longer hair in the middle into the usual spikes. They fell over as soon as he turned away from the mirror. Elliot reached out and pulled them upright again.

"So, Elliot, you have a bed around here somewhere?"

Elliot ran a hand through his hair and scratched at the back of his neck. "Of course, but, I'm sorry, I don't know if—" He scratched again. "I might be done for a bit."

"Then I'll get my nap in." Their bodies brushed when Cade walked past and into the hall, picking up the bag he'd brought.

Cade's lack of concern was kind of annoying. Elliot had been so convinced that this was going to be it, and now Cade was talking about naps? *Trust me*, wasn't that what he'd said?

Naked except for the bag over his shoulder, Cade followed him into the bedroom. It should have looked ridiculous but when Cade bent over and Elliot saw that gorgeous ass, he remembered how it felt under his hands, and it just looked hot.

"You make your bed? That's fucking adorable, kid."

Elliot's annoyance began to spiral into anger. He didn't want to be adorable and he didn't want to be "kid". He wanted to be losing his virginity.

Cade dropped the bag and pulled back the covers. Elliot came up from behind and dragged Cade down onto the bed.

"Whoa. Feeling a little less done?" Cade twisted around and stroked a hand down Elliot's chest.

He was. He wasn't exactly getting hard, but it no longer seemed out of the picture.

Cade's hands wrapped around Elliot's waist. "Anger boosts your testosterone levels."

"You were trying to make me mad?"

Cade grinned and leaned up to kiss him. "Maybe a little."

Elliot felt the recoil of desire along his spine. He thought they should get a few things cleared up while his brain was still functioning. "So, how should we—is there a position you'd prefer?"

"I'm not trying to piss you off now, but you are adorable." Cade ran his hand along the side of Elliot's face. "I'm pretty flexible. I love getting fucked."

Elliot's dick loved hearing that. He thought of some of his favorite videos. "On your knees?"

"Sure."

That was good. He wasn't sure he could do this if he had to see Cade's grin.

Cade pulled away and leaned over the side of the bed. "Two rules. There's no such thing as too much lube, and you've got to wear a rubber." He tossed a bottle on the bed. "I'm glad I made a trip to the drugstore yesterday." A box of large-sized condoms ended up next to the lube. "I don't think the regular's gonna fit you."

"Yesterday? You were planning—"

"I was hoping. Is that bad?"

"No, it's..." Elliot's lips twisted. "Adorable."

Flashing that unnerving grin, Cade crawled to the middle of the bed on all fours. "It's all yours, kid." He arched his back, exposing his perfectly round ass.

Elliot curved a hand around the tempting skin. "Just like that?"

"If you do anything I don't like, believe me I'll let you know."

Elliot remembered how they started out in porn videos, but he wasn't sure he was ready to use his mouth on Cade there yet. Since it had felt so good in the shower, Elliot ran his hands up the backs of Cade's thighs. He repeated the stroke with the flat of his tongue and watched Cade jump.

Cade wouldn't enjoy this unless he was turned on, so Elliot reached around Cade's hips to palm his cock. The shaft filled and lengthened in his hand. Elliot licked up the back of Cade's thigh again, jacking him at the same time. Groaning, Cade buried his face in his forearms.

Excitement pulsed from Elliot's stomach, pooling in his sac when he leaned in and lapped around Cade's balls. Elliot kissed and sucked until he felt a drop of precome well up in Cade's slit. Releasing Cade's dick, Elliot got both hands on his ass, stretching and pulling at the tight muscles. Cade was panting, groaning on every breath. That got Elliot ready to try something new. He took a deep breath and held Cade open while licking from Cade's balls to the top of his ass.

"Holy fuck." Cade sounded shocked, but it couldn't be the first time anyone had ever done that to him.

"Bad?"

"Oh no. Just a surprise."

Elliot loved the way Cade's smooth voice had turned rough as if the moans had turned his voice hoarse.

"You can keep doing whatever the fuck you want, kid."

Elliot licked the crease again. Cade tasted like soap and a little sweat and spice, just like when Elliot had licked Cade's balls. This time Elliot stopped at the hole, circling the rim with his tongue while Cade cursed until Elliot was convinced God either had a sense of humor or was wearing earplugs because Cade should have been struck by lightning.

It was a lot like the skin around his balls, but the muscle underneath was hard, resisting Elliot's tongue as he tried to push it inside. He filled his mouth with spit and left a long, wet kiss. The moan from Cade didn't even sound human.

Holding Cade wide open, Elliot dipped a thumb into the spit-slick hole and, pushing against the tight muscle until it yielded, he slid inside to find hot, squeezing, smooth pressure. Elliot's cock jumped against his belly, and he pressed against the mattress to ease the ache.

Sliding his thumb free, he licked again with his tongue, this time managing to stab it inside. Cade let out a long moan, and then Elliot got lost in the overwhelming sensation of knowing his tongue was in Cade's ass. Elliot groaned and pushed in deeper, the blood in his cock pounding, demanding he take Cade hard, now.

Elliot pulled away, gasping, his breath sounding as ragged as Cade's.

Cade got his breath back first. "Remember the first rule."

Elliot fumbled for the bottle and poured some of the gel over his fingers. He traced two down the crease before lining them up and pressing in. Cade jumped forward with a grunt.

"Was that wrong?"

Cade rocked back onto Elliot's fingers. "No, just a little quick."

Slow, Elliot told himself. He didn't just want to do this. He wanted to do this right. He wanted to fuck that cheating ex-lover and the whole long list of other exes right out of Cade McKeun's head.

Elliot held his fingers still for a minute and then moved them carefully in and out. Cade started repeating "Yeah" in a strangled whisper. "Twist them."

Elliot did, turning his wrist, and Cade looked over his shoulder. "Fuck yeah, do that again." Another twist, and there was that deep whine Elliot had heard when Cade came in the shower, in the car. "There, feel that?" Cade gasped.

Elliot was starting to think maybe he wanted some rules of his own, like no looking back and distracting him with talking.

"There," Cade said again.

Elliot did feel it. A swelling in the smooth passage.

"Rub it," Cade whispered.

Elliot did, rolling the balls of his fingers over that spot. Cade wasn't looking over his shoulder anymore. His head was back on his forearms, and it looked like he was chewing on himself. Elliot wondered if he could get the condom on with one hand.

"Three." Cade's voice was so hoarse Elliot wasn't sure he understood.

"Huh?"

"Put another finger in me. I'm going to need it."

Elliot remembered rule one without prompting and poured more lube on his hand. He took it slowly this time, and when his three fingers sank deep inside Cade's body, Cade sighed and started rocking back and forth, fucking himself on Elliot's hand. Since Cade came into Elliot's world, he kept having to reevaluate his definition of hot, and that was the hottest thing he had ever seen. He dropped the box of condoms and just worked his cock, watching while Cade sank down to the knuckles.

Cade looked back over his shoulder. "You ready, man?"

If Elliot got more ready, he'd be wasting himself on his hand again. Cade turned around and grabbed the lube. He rubbed a drop around the head of Elliot's cock while Elliot fought to keep from shoving Cade back on his stomach and driving into the heat that had been swallowing Elliot's hand.

Cade ripped open the box and tore into the condom wrapper with his teeth. That moved up to number two on the hottest-things-ever list. He rolled the condom over Elliot's dick and sucked the head into his mouth.

Elliot's fingers twisted in the sheets. "Cade, please."

Cade pulled off with a grin and rubbed some lube over the top of the condom. Then he dropped back onto all fours. "Let's go."

Elliot knee-walked until he was behind Cade, took his own cock in hand and lined it up, resting it at the opening to Cade's body. It seemed like he'd been waiting to do this for half his life. What if it didn't live up to—?

"I can hear you thinking. Stop. Just fuck me." Cade's hand covered Elliot's as Cade pressed back, and the tight ring of muscle slipped over the head of Elliot's cock.

Cade's breath came in shallow, quick hisses between his teeth as his hand gripped Elliot's harder.

"Should I..." *God, please don't let me be hurting him.*

"No. Just take it slow."

Elliot pressed forward. Cade's muscles shifted and gripped him, tighter than a fist, smoother than a mouth. Even through the latex Elliot could feel Cade's ass along every millimeter of his cock.

This was better than amazing.

"More," Cade panted. His hand fell away.

Elliot didn't need to hold his cock anymore so he rested his hands on Cade's hips where they just naturally started pulling him back and down as Elliot pressed deeper.

"Oh fuck. Wait. Just—" Cade's voice was almost a whine.

Cade's muscles pulsed around him, so hot they felt like they'd burned his skin. Elliot knew the rubber was still on, he could see it since he wasn't all the way in, but his dick was wet from the lube Cade had put under the condom. Need built from the base of Elliot's spine, taking over his brain with the command to snap his hips. He had to, had to—

"Please, Cade, can...can I move?"

"Yeah, man, fuck me."

That was it. His hands dug into Cade's hips and just like he'd said, biology took over. It *was* as easy as breathing for Elliot to flex his hips faster and faster, to arch and plunge back into all that clinging heat. Cade's body fought Elliot's thrusts on the upstrokes, trying to keep him in, then sucked him back down into perfect pressure. When Cade groaned, the vibrations ran all the way down to Elliot's cock.

He was slamming forward so hard his thighs were pounding into Cade's ass, but all Cade did was throw his head back and say, "Yeah, do it."

Elliot slowed enough to lean down, to kiss Cade's shoulders, trying to show him how damned good it felt to be in his body. Cade turned his head, and their mouths met in a sloppy kiss. Both of them were short of breath and full of moans so it only lasted a few seconds, but Cade's mouth was as open as his body.

Elliot tightened his grip on Cade's hips and let instinct take over. Rolling his hips, Elliot shifted their angle so that Cade tightened and pulsed around him again.

"Fuck." Sometimes there was really only one word that would do.

"Yeah, c'mon." Cade collapsed onto his stomach, and Elliot followed, pressing up on his toes, bracing his leg across Cade's for the leverage to keep up the deep penetration Elliot's body demanded. Cade's voice broke and shattered around one long moan.

Elliot looped an arm around Cade's shoulder, wrapping it under his neck, and dropped openmouthed kisses across his back.

The shift in position forced Elliot to move up and down as well as in and out and that was evidently a good thing because Cade's hands gripped the edge of the mattress. "There, yeah, motherfucking hell, don't stop."

When Cade shifted again, he was impossibly tighter, as tight as he'd been at that first thrust. It was too much, Elliot couldn't last with that incredible pressure.

"Cade—it's too—I—"

"I know." Cade's voice was soft and reassuring.

Elliot ground his teeth, trying to force out a few extra minutes of that soul-deep pleasure.

And then he heard the low, harsh whine that meant Cade was coming.

The pressure Elliot had felt before was nothing compared to the way Cade's ass squeezed now as his body locked down hard, muscles rigid until the whine ended in a few short cries.

Knowing he'd fucked Cade into coming made it even harder to hang on. Elliot didn't want to come, he wanted to ride this forever, power and pleasure pounding in his blood, pulsing in his balls.

Cade groaned again and his white-knuckled fingers tore the sheet off the mattress. "Come in me, Elliot. Wanna feel you come."

Elliot wanted it too, he just didn't want this to end. Then Cade tightened again, and Elliot couldn't fight it. His body jerked, back arched. He knew his fingers were leaving bruises where they gripped Cade's shoulders but Elliot's body had gone out of control as bolt after bolt of electricity shot out of his cock.

"Damn, damn, damn," Cade panted.

Elliot realized he could see now, though he'd squeezed his eyes so tightly he was seeing little sparks around the edges of his vision. He'd paid enough attention in sex ed to know he was supposed to hold onto the base of the condom when he slid out. Cade didn't have to issue a reminder to go slow. Elliot could see the need in the quiver of Cade's muscles, as if every touch was magnified. His own cock got like that sometimes when he jerked off, so sensitive he couldn't even stand to put his pants back on.

Cade seemed to be feeling that sensitivity everywhere. He flinched as Elliot untangled their legs and peeled his hands off Cade's shoulders, but he didn't complain. Elliot rolled away, still holding the condom. Cade sighed and settled deeper into the mattress.

Elliot slipped off the condom and got to his feet. His legs were shaking but they should hold him long enough to get to the bathroom.

"Might want to grab a towel." Cade's voice was muffled since his head was buried in Elliot's pillow.

Elliot stopped in the doorway on his way back to the bedroom and had to lean against the frame. It wasn't that his legs were giving out, though that did seem to be a possibility, but he had to stare at the sight of the man in his bed.

Cade was sprawled on his belly, long stretch of inked spine curving into his ass—the ass Elliot had just fucked. Against the pale skin, Elliot could see the red marks his grip had left on Cade's shoulders and hips. Elliot should have felt guilty, but instead he felt proud. No one would see them, but they'd be on Cade's body, even after he left. A part of Elliot that Cade wouldn't be able to wash away.

Cade turned and grinned. "Thinking again?"

Elliot shook his head. "Just looking."

"That's about all we've got time for. I've got to get cleaned up for work soon, so if you're looking for pillow talk you'd better get your ass back in here."

Elliot sat on the bed and handed Cade the towel.

Cade lifted up to scrub at his belly and the wet spot, then flopped back on top of the towel. "Man, I think I'm going to be feeling you for days."

"Sorry."

Cade rolled on his side and winked. "No, you're not."

He wasn't. And pride wasn't the right word for it either. A mixture of rough tenderness and possessiveness warmed his gut as he stretched out next to Cade. Should Elliot kiss him? Would Cade laugh if Elliot pulled Cade into his arms? The sweat drying on Elliot's skin was starting to make him cold so he tugged the sheet over them both. Cade moved until his chin rested on Elliot's chest. It was probably going to get uncomfortable in a few minutes, but right now he liked the way Cade was looking up at him.

After a few minutes, Elliot's intent stare started to make Cade a little nervous. "Man, I cannot believe you rimmed me."

"Did I do it wrong?" The kid was so fucking earnest.

"Hell no, it was great, you were great." Cade winked. "I just was surprised, first time out of the gate and everything. I loved it."

"I liked doing it to you."

Experienced or not, Elliot had driven Cade crazy with that rim job. He was lucky he hadn't freaked the kid out wriggling onto his tongue like that, carrying on like he was the damned virgin. Cade didn't mind letting his partner know what he liked, but grinding into the kid's face the first time he tried rimming was majorly lacking cool points.

"Seriously, man, you were hot. I think I need to start turning more virgins 'cause that was a hell of a ride."

Elliot moved away, and Cade had to catch himself on his forearm.

"So what, this was another one of your adventures? Like jumping a freight train to get to an Alice in Chains concert?"

Cade pushed up and sat back on his legs, stunned. "Elliot, what the fuck? Did I say that?"

"Sounded like it."

All Cade's muscles got tight. His legs and feet ached from curling them so hard. His skin was even too tight. He tried to find the calm center everyone was always talking about but gave up. "I was kidding. I'm not going to run out and jump in bed with the next ten virgins I can find." At least he managed not to yell.

"I don't know. Could be fun. Do you think you could find ten virgins?" Elliot smiled, but Cade could tell the kid was pissed.

"Elliot, I'm glad you were honest with me, and I wasn't making fun of you." Cade glanced at his watch. "But I've got to get to work, and I need another shower."

Elliot looked like he'd just figured out that Santa Claus was a malicious fantasy used to torment children. "Okay."

"Don't worry about driving me, I'll walk."

"No. I'll drive you."

"I need the walk. You need to stay here."

"I'm not angry."

Cade snorted. "So much for honesty."

Chapter Six

Waiting tables on a Saturday night should have kept Cade busy enough so he didn't have to think about Elliot. Fuck, he shouldn't have needed to think about Elliot at all. So they'd had sex—awesome sex. Elliot was a natural top, fucked like a steam drill without all the annoying cockiness. Even with all that tension of his first time, he still had tried to make sure Cade was enjoying himself.

Cade dropped two plates in the kitchen when his mind kept wandering back to Elliot coming, his powerful body snapping and jerking, a deeper and sexier growl than Cade's favorite heavy-metal singer rumbling in that broad chest. He had to get control or he'd be showing the customers a lot more than they expected to see at La Pomme D'Orée. And being conscious of his breathing wasn't doing a damned thing to help.

He dropped a third plate when Rick came in from having a cigarette and said he'd heard Cade's phone ringing in the back. Cade nodded and turned away before he smiled. He'd left the numbers for his cell and Steve's apartment on the table in Elliot's hall before leaving.

Cade didn't drop another dish.

He couldn't take a break until an hour before he cashed out, so he didn't bother checking his phone, saving it for an after-work treat. If Elliot was calling to tell Cade he was an asshole, he'd rather wait until after work to deal with it.

The screen showed two missed calls and three voice mails.

The missed calls were from the same unknown number—Elliot's, Cade hoped. The first voice mail left him colder than the snowflakes melting into his neck as he walked home.

"How you liking community service, baby?" Mike's words were a little slurred but long experience had left Cade fluent in every kind of speech from Mike's lips. The noise in the background made Cade think Mike was calling from a bar. Mike sighed. "I still miss you, you son of a bitch."

"I'm not the one who blew it, asshole," Cade muttered into the dead air. He did not fucking need this now. If he wasn't hoping one of those messages was from Elliot, Cade would have deleted everything in case drunk dialing him was Mike's idea of an entertaining night.

The next message started. "My bed smells like sex and I can't sleep." Elliot didn't sound drunk or desperate, just a little nervous. As booty calls went, he had a hell of a line. Cade turned and headed back toward Elliot's apartment.

The last message played as Cade crossed Loomis Street. Elliot's tone was plaintive as he asked, "Who was that guy who answered the other phone?" Cade started laughing as he jogged down Park Street.

Elliot had apparently been telling the truth when he said he couldn't sleep. The door swung open less than a minute after Cade's soft knock.

"Hey."

"Hi." Elliot's eyes searched Cade's face.

Cade offered up a grin. "You know you could always change the sheets."

"Cade, I'm sorry."

"Don't be sorry. Do what you mean."

Elliot pulled Cade in and kissed the chill off his lips.

In five minutes their clothes were on the floor and they were on the bed.

Elliot sucked the bar on Cade's nipple into heat that made him shiver and the tug of it went all the way down to his dick. Elliot lifted his head. "Cade, can I—can I fuck you again?"

He'd definitely been feeling Elliot all night. He was as thick as Cade's wrist and he'd only been fucked a couple times since he'd left Mike. If Cade didn't want to be walking funny tomorrow, he ought to say no, but the memory of how good it felt was kicking the idea of restraint in its well-fucked ass.

"Yeah."

Elliot kissed him, long and hard. The kid was already more confident, taking what he wanted, and Cade's dick jumped.

"Don't forget the rules."

Elliot reached into the drawer next to them and came out with the lube and the condoms. While he was busy, Cade dragged a pillow down under his hips and laid on his back, leaving himself some room so that his head didn't get fucked all the way into the headboard.

When Elliot slicked his finger and touched Cade lightly, the skin was so tender he couldn't keep still.

Elliot looked alarmed.

"It's okay. I want to. Just go slow."

Elliot's finger eased so gently inside Cade, he had to choke back a laugh. "Okay. Not that slow."

As Elliot slipped another finger inside, he watched Cade's face. The earnest concern was heartbreakingly intense.

"Help me along, man."

Elliot thought about that for a second and then his lips parted and he went down on Cade. The wet suck relaxed him until that warm mouth took him deeper and he bucked up against the back of Elliot's throat.

Elliot didn't gag, just kept right on sucking. When Cade sank back on the mattress, Elliot had three fingers inside, curling up against Cade's prostate. Fuck, the kid was a fast learner. Elliot rubbed while he sucked, the burning stretch and the so-good pressure leaving Cade balanced on a knife-edge of pleasure and pain.

He tugged on Elliot's hair until he lifted off Cade's dick. "C'mon."

He thought he remembered what to expect but when Elliot suited up and pressed in, Cade forgot how to breathe. Elliot filled Cade's ass in one long stroke, and he grabbed Elliot's hips hard enough to bruise.

"God, I'm sorry. I—it just—" Elliot's eyes were wide and apologetic.

"Don't fucking move."

Elliot nodded and rested his forehead against Cade's. Elliot's breath was shallow and fast. Cade was still trying to catch his. All his muscles seemed paralyzed by that sting.

Elliot's arms shook as they held him off Cade's chest. Letting go of Elliot's hips, Cade braced his hands on those trembling shoulders. The warm skin seemed to shiver to life as he touched it.

"Okay," Cade murmured.

Elliot arched back, just moving an inch, and that was enough. It flipped a switch in Cade's body, and the nerves that had been screaming were singing.

"Yeah, go." Cade flung his neck back into the mattress, and Elliot reared up and started to fuck him, deep hard thrusts Cade swore hit his guts, forcing groan after groan from his chest.

He watched the deep red flush spill down Elliot's throat and chest, and heard the first of his beautiful growls.

"Feel so good, Cade."

"Yeah, you do." Cade's insides were melting, gone liquid around the thrusts that were driving him up onto the bed.

Elliot grabbed Cade's shoulders in time to pull him back from the headboard, and he reached up to drag Elliot down for a kiss. Their bodies ground together as Elliot's mouth stole what was left of Cade's mind. Cade hiked his knees higher, and Elliot lost the kiss in a moan as he rocked in deeper.

"Oh, fuck." The kid was so sexy when he swore, the word all strange on his lips, but knowing Cade had made Elliot lose control like that was what sent Cade slamming up toward the edge.

Elliot arched his back, hips stuttering and then pistoning against Cade faster and faster, those deep growls making Cade feel like he was turning inside out, as if by the time Elliot was done Cade would be all soft on the outside, nothing to keep him safe from the world.

Elliot's hands moved to cup Cade's ass, and the motion dragged the ridge of Elliot's dick against the perfect spot, pounding white-hot pleasure through him. Cade had to come, now, before Elliot fucked any deeper inside. Cade reached down and grabbed his dick, pulling hard and long, turning his wrist to burn under the crown with friction.

Elliot knocked Cade's hand away and took up the motion, jerking just fast enough to drag him so high and tight he had to come or die. The next deep slam into his body pushed him over, his muscles tensing and jerking as he shot up onto Elliot's stomach. Elliot fucked Cade through it until he didn't think he'd ever stop coming. The contractions went on and on as Elliot kept rocking them and then he froze with the deepest growl Cade had heard yet, eyes screwing shut as the kid arched and bucked.

Elliot's face was gorgeous when he came, eyes slits, cheeks stretched as his mouth dropped open. Cade's heart was still pounding as Elliot eased back.

When Elliot climbed back in bed, Cade remembered Elliot's earlier question.

"Steve." Cade snugged his ass back against Elliot's warm belly.

"What?"

"The guy who answered the phone. His name's Steve. I've been crashing at his place for five months."

"That's not crashing; that's moving in." Elliot's body went still. "Do you and Steve...?"

"Steve? No. He's cute and funny but we don't click like that."

"Oh." With an arm around Cade's chest, Elliot pulled them closer. They fell asleep tangled together.

&

Cade woke to a happy fucked-out body and the smell of really good coffee. He leaned up on his elbow and saw Elliot at the foot of the bed in a sweater and jeans, a large cup of Café Heaven coffee and a bundle of newspapers in his hands.

He brought the coffee to the nightstand and put the newspapers on the foot of the bed. "I got *The Globe* and *The Times*. I wasn't sure which one you read."

Elliot had come a long way from assuming Cade had never heard of Haydn to assuming he read the *Sunday Times*. He looked from the coffee to the papers. With anyone else, he would say they were trying too hard, but that was just Elliot. He really was a bring-you-coffee-and-papers-in-bed kind of guy. Cade had to remind himself not to get used to it.

&

"You can't be serious. You've never seen *Casablanca*? All this time I thought you were doing a bad Humphrey Bogart impersonation." Elliot sounded as if not watching some overhyped classic piece of war propaganda was the greatest sin known to man.

Cade poked Elliot with a toe and unfolded *The Globe's* opinion section across the bed. "I call you a kid because you are one. And I don't watch movies or TV."

"How can you not watch movies?"

Cade turned a page, ignoring the incredulous look on Elliot's face. "I just don't."

Elliot pulled out the travel section and opened it on Cade's back. "Even the artsy kind with subtitles?"

"If I were going to go to the movies, it wouldn't be for that pretentious shit." He looked over at the snow-splattered window, glad he wasn't working brunch. Nothing but collecting dirty buffet dishes and getting lousy tips.

"I went with you to that so-called concert. You can come to a movie with me."

"I work almost every night."

"You're not working the night of the Academy concert, are you? I thought we'd—"

Cade rolled over and pinned Elliot to the bed, the papers sliding under and crumpling between them. "Damn, man, all that suffering and hard work to get me to give it up and you're just going to give the ticket back?"

"Give it up? You're sure you can handle giving it up again?" Elliot's brows arched. The steady confidence in those blue eyes made Cade's heart kick, speed up production to get ready for another round, even as his sore body protested.

He kept Elliot flat on the bed, hands pinning his shoulders, and arched up into cobra pose. "I'm not giving anything up. You're going to have to work for it."

Elliot jabbed fingers into Cade's ribs. His pose collapsed in helpless laughter. Elliot rolled Cade under him, destroying any hope of reading the rest of the paper.

"That is not fucking fair, man," Cade choked out through his laughter.

"I think I've been learning from you."

80

Elliot's community service finished up the next Saturday, but Cade's wouldn't until March so Elliot had to wait until Cade had another free Sunday before being able to drag him to the closest theater showing an action movie. Although Cade's soft murmur mocked the obviousness of the plot and the predictability of the dialogue, Elliot felt Cade's muscles tense during the action sequences.

The Wednesday before the concert, Elliot woke to the warm slide of flesh against his body. He'd given Cade a key to the apartment at the end of the first week in February. Elliot had thought about it for the whole week before and couldn't come up with a single reason why it wouldn't be easier for Cade to just show up without knocking or calling on the nights he came over.

Elliot kept the hall light on for Cade. Even on the nights he didn't show up, Elliot found himself waking around one and drifting back to sleep. Sometimes when Cade climbed into bed, Elliot rolled Cade onto his back and fucked him into the mattress so that they fell asleep sticky and sweaty. Some nights Cade would slip in so quietly he'd have Elliot blown halfway to heaven before he woke up.

Cade still hadn't left so much as a single sock at Elliot's apartment even though while he was there he scattered his stuff all around. Elliot wondered how moving in together happened. Did you just stop keeping separate addresses or did there have to be some kind of discussion?

He wasn't going to get into any discussion now. The covers were down to his thighs, and the light from the hall showed Cade's lips pursed in a frown. "I told you to stop wearing underwear to bed."

Cade tugged, and Elliot lifted his hips to help Cade slide the cotton free. As soon as Elliot had kicked the briefs off his ankles, Cade had Elliot's cock in his mouth, sucking him from zero to *oh fuck* in five seconds. Taking him all the way in a few quick bobs, Cade swallowed around the head before pulling off with a grin that made his teeth flash in the dark.

Cade straddled Elliot and crawled up his body until Cade's half-hard cock was teasing Elliot's lips. Cade's legs pinned Elliot's shoulders, so he had to lift his head just to get a good lick around the crown. He wanted more, wanted the weight and the taste on his tongue, wanted the sting of Cade's frantic grip in his hair.

But Cade dug in the nightstand, pulling out the lube and the new box of condoms. Elliot had never realized how expensive keeping a stock would be.

Cade didn't roll to his back or drop to his knees; he just reached behind himself. And when Elliot heard the wet sound of Cade stretching himself on his own fingers, Elliot's cock kicked against his belly like it was starting its own soccer match.

Cade's eyes squeezed shut in something like a grimace. "Remind me to…ah…get a dildo or do more yoga…because…my shoulder…uh."

The mention of a dildo whited out Elliot's brain for a minute. He could fuck Cade with it and suck him at the same time. Elliot's cock won the kick off and was really going to town now, twitching and leaking against his stomach.

Cade lifted off and rolled the condom down Elliot's too-eager cock. Cade's touch as he slicked the latex was almost too much. Elliot hoped Cade was ready for a fast ride because Elliot didn't know how long he was going to be able to go. Especially with the way Cade looked as he eased onto Elliot's cock, the way Cade's legs quivered around his hips.

Elliot arched up as Cade sank down. When Elliot's balls hit Cade's ass, he shuddered. Cade rocked up and down, squeezing and flexing, pushing off Elliot's shoulders, fucking himself on Elliot's cock. That took over the number one spot on the list of the hottest things he'd ever seen. Elliot was grabbing Cade's hips to roll him under when Cade whispered, "Wait. Can you go longer?"

Elliot could. It might kill him, but he would. He nodded. Cade eased up, letting Elliot slide from that perfect heat, and turned on his side.

"Got it?" Cade asked.

Basic biology. Elliot lifted one of Cade's legs over his own and slid back in with a groan. "Yeah, I think so."

"Yeah, you do."

It was hard to get as much momentum this way, but the sounds from Cade suggested Elliot was doing just fine. He held Cade's legs wide open and rocked as hard as the angle permitted. It was easy to kiss Cade like this too. Cade's head twisted up, mouth wet, sloppy and hungry.

Elliot recognized the sound Cade made as he pulled away from Elliot's kiss. It was the one just before the *I'm-coming* whine. He leaned down to pant in Cade's ear. "If you wait, I'll finish you in my mouth."

"Fuuuck." Cade dragged the word out to five syllables and he was gone. The first shot of come landed almost on the edge of the bed, the next thick rope on Elliot's thigh. "Goddamn it. Next time tell me sooner."

Elliot smiled. "Next time, I will."

Cade's ass pulsed around Elliot's cock. "I can still finish you like that."

Elliot rolled away and dropped the condom into the wastebasket he'd moved next to the bed.

Cade was on his back. "Why don't you climb up here and fuck my face."

Elliot's heart was hammering a hole in his rib cage as he straddled Cade's shoulders.

"That's it. Give it to me. C'mon, Elliot." Cade almost always called him kid when they were in bed. The sound of Cade purring his name just as Elliot rolled his cock across those warm, slick lips brought him almost to the brink.

Cade's mouth was always skilled, that piercing quick to press and tease on all kinds of sensitive parts, but when Cade winked at him, when he smiled around his mouthful of cock and fucking winked at him, that's when Elliot lost it. He knew he was pushing hard into Cade's throat but couldn't stop. Everything just felt too good.

Elliot collapsed onto his side, hit a wet spot and wiggled out of it.

"That was fucking hot, man. Thanks." Cade's voice was thick with satisfaction.

"You're thanking *me*?"

Cade turned on his side and rolled closer. "Yeah. Thanks for my birthday present."

"You never said—Happy Birthday."

"Thanks."

"Cade, your birthday is Valentine's Day?"

Cade dropped his gaze. "Yeah."

"That's just adorable," Elliot teased.

"You see now why I didn't mention it."

"You should have."

Cade rubbed a thumb over Elliot's lips and down his jaw to his ear. "I already got just what I wanted. And I get to go to the concert."

"How old are you?"

Cade looked at Elliot a long time before answering. "Thirty-four."

Elliot knew Cade was watching for his reaction, knew that it was really important he keep the surprise off his face. He'd known Cade was older, just not by how much. Ten years. Elliot had never been good at hiding his emotions.

Cade's lips twisted in the cynical sneer Elliot hadn't seen since the day they met. "And you're what—twenty-two?"

"Twenty-three."

It didn't matter. Would matter less the older he became, but he could tell Cade was waiting for some kind of reaction. Elliot didn't know what reaction was the right one.

He kissed him. "Happy Birthday," he said again. "And Happy Valentine's Day," he added softly.

Cade's hand was still resting on Elliot's jaw, thumb behind his ear. Cade swallowed hard and bit his lip. "You got any ice cream?"

Elliot thought for a second that Cade wanted ice cream for some kind of birthday ritual, then he remembered how hard he'd been going at Cade's throat. "Oh my God." Elliot rolled on his back and covered his face with his hands. The blush leaked out under his fingers, to his ears, his neck. He couldn't believe he'd lost control like that. "I am so sorry."

"Don't be sorry. Just get me some damn ice cream."

Chapter Seven

Cade expected any venue that could score Academy of St. Martin in the Fields would have more taste, but the music hall had gone overboard with the decorations for Valentine's Day in a way that turned his stomach. It looked like the worst possible high school dance. Heart-shaped fucking Mylar balloons decorated the lobby and if he saw another rose, he was going to puke into the pocket of the suit jacket Elliot had forced Cade to wear. He never should have promised Elliot he could play dress up as revenge for Cade's extreme makeover when he'd taken Elliot to Lizzie Borden's Sofa. The kid had even managed to get Cade into a tie.

Elliot's jacket hung loose over slacks borrowed from Steve. The only dress shirts Cade owned were the ones he wore to work, so he was in black and white relieved only by a purple-and-blue checked—not red and white, or he'd have died—tie.

Their seats were perfect, center orchestra, on the aisle. Cade checked the program as they settled in. "Boyce first. This is good."

"Why? I though you liked him better."

"Boyce makes me all emotional. Haydn makes me horny."

Elliot's cheeks darkened, and he glanced around. Cade winked at him, and Elliot settled back in his seat. "You do that to drive me nuts."

"I do it because you have a sexy blush."

Elliot had a sexy everything. It was getting harder and harder to think of the time when Elliot would get tired of his trip to Adventureland and give someone else the benefit of his newly honed skills. Twenty-three and just discovering sex—why wouldn't he want to try out everything that was out there?

Elliot's forearm covered Cade's on their shared armrest, and he interlaced their fingers. "Need me to hold your hand through the sad parts?"

Cade turned his hand until his knuckles were rubbing across Elliot's palm. The hitch in Elliot's breathing was barely audible.

Elliot pulled his hand away. "I would have thought you'd save that for Haydn."

"Don't tempt me, kid."

The house lights went down, and Cade turned his hand palm up. Elliot looked down and then rested his own on top.

At intermission, Cade offered to get them bottled water to sip against the hot dry air. He tried to avoid looking at the tacky decorations, but there wasn't much else to look at as he stood in line.

He peered around the long line of customers. One of the guys selling drinks looked up, and Cade caught his eye. Orlando, his favorite barista at Café Heaven, jerked his chin, and Cade went around the back of the stand where Orlando passed him two waters under the guise of checking the coolers.

Cade tucked them under his arm and decided to enjoy stretching his legs for a few more minutes. He leaned against the railing of the balcony stairs and opened one of the waters.

"I should have known you'd find a way around the line." Mike leaned against the newel post.

Cade waited to feel the customary anger, betrayal, or hell, even an old flash of longing, but he just felt annoyed. Like when he got a table he knew would calculate fifteen percent before tax down to the penny. He shrugged and took a gulp of water.

"Could never get you to dress up for me. Saw the new boy. Pretty. And you thought I liked 'em young."

"Did you have a point, Mike, or is this just a convenient place to cruise the few legislative pages you haven't fucked?"

"You know there was only the one. I just said that to make you angry."

"Good job. Congratulations. Now fuck off." Cade pushed away from the railing.

"It won't work, you know."

Cade should have walked away. Why didn't he walk away? "What?"

"Training a replacement. He's such a baby version of me I think I'm flattered."

Cade could have spit the water in Mike's face, but probation didn't sound like fun.

"Must be rich to have scored those seats, too. Connected. But even getting him young won't change the fact that he'll get just as bored with your look-at-me shit as I did."

The nausea spinning in Cade's stomach had nothing to do with the frantically romantic décor or the smell of the rose in Mike's boutonniere. Cade tightened his jaw and leaned forward to put a hand on Mike's lapel. "Oh, baby, you've got it all wrong. I was just desperate for someone who could give me more than five inches." He sighed. "It'd be really hard to mistake him for you."

He forced a saunter in his steps as he moved back into the orchestra seats.

Elliot stood when Cade got to their aisle. Until Elliot had to pry the water out from under his arm, Cade had no idea he was holding it that tightly. Or even that he had it at all.

Cade slid into his seat, and Elliot sat back down next to him. Cade took a long swig of water.

"So that was him, huh?"

Cade didn't bother to play the "who" game. Cold sweat was soaking down the back of his shirt. At least the jacket would hide it. He looked over at Elliot.

"I had to piss." Elliot shrugged. "Cade?" Elliot was looking at him with concern—and fuck, was that pity?

The tie was tight enough to choke, and it was too goddamned hot in here.

And Elliot was nothing like Mike.

"What did he say?" Elliot asked.

"Same old shit."

"Do you want to go?"

"No. Don't look at me like that. I'm hot and these clothes are fucking uncomfortable."

Elliot's gaze still searched Cade's face as the house lights flashed off and on in warning.

"He's just an asshole, all right? And he's taken up too much of my time. And I told you Boyce makes me fuck-all emotional." Cade managed a grin.

"I can't wait to see what Haydn does for you."

℘

Elliot had never been a violent sort of person. His last physical fight had been at around age twelve over some arcane rule of a street game invented by the kids in whatever neighborhood they were in that year. But right now, if Cade's bastard of an ex had showed his face, Elliot wouldn't have had the slightest hesitation about seeing if he could still land a punch. The streetlights made Cade paler than usual, but he hadn't been right since the intermission. Elliot didn't know how many years Cade and Mike had been together, but Mike still had the power to hurt Cade badly. Which led to the disappointing conclusion that Cade was still in love with the jerk.

Cade was leaning against the window, and Elliot wished now he hadn't insisted they take his car. At the time, actually making it to the concert had seemed important, but now it would have been better if they'd left transportation up to the whims of Bucky's electrical system. At least in the Plymouth, they'd be a lot closer.

"Drop me off at Steve's. I'll bring over the jacket tomorrow."

"But it's your birthday."

"Yeah, well, I'm tired. And I already got my present." Cade's grin fell so short of his usual style Elliot started thinking about punching again.

"We could go out."

"I'm not going anywhere dressed like this."

"We'll stop and you can change."

"I'm tired and hot. I just want to crash."

Cade could crash just as easily at Elliot's apartment. He turned down Loomis Street.

"Elliot. If you don't take me to Steve's, I'm walking there."

"Cade—"

"Fine. Stop the car. I'll walk."

Valentine's Day was a stupid holiday. Just ask anyone who's ever suffered through the onslaught of forced romance in a prolonged state of unattachment. Personally, Elliot thought the whole thing had been invented by a secret cabal of merchants to boost slumping winter sales. However, the fact that he couldn't see himself ever spending a hundred bucks on a dozen roses didn't mean he hadn't thought that his first Valentine's Day with a boyfriend—his first any holiday with a boyfriend—would end at least in a kiss. Cade could say it wasn't a big deal all he wanted, but it was his birthday and he shouldn't have to spend it feeling miserable because of that bastard.

"Stop the fucking car."

Elliot sighed. "I'm turning around, okay? You don't have to walk." He drove around the block and headed north. "How many years were you together?"

"Six. Just stop the car for a second. I won't jump out."

Elliot pulled over as soon as he found a space and turned to look at Cade.

"This isn't about Mike. It's about me. I just need a walk to clear my head. I feel like shit."

That sounded perilously close to the *it's-not-you-it's-me* kiss of death. Elliot didn't want Cade to get out of the car. But Elliot's mind had frozen and he couldn't think of a damned thing that would keep Cade from walking away.

Cade opened the door. "Elliot, I promise I'll see you tomorrow."

Elliot wished Cade had called him kid.

The walk kept a lid on Cade's temper. He stripped out of the jacket and tie as soon as he cleared Steve's apartment door.

"Didn't expect you back, dude," Steve called from where he was twisting around with a game controller on the couch.

"Did you have plans?"

"Nope. Just didn't expect you."

Cade went to the kitchen and looked in the fridge. He almost grabbed a beer, decided it was too cliché, and made himself green tea. He brought his mug out and flopped next to Steve on the couch to watch the little skateboarder figure do flips and spins on the TV. They bumped shoulders as Steve gyrated all over the couch guiding his digital avatar over the ramps.

The door buzzing startled them both.

"Son of a bitch." The skateboarder wiped out. "'S for you, dude."

"Better not be."

The only person it could be was Mike, and if he showed up here tonight, Cade was going to find out what the inside of Washington County Jail looked like. It couldn't be Elliot. He'd take at least a week to think things through.

The doorbell buzzed again.

"Dude." Steve sighed and pushed to his feet. Cade held his mug against his mouth and listened to Steve's big feet thump down the stairs.

The door opened. And then Elliot's deep voice said, "Sorry, I—"

"You must be Elliot. Nice to finally meetcha, dude." Steve came back up the stairs with Elliot in tow.

Cade looked over his mug. Elliot's eyes were wide under a furrowed brow. His hand jangled keys in his pocket.

Steve looked from Elliot hovering in the hall to Cade frozen on the couch. Cade's so-called friend rolled his eyes and began an immediate desertion by grabbing his jacket from the chair. "You dudes feel free to get as loud as you want. I'm heading out." Steve stood next to the couch as he shrugged into his jacket. Folding his lanky frame down, he muttered, "You, my man, are a major fucking ass." Steve nodded at Elliot. "I suggest you kick his." With a slap on Cade's shoulder, he headed for the door. "Later, dudes."

Cade was so happy to see Elliot it made him feel a million fucking times worse. He shouldn't have burned off his temper walking. He needed it now, angry armor against the look on Elliot's face—a look Cade was afraid to put a label on.

He didn't stand, just swung his sock-covered feet up onto the coffee table and drank his tea while the skateboarder thrashed around after his wipeout.

"It's tomorrow," Elliot said.

Cade checked his watch. 12:02. "Yup."

"Are you going to tell me what happened?" Elliot stopped jangling his keys and folded his arms across his chest.

"Elliot, look." Cade downed enough tea to burn his throat. He stretched his ankles back and forth and then looked up. "I think we should back off."

"Back off what? Fucking?" The word in Elliot's mouth sounded bitter. Nothing like the sexy way he growled it when he was balls-deep inside Cade's body.

It'd be easier to do if it was just fucking. But it was coffee at Café Heaven. Elliot trying to make him sit through his DVDs of some gay soap opera with that one guy Cade would never admit was kind of hot. Watching Elliot struggle not to laugh or blush when Cade said something outrageous.

"Yeah, I guess. I don't know how much longer I'm going to be around. I'm thinking of applying to school again. Finish up. Maybe down in North Carolina." Cade looked down at his socks. Elliot's socks. He didn't own a dressy enough pair.

"You're going to let him win? Chase you out of town?"

"It's not about Mike."

"That's a load of crap. Are you still in love with him?"

"No. Fuck no. I just... I'm feeling like I need to—"

"Run away?"

"What the fuck would you know about it? You're so goddamned scared to have fun you plan other people's vacations while your ass sits in Montpelier."

Anyone with sense would have left then. Elliot's eyes went wide, and Cade knew he'd hurt the kid. But he hadn't backed down from a single challenge Cade had flung his way since the day they met. Elliot crossed the room and sat next to Cade.

"I think you're just scared. And you are not leaving." The force in that deep voice made the hair on Cade's arms stand up.

Cade got off the couch and went to the window. Snow was spinning down through the black sky. Big surprise. He'd bet it was just starting to warm up in North Carolina. "Just because I let you fuck my ass doesn't mean you own it, kid."

"That's bullshit too." Elliot came over to stand in front of Cade. "You love not having control. Your whole life—your car, your bands. Nothing's your fault because you're not in charge. And that's just the way you want it."

Anger flowed through Cade. Good hard tension in his muscles, curling his hands to fists. "What the fuck gives you the right to say that shit to me?"

"I love you, that's what."

The anger drained away in shock and fear. "Elliot, man, you're just a kid."

"For God's sake will you stop saying that? You think I don't know what I feel, what I want? You think I wanted to fall in love with you? This is so far from anything I ever thought would happen. But it did."

"Elliot." Cade reached for Elliot, but he ducked away. "I'm your first boyfriend—your first fuck, and I know that means something to you—it does to me, too, but sooner or later you're going to want to try someone else out."

"So you are scared? Scared I'm going to do what Mike did?"

Cade shook his head. "Nah. You're a lot of things ki—man, but you're not an asshole like that."

"Thanks." Elliot rolled his eyes. "Cade, I can't tell what's going to happen in five years—"

Cade started to explain the inevitable, but Elliot ran right over the words before Cade could spit them out.

"—and neither can you. But I know this, being with you feels like what I've always wanted. And even if I couldn't have that hot ass of yours I'd still want you."

Cade quirked a half smile. "I have a hot ass?"

"You already know that. Shut up and let me finish."

Cade shifted against the cold glass of the window.

Elliot went on, his voice softer. "You know, if you're serious about wanting to go back to school, the University of Vermont is right here. Or you could take online classes."

Cade hadn't minded the learning part of school. It was the tedium of actually going to class, putting up with all those other assholes who had chafed him to the point where he couldn't stand it anymore.

"I love you, Cade. I'm not Mike. I'm going to be honest with you. Even about your scary fashion choices."

"Well don't think you're going to change them." Shit, was he giving in? "I'm going to burn that goddamned tie."

"You'd be doing me a favor. My mother gave it to me, and I hate it."

Lizzy Borden's Sofa probably didn't make it down to North Carolina much. And Cade did like snowboarding.

Elliot looked like he was ready to go ten more rounds, relentless in turning around every argument Cade could pose. He'd swear Elliot had been thinking this through, but there was no way Elliot could have known Mike would pick tonight to be such a prick. It had taken serious balls to chase Cade here, and Elliot had needed to make some pretty quick decisions.

Ever since Mike had made that crack about Elliot, Cade's stomach had been spitting out cold fear like a snow machine. Now he stared at the man in front of him.

He hadn't tried to make Elliot into anything. Cade had given Elliot every chance to get rid of him, and Elliot had chosen Cade every step of the way. Elliot was strong and funny and smart and ballsy enough to stand up to Cade at his worst.

Elliot's voice shook a little. "Or was I right before? Was I was just another adventure? How I Seduced an Uptight Virgin."

Cade tucked his hand around Elliot's neck and pulled him in until their foreheads touched. "No. God, no. Shit, don't ever think that again."

Elliot wrapped his arms around Cade's waist. "So I don't have to get you busted for the felony of stealing mail to keep you in Montpelier?"

"Stealing mail?"

"The tickets."

"There was no address on the envelope."

"The outer envelope was stuck to the bottom."

"But already open."

"My word against yours." Elliot leaned back to give Cade an appraising stare, gaze flicking over Cade's ears, his eyebrow.

"You'd be balls-deep in it too." Cade stuck out his tongue.

"Sounds like fun." Elliot sucked Cade's tongue into his mouth.

"Damn, have you always had such a dirty mind?"

"Had to amuse myself somehow until I found a guy cute enough to fuck."

"Cute enough?"

"Hot enough."

"Better."

Elliot kissed him with more force, strong hands coming up to pin Cade's head between them while taking control of Cade's mouth. Cade held on to Elliot's neck and let him have it.

Breathing hard, Elliot broke away. "So can I?"

Could he what? Love him? Cade could. He was half there already. "Yeah."

Elliot dragged Cade to the couch.

"Wait. Can you what?" After that kiss, Cade couldn't remember what he'd just agreed to.

"Get balls-deep." With a smile, Elliot pushed Cade back against the armrest.

"Oh. Hell yeah."

Elliot kissed Cade again, hands already unfastening the belt holding up Steve's pants. "I think your friend would appreciate it if we got these off."

Cade kicked the pants off his ankles. "Fuck. Wait. I don't have anything."

"I do." Elliot stood and produced a condom and lube from his coat pocket. He stripped then climbed back on top of Cade, fingers reaching for the buttons on his shirt.

"Were you planning—?"

"I was hoping."

Wiggling beneath Elliot's weight, Cade turned onto his stomach, bracing himself over the armrest.

Elliot's hand slid under the shirt, stroking up Cade's spine and then down over his ass. "Roll back over. I want to watch you."

The snow machine gave another little spurt in his stomach as he complied, then Elliot's dark blue eyes were steady on his and there was nothing but warmth. Cade grinned.

"Steve'll be happy. Less chance of a come stain this way."

"Oh by all means, let's make Steve happy."

Cade shifted his shoulders against the lumpy cushions. "I think I'm going to like fucking on this couch a lot better than sleeping on it."

"You don't have to anymore, you know. I want you to move in with me."

It was on the tip of Cade's tongue to say "We'll see," but when he looked up at Elliot, Cade knew he didn't want to wait. "I'm a slob."

"I'll deal."

Cade couldn't tell who moaned louder when Elliot's fingers pressed inside Cade's ass.

Elliot licked up Cade's neck to murmur in his ear, "You are so hot."

Elliot scissored his fingers, and Cade's back arched off the couch.

"Oh, got it," Cade panted.

Elliot slid his hand back. "Got what?"

"My six-month blood test. I'm still negative."

Elliot stopped and held up the condom wrapper. "And?"

"It's up to you. You can do me bare if you want."

"What about me?"

"There something you haven't told me?"

"No."

"And you're going to be honest?"

"I told you that."

"Do you want to fuck other guys?"

"No."

"Then it's up to you."

Elliot put the condom on the coffee table. He rubbed up against Cade, skin to skin.

"Rule one is still in effect."

"Oh." Elliot's eyes popped open. He grabbed the lube. The deep moan he made as he slicked himself made Cade's own dick leak against his stomach. If he got much harder, he was going to split the fucking skin off.

Cade swung a leg over the back of the couch and arched his back. Elliot took his lead, dragging Cade forward so his ass came to rest on those thick-muscled thighs. As those huge hands held him open and ready, anticipation sent a jolt through his cock.

"If you don't get in me, I'm going to come thinking about it."

The head of Elliot's dick slipped around Cade's opening, and then Elliot held himself still.

"Elliot, man, if you changed your mind I won't be mad. Get the rubber."

"No. I trust you."

"Oh." Cade lifted his head so he was looking right into the kid's eyes. Locking a hand around Elliot's wrist, Cade nodded.

Elliot arched and pressed forward, all the way in, a long hard thrust that burned every nerve in Cade's body.

"Oh God." Elliot's eyes got wide and dark. His teeth gnawed on his bottom lip.

Cade grinned. "Oh yeah."

Elliot pulled out far enough to stretch the rim with his crown and then sank deep again. His hand tightened around Cade's wrist.

"Fuck me. I can't wait to feel you go inside me."

Elliot took another long stroke and shuddered. "Gonna be soon, damn it. The way you feel on me..."

"S'okay. There's a lot of good that can come out of you being twenty-three."

When Elliot laughed buried deep inside Cade, the echo rumbled up his spine.

"C'mon. Show me what you've got."

Elliot's hips picked up speed, the strokes firing so-good friction along Cade's nerves. Cade pressed forward to meet each thrust until the sound of their bodies coming together drowned out the soundtrack from the video game.

Elliot swiveled his hips and cupped Cade's ass, rubbing inside on just the right place. It was already there, boiling in his balls.

Cade's fingers dug into the couch. "Now."

"Oh, thank God." Elliot grabbed Cade's cock and jacked him once, twice and the pressure inside was enough.

Cade spilled hard and fast, muscles locking down so tight he shook through it. He thought he was done when he felt Elliot swell inside him, and then the flood of warmth deep in his guts triggered another spurt from his cock. He managed to pry his eyes open in time to watch Elliot jerk through the last of his orgasm.

Elliot's shoulders slumped, but he grabbed a napkin off the coffee table and wiped off his hand and Cade's belly. "Um." He looked down.

Cade laughed. "Yeah. So much for no come stains. I'm half on my shirt. Just hand me a napkin after you pull out. Or that goddamned tie if you can reach it."

Elliot collapsed on top of Cade convulsing in laughter.

When he quieted, he kissed Cade's neck before raising his head. "This is going to be fun, isn't it?"

"Yeah." Cade rubbed his thumb across Elliot's lips. "Yeah, kid, it is."

About the Author

K.A. Mitchell discovered the magic of writing at an early age when she learned that a carefully crayoned note of apology sent to the kitchen in a toy truck would earn her a reprieve from banishment to her room. Her career as a spin-control artist was cut short when her family moved to a two-story house, and her trucks would not roll safely down the stairs. Around the same time, she decided that Chip and Ken made a much cuter couple than Ken and Barbie and was perplexed when invitations to play Barbie dropped off. An unnamed number of years later, she's happy to find other readers and writers who like to play in her world.

To learn more about K.A. Mitchell, please visit www.kamitchell.com. Send an email to K.A. Mitchell at authorKAMitchell@gmail.com.

Look for these titles by
K. A. Mitchell

Now Available:

Custom Course
Diving in Deep
Regularly Scheduled Life
Collision Ride

Print Anthology:
Midsummer Night's Steam: Temperature's Rising

Welcome to Fantasm Island! Leave your inhibitions at the door and let your fantasies soar.

Fantasmagorical
© 2007 Annmarie McKenna

That's what the brochure said anyway. A week long fling with a stranger. Where's the harm in that? Take a compatibility quiz and a slew of other health tests, sign a strict privacy agreement and give license to any sexual fantasy you've ever had. Evan Knight couldn't wait.

Gabe and Lance have been searching for their perfect third for what seems like forever. One look at the woman he and his best friend and lover Lance have chosen to claim during her time on the island, and Gabe thinks they may have finally found her.

But what if Evan isn't interested in more than the fling she signed up for? Or worse, what if she can't handle two men who are into each other too? Gabe and Lance have one week to convince Evan that the three of them belong together...and they'll use every bit of seduction in their arsenal to make sure when the fantasy ends, their reality together will only just be beginning.

Warning, this title contains the following: explicit fantasmagorical sex, graphic language, ménage a trois, and hot nekkid man-love.

Available now in ebook and in the print anthology
Sins of Summer from Samhain Publishing.

Life's not always about the journey,
but who takes you on the ride.

Custom Ride

© 2007 K.A. Mitchell

A stint in the Air Force left Ryan MacRae with a bitter memory of life in the closet. Jeff Allstein is a mechanic who has too much to lose if his private life becomes public. The heat of their attraction boils over on a stormy summer night, but satisfying that need only makes them both crave more.

Their searing connection makes it hard for Ryan to understand the road blocks Jeff continually puts down. Ryan will have to buckle up if he's going to find love at the end of his custom ride.

Warning, this title contains the following: explicit male/male sex, graphic language.

Available now in ebook and in the print anthology
Temperature's Rising from Samhain Publishing.

GET IT
NOW

MyBookStoreAndMore.com
GREAT EBOOKS, GREAT DEALS . . . AND MORE!

Don't wait to run to the bookstore down the street, or
waste time shopping online at one of the "big boys." Now,
all your favorite Samhain authors are all in one place—at
MyBookStoreAndMore.com. Stop by today and discover
great deals on Samhain—and a whole lot more!

WWW.SAMHAINPUBLISHING.COM

GREAT
CHEAP
FUN

Discover eBooks!

THE FASTEST WAY TO GET THE HOTTEST NAMES

Get your favorite authors on your favorite reader, long before they're out in print! Ebooks from Samhain go wherever you go, and work with whatever you carry—Palm, PDF, Mobi, and more.

Samhain
Publishing, ltd

WWW.SAMHAINPUBLISHING.COM

Printed in the United States
210102BV00004B/103-111/P

9 781599 989983